The dead girl, her skin glowing with a bluish pallor, comes toward me, and the crowd between us parts swiftly and unconsciously.

They may not be able to see her but they can *feel* her, even if it lacks the intensity of my own experience. Electricity crackles up my spine—and something else, something bleak and looming like a premonition.

She's so close now I could touch her. My heart's accelerating, even before she opens her mouth, which I've already decided, ridiculously, impossibly, that I want to kiss. I can't make up my mind whether that means I'm exceedingly shallow or prescient. I don't know what I'm thinking because this is such unfamiliar territory: total here-be-dragons kind of stuff.

She blinks that dead person blink, looks at me as though I'm some puzzle to be solved. Doesn't she realize it's the other way around? She blinks again, and whispers in my ear, "Run."

DEATH MOST DEFINITE

DEATH WORKS
BOOK ONE

TRENT JAMIESON

www.orbitbooks.net

This book is a work of fiction. Names, characters, places, and incidents are the product of the author's imagination or are used fictitiously. Any resemblance to actual events, locales, or persons, living or dead, is coincidental.

Orbit
Hachette Book Group
237 Park Avenue
New York, NY 10017
Visit our website at www.orbitbooks.net

Orbit is an imprint of Hachette Book Group. The Orbit name and logo are trademarks of Little, Brown Book Group Limited.

Printed in the United States of America

Originally published in paperback by Hachette Australia: 2010
First North American Orbit edition: August 2010

10 9 8 7 6 5 4 3 2 1

For Diana

But lo, a stir is in the air!
EDGAR ALLAN POE, "THE CITY IN THE SEA"

Brace yourselves.
OLD RM HUMOUR

PART ONE

THE SCHISM

1

i know something's wrong the moment I see the dead
girl standing in the Wintergarden food court.

    She shouldn't be here. Or I shouldn't. But no
one else is working this. I'd sense them if they were. My
phone's hardly helpful. There are no calls from Number Four, and that's a serious worry. I should have had a
heads-up about this: a missed call, a text, or a new schedule. But there's nothing. Even a Stirrer would be less peculiar than what I have before me.

    Christ, all I want is my coffee and a burger.

    Then our eyes meet and I'm not hungry anymore.

    A whole food court's worth of shoppers swarm
between us, but from that instant of eye contact, it's just
me and her, and that indefinable something. A bit of *deja
vu*. A bit of lightning. Her eyes burn into mine, and there's
a gentle, mocking curl to her lips that is gorgeous; it hits
me in the chest.

    This shouldn't be. The dead don't seek you out unless
there is no one (or no thing) working their case: and that

just doesn't happen. Not these days. And certainly not in the heart of Brisbane's CBD.

She shouldn't be here.

This isn't my gig. This most definitely will not end well. The girl is dead; our relationship has to be strictly professional.

She has serious style.

I'm not sure I can pinpoint what it is, but it's there, and it's unique. The dead project an image of themselves, normally in something comfortable like a tracksuit, or jeans and a shirt. But this girl, her hair shoulder length with a ragged cut, is in a black, long-sleeved blouse, and a skirt, also black. Her legs are sheathed in black stockings. She's into silver jewelery, and what I assume are ironic brooches of Disney characters. Yeah, serious style, and a strong self-image.

And her eyes.

Oh, her eyes. They're remarkable, green, but flecked with gray. And those eyes are wide, because she's dead— newly dead—and I don't think she's come to terms with that yet. Takes a while: sometimes it takes a long while.

I yank pale ear buds from my ears, releasing a tinny splash of "London Calling" into the air around me.

The dead girl, her skin glowing with a bluish pallor, comes toward me, and the crowd between us parts swiftly and unconsciously. They may not be able to see her but they can *feel* her, even if it lacks the intensity of my own experience. Electricity crackles up my spine— and something else, something bleak and looming like a premonition.

She's so close now I could touch her. My heart's accelerating, even before she opens her mouth, which I've already decided, ridiculously, impossibly, that I want to kiss. I can't make up my mind whether that means I'm exceedingly shallow or prescient. I don't know what I'm thinking because this is such unfamiliar territory: total here-be-dragons kind of stuff.

She blinks that dead person blink, looks at me as though I'm some puzzle to be solved. Doesn't she realize it's the other way around? She blinks again, and whispers in my ear, "Run."

And then someone starts shooting at me.

Not what I was expecting.

Bullets crack into the nearest marble-topped tables. One. Two. Three. Shards of stone sting my cheek.

The food court surges with desperate motion. People scream, throwing themselves to the ground, scrambling for cover. But not me. She said run, and I run: zigging and zagging. Bent down, because I'm tall, easily a head taller than most of the people here, and far more than that now that the majority are on the floor. The shooter's after me; well, that's how I'm taking it. Lying down is only going to give them a motionless target.

Now, I'm in OK shape. I'm running, and a gun at your back gives you a good head of steam. Hell, I'm sprinting, hurdling tables, my long legs knocking lunches flying, my hands sticky with someone's spilt Coke. The dead girl's keeping up in that effortless way dead people have: skimming like a drop of water over a glowing hot plate.

We're out of the food court and down Elizabeth Street. In the open, traffic rumbling past, the Brisbane sun a hard light overhead. The dead girl's still here with me, throwing glances over her shoulder. Where the light hits her she's almost translucent. Sunlight and shadow keep revealing and concealing at random; a hand, the edge of a cheekbone, the curve of a calf.

The gunshots coming from inside haven't disturbed anyone's consciousness out here.

Shootings aren't exactly a common event in Brisbane. They happen, but not often enough for people to react as you might expect. All they suspect is that someone needs to service their car more regularly, and that there's a lanky bearded guy, possibly late for something, his jacket bunched into one fist, running like a madman down Elizabeth Street. I turn left into Edward, the nearest intersecting street, and then left again into the pedestrian-crammed space of Queen Street Mall.

I slow down in the crowded walkway panting and moving with the flow of people; trying to appear casual. I realize that my phone's been ringing. I look at it, at arm's length, like the monkey holding the bone in *2001: A Space Odyssey*. All I've got on the screen is Missed Call, and Private Number. Probably someone from the local DVD shop calling to tell me I have an overdue rental, which, come to think of it, I do—I always do.

"You're a target," the dead girl says.

"No shit!" I'm thinking about overdue DVDs, which is crazy. I'm thinking about kissing her, which is crazier still, and impossible. I haven't kissed anyone in a long time. If I smoked this would be the time to light up, look into the middle distance and say something like: "I've seen trouble, but in the Wintergarden, on a Tuesday at lunchtime, c'mon!" But if I smoked I'd be even more out of breath and gasping out questions instead, and there's some (well, most) types of cool that I just can't pull off.

So I don't say anything. I wipe my Coke-sticky hands

on my tie, admiring all that *je ne sais quoi* stuff she's got going on and feeling as guilty as all hell about it, because she's dead and I'm being so unprofessional. At least no one else was hurt in the food court: I'd feel it otherwise. Things aren't *that* out of whack. The sound of sirens builds in the distant streets. I can hear them, even above my pounding heart.

"This is so hard." Her face is the picture of frustration. "I didn't realize it would be so hard. There's a lot you need—" She flickers like her signal's hit static, and that's a bad sign: who knows where she could end up. "If you could get in—"

I reach toward her. Stupid, yeah, but I want to comfort her. She looks so pained. But she pulls back, as though she knows what would happen if I touch her. She shouldn't be acting this way. She's dead; she shouldn't care. If anything, she should want the opposite. She flickers again, swells and contracts, grows snowy. Whatever there is of her here is fracturing.

I take a step toward her. "Stop," I yell. "I need to—"

Need to? I don't exactly know what I need. But it doesn't matter because she's gone, and I'm yelling at nothing. And I didn't pomp her.

She's just gone.

2

That's not how it's meant to happen. Unprofessional. So unprofessional. I'm supposed to be the one in control.

After all, I'm a Psychopomp: a Pomp. Death is my business, has been in my family for a good couple of hundred years. Without me, and the other staff at Mortmax Industries, the world would be crowded with souls, and worse. Like Dad says, pomp is a verb and a noun. Pomps pomp the dead, we draw them through us to the Underworld and the One Tree. And we stall the Stirrers, those things that so desperately desire to come the other way. Every day I'm doing this—well, five days a week. It's a living, and quite a lucrative one at that.

I'm good at what I do. Though this girl's got me wondering.

I wave my hand through the spot where, moments ago, she stood. Nothing. Nothing at all. No residual electrical force. My skin doesn't tingle. My mouth doesn't go dry. She may as well have never been there.

The back of my neck prickles. I turn a swift circle.

Can't see anyone, but there are eyes on me, from somewhere. Who's watching me?

Then the sensation passes, all at once, a distant scratching pressure released, and I'm certain (well, pretty certain) that I'm alone—but for the usual Brisbane crowds pushing past me through the mall. Before, when the dead girl had stood here, they'd have done anything to keep away from her and me. Now I'm merely an annoying idiot blocking the flow of foot traffic. I find some cover: a little alcove between two shops where I'm out of almost everyone's line of sight.

I get on the phone, and call Dad's direct number at Mortmax. Maybe I should be calling Morrigan, or Mr. D (though word is the Regional Manager's gone fishing), but I need to talk to Dad first. I need to get this straight in my head.

I could walk around to Number Four, Mortmax's office space in Brisbane. It's on George Street, four blocks from where I'm standing, but I'm feeling too exposed and, besides, I'd probably run into Derek. While the bit of me jittery with adrenaline itches for a fight, the rest is hungry for answers. I'm more likely to get those if I keep away. Derek's been in a foul mood and I need to get through him before I can see anyone else. Derek runs the office with efficiency and attention to detail, and he doesn't like me at all. The way I'm feeling, that's only going to end in harsh words. Ah, work politics. Besides, I've got the afternoon and tomorrow off. First rule of this gig is: if you don't want extra hours keep a low profile. I've mastered that one to the point that it's almost second nature.

Dad's line must be busy because he doesn't pick up.

Someone else does, though. Looks like I might get a fight after all.

"Yes," Derek says. You could chill beer with that tone.

"This is Steven de Selby." I can't hide the grin in my voice. Now is not the time to mess with me, even if you're Morrigan's assistant and, technically, my immediate superior.

"I know who it is."

"I need to talk to Dad."

There are a couple of moments of uncomfortable silence, then a few more. "I'm surprised we haven't got you rostered on."

"I just got back from a funeral. Logan City. I'm done for the day."

Derek clicks his tongue. "Do you have any idea how busy we are?"

Absolutely, or I'd be talking to Dad. I wait a while: let the silence stretch out. He's not the only one who can play at that. "No," I say at last, when even I'm starting to feel uncomfortable. "Would you like to discuss it with me? I'm in the city. How about we have a coffee?" I resist the urge to ask him what he's wearing.

Derek sighs, doesn't bother with a response, and transfers me to Dad's phone.

"Steve," Dad says, and he sounds a little harried. So maybe Derek wasn't just putting it on for my benefit.

"Dad, well, ah..." I hesitate, then settle for the obvious. "I've just been shot at."

"What? Oh, Christ. You sure it wasn't a car backfiring?" he asks somewhat hopefully.

"Dad...do cars normally backfire rounds into the Wintergarden food court?"

"That was you?" Now he's sounding worried. "I thought you were in Logan."

"Yeah, I was. I went in for some lunch and someone started shooting."

"Are you OK?"

"Not bleeding, if that's what you mean."

"Good."

"Dad, I wouldn't be talking to you if someone hadn't warned me. Someone not living."

"Now that shouldn't be," he says. He sounds almost offended. "There are no punters on the schedule." He taps on the keyboard. I could be in for a wait. "Even factoring in the variables, there's no chance of a Pomp being required in the Wintergarden until next month: elderly gentleman, heart attack. There shouldn't be any activity there at all."

I clench my jaw. "There was, Dad. I'm not making it up. I was there. And, no, I haven't been drinking."

I tell him about the dead girl, and am surprised at how vivid the details are. I hadn't realized that I'd retained them. The rest of it is blurring, what with all the shooting and the sprinting, but I can see her face so clearly, and those eyes.

"Who was she?"

"I don't know. She looked familiar: didn't stay around long enough for me to ask her anything. But Dad, I didn't pomp her. She just disappeared."

"Loose cannon, eh? I'll look into it, talk to Morrigan for you."

"I'd appreciate that. Maybe I was just in the wrong place at the wrong time, but it doesn't feel like that. She was trying to save me, and when do the dead ever try and look after Pomps?"

Dad chuckles at that. There's nothing more self-involved than a dead person. Talking of self-involved...

"Derek says you're busy."

"We're having trouble with our phone line. Another one of Morrigan's 'improvements'," Dad says, I can hear the inverted commas around improvements. "Though... that seems to be in the process of being fixed." He pauses. "I *think* that's what's happening, there's a half-dozen people here pulling wiring out of the wall." I can hear them in the background, drills whining; there's even a little hammering. "Oh, and there's the Death Moot in December. Two months until everything's crazy and the city's crowded with Regional Managers. Think of it, the entire Orcus here, all thirteen RMs." He groans. "Not to mention the bloody Stirrers. They keep getting worse. A couple of staffers have needed stitches."

I rub the scarred surface of the palm of my free hand. Cicatrix City as we call it, an occupational hazard of stalling stirs, but the least of them when it came to Stirrers. A Pomp's blood is enough to exorcise a Stirrer from a newly dead body, but the blood needs to be fresh. Morrigan is researching ways around this, but has come up with nothing as of yet. Dad calls it time-wastery. I for one would be happy if I didn't have to slash open my palm every time a corpse came crashing up into unlife.

A stir is always a bad thing. Unsettling, dangerous and bloody. Stirrers, in essence, do the same thing as Pomps, but without discretion: they hunger to take the living and the dead. They despise life, they drain it away like plug-holes to the Underworld, and they're not at all fond of me and mine. Yeah, they hate us.

"Well, I didn't see or sense one in Logan. Just a body, and a lot of people mourning."

"Hmm, you got lucky. Your mother had two." Dad sighs. "And here I am stuck in the office."

I make a mental note to call Mom. "So Derek wasn't lying."

"You've got to stop giving Derek so much crap, Steve. He'll be Ankou one day, Morrigan isn't going to be around forever."

"I don't like the guy, and you can't tell me that the feeling isn't mutual."

"Steven, he's your boss. Try not to piss him off too much," Dad says and, by the tone of his voice, I know we're about to slip into the same old argument. Let me list the ways: My lack of ambition. How I could have had Derek's job, if I'd really cared. How there's more Black Sheep in me than is really healthy for a Pomp. That Robyn left me three years ago. Well, I don't want to go there today.

"OK," I say. "If you could just explain why the girl was there and, maybe, who she was. She understood the process, Dad. She wouldn't let me pomp her." There's silence down the end of the line. "You do that, and I'll try and suck up to Derek."

"I'm serious," Dad says. "He's already got enough going on today. Melbourne's giving him the run-around. Not returning calls, you know, that sort of thing."

Melbourne giving Derek the run-around isn't that surprising. Most people like to give Derek the run-around. I don't know how he became Morrigan's assistant. Yeah, I know *why*, he's a hard worker, and ambitious, almost as ambitious as Morrigan—and Morrigan is Ankou, second only to Mr. D. But Derek's hardly a people person. I can't think of anyone who Derek hasn't pissed off over the years: anyone *beneath* him, that is. He'd not dare with

Morrigan, and only a madman would consider it with Mr. D—you don't mess with Geoff Daly, the Australian Regional Manager. Mr. D's too creepy, even for us.

"OK, I'll send some flowers," I say. "Gerberas, everyone likes gerberas, don't they?"

Dad grunts. He's been tapping away at his computer all this time. I'm not sure if it's the computer or me that frustrates him more.

"Can you see anything?"

A put-upon sigh, more tapping. "Yeah...I'm...looking into...All right, let me just..." Dad's a one-finger typist. If glaciers had fingers they'd type faster than him. Morrigan gives him hell about it all the time; Dad's response requires only one finger as well. "I can't see anything unusual in the records, Steve. I'd put it down to bad luck, or good luck. You didn't get shot after all. Maybe you should buy a scratchie, one of those $250,000 ones."

"Why would I want to ruin my mood?"

Dad laughs. Another phone rings in the background; wouldn't put it past Derek to be on the other end. But then all the phones seem to be ringing.

"Dad, maybe I should come into the office. If you need a hand..."

"No, we're fine here," Dad says, and I can tell he's trying to keep me away from Derek, which is probably a good thing. My Derek tolerance is definitely at a low today.

We say our goodbyes and I leave him to all those ringing phones, though my guilt stays with me.

3

I take a deep breath. I feel slightly reassured about my own living-breathing-walking-talking future. If Number Four's computers can't bring anything unusual up then nothing unusual is happening.

There are levels of unusual though, and I don't feel that reassured by the whole thing, even if I can be reasonably certain no one has a bead on me. Something's wrong. I just can't put my finger on it. The increased Stirrer activity, the problems with the phones . . . But we've had these sorts of things before, and even if Stirrers are a little exotic, what company doesn't have issues with their phones at least once a month? Stirrers tend to come in waves, particularly during flu season—there's always more bodies, and a chance to slip in before someone notices—and it's definitely flu season, spring is the worst for it in Brisbane. I'm glad I've had my shots, there's some nasty stuff going around. Pomps are a little paranoid about viruses, with good reason—we know how deadly they can be.

Still, I don't get shot at every day (well, ever). Nor do I

obsess over dead girls to the point where I think I would almost be happy to be shot at again if I got the chance to spend more time with them. It's ridiculous but I'm thinking about her eyes, and the timbre of her voice. Which is a change from thinking about Robyn.

My mobile rings a moment later, and I actually jump and make a startled sound, loud enough to draw a bit of attention. I cough. Pretend to clear my throat. The LCD flashes an all too familiar number at me—it's the garage where my car is being serviced. I take the call. Seems I'm without a vehicle until tomorrow at least, something's wrong with something. Something expensive I gather. Whenever my mechanic sounds cheerful I know it's going to cost me, and he's being particularly ebullient.

The moment I hang up, the phone rings again.

My cousin Tim. Alarm bells clang in the distant recesses of my mind. We're close, Tim's the nearest thing I have to a brother, but he doesn't normally call me out of the blue. Not unless he's after something.

"Are you all right?" he demands. "No bullet wounds jettisoning blood or anything?"

"Yeah. And, no, I'm fine."

Tim's a policy advisor for a minor but ambitious state minister. He's plugged in and knows everything. "Good, called you almost as soon as I found out. You working tomorrow?" he asks.

"No, why?"

"You're going to need a drink. I'll pick you up at your place in an hour." Tim isn't that great at the preamble. Part of his job: he's used to getting what he wants. And he has the organizational skills to back it up. Tim would have made a great Pomp, maybe even better than Morrigan, except he decided very early on that the family trade wasn't for him. Black Sheep nearly always do. Most don't even bother getting into pomping at all. They deny the family trade and become regular punters. Tim's decision had caused quite a scandal.

But, he hadn't escaped pomping completely; part of his remit is Pomp/government relations, something he likes to complain about at every opportunity: along the lines of every time I get out, they pull me back in. Still, he's brilliant at the job. Mortmax and the Queensland government haven't had as close and smooth a relationship in decades. Between him and Morrigan's innovations, Mortmax Australia is in the middle of a golden age.

"I don't know," I say.

Tim sighs. "Oh, no you don't. There's no getting out of this, mate. Sally's looking after the kids, and I'm not going to tell you what I had to do to swing that. It's her bridge night, for Christ's sake. Steve, how many other thirty-year-olds do you know who play bridge?"

I look at my watch. "Hey, it's only three."

"Beer o'clock." I've never heard a more persuasive voice.

"Tim, um, I reckon that's stretching it a bit."

There's a long silence down the other end of the phone. "Steve, you can't tell me you're busy. I know you've got no more pomps scheduled today."

Sometimes his finger is a little too on the pulse. "I've had a rough day."

Tim snorts. "Steve, now that's hilarious. A rough day for you is a nine o'clock start and no coffee."

"Thanks for the sympathy." My job is all hours, though I must admit my shifts have been pretty sweet of late.

And no coffee *does* make for a rough day. In fact, coffee separated by more than two-hourly intervals makes for a rough day.

"Yeah, OK, so it's been rough. I get that. All the more reason..."

"Pub it is, then," I say without any real enthusiasm.

I've a sudden, aching need for coffee, coal black and scalding, but I know I'm going to have to settle for a Coke. That is, if I want to get home and change in time.

"You're welcome," Tim says. "My shout."

"Oh, you'll be shouting, all right."

"See you in an hour."

So I'm in the Paddo Tavern, still starving hungry, even after eating a deep-fried Chiko Roll: a sere and jaundiced specimen that had been mummifying in a nearby cafe's bain-marie for a week too long.

I had gone home, changed into jeans and a Stooges T-shirt—the two cleanest things on the floor of my bedroom. The jacket and pants didn't touch the ground, though, they go in the cupboard until I can get them dry-cleaned. Pomps know all about presentation—well, on the job, anyway. After all, we spend most of our working day at funerals and in morgues.

I might have eaten something at home but other than a couple of Mars Bars, milk, and dog food for Molly there's nothing. The fridge is in need of a good grocery shop; has been for about three years. Besides, I'm only just dressed and deodorized when Tim honks the horn out the front. Perhaps I shouldn't have spent ten minutes working on my hair.

Getting to the pub early was not such a good idea. Sure,

we avoided peak-hour traffic, but my head was spinning by the first beer. Chiko Rolls can only sop up so much alcohol—about a thimbleful by my calculations.

"Why bulk up on the carbs?" Tim had declared—though I'm sure he'd actually had something for lunch. "You need room for the beer."

I end up sitting at the table as Tim buys round after round. He comes back each time a little bit drunker. His tie slightly looser around his neck. A big grin on his face as he slides my beer over to me. "Now, isn't this perfect?"

We've always been like this. Get us together and the drinks keep coming.

He's already bought a packet of cigarettes. We used to sneak off at family parties and sit around smoking whatever cigarettes we could afford, listening to the Smiths on cassette. Things haven't changed for Tim. If Sally knew about those cigarettes he'd be a dead man. To be honest, I'm not that keen on them either. The last thing you ever want to do is pomp a family member.

"Look," he says, well into our fifth pint. He nurses his beer a while, staring at me like I'm some poor wounded pup. "We're worried about you. Look at you there, all miserable."

"Yeah, but I don't get shot at every day. This is new."

"You know that's not what I'm talking about."

"Don't you mention her. It was three years ago."

"Exactly."

"I'm over her."

Tim drops his glass onto the table. It makes a definitive and sarcastic crack. "If Sally were here she'd be laughing right now. Just because we've stopped setting you up on dates doesn't mean we agree with you." He raises his

hand at my glare. "OK. So how about work? Is that going
well? I hear there's been a few issues lately."

"What are you fishing for?"

"Nothing—that's Mr. D. He's been away the last few
days, fishing, hasn't he?"

I raise an eyebrow. "I didn't think these were work
drinks. You trying to claim this on your tax?"

Tim shakes his head. "Of course not. I suppose I just
get a bit nervous when Mr. D is away for so long. The
whole department does."

"Shit, you *are* fishing."

"Not at all."

"You're going to have to be more subtle than that. Morrigan doesn't like you that much, Tim."

Tim's face darkens. "It's not my job to be liked. Besides,
he doesn't like your dad all that much, either."

"Morrigan loves my father. He just never agrees with
him. That, my dear cousin, is the very definition of a
friendship. Mutual admiration orbiting mutual contempt."

Tim grins. "Certainly what we have, eh? And may it
always be so." He raises his pint glass. "To immortality."

I crack my pint against his. "Immortality." We're
both aware of how ridiculous we sound. Grow up around
Pomps and ridiculous is all you've got.

I want to tell Tim about the dead girl but I can't quite
bring myself to. Truth is, I'm a bit embarrassed. I'm not
sure if my feelings for her show that I'm finally over
Robyn or that I'm in deeper than ever. Besides, it's just not
the done thing. You don't fall for a punter. No one's that
unprofessional. No one's that stupid.

By mid evening there's a pretty decent cover band belt-
ing out versions of pub rock standards from The Doors

to Wolfmother. They've only started into the first bars of Soundgarden's "Black Hole Sun" when I see the dead guy. I look at Tim, who's just ducked back from a smoke.

"That's odd," I say, all the while wondering how sober I am.

Tim raises an eyebrow. He's not a Pomp but he knows the deal. He can recognize the signs. And they're very obvious in a crowded pub. Some people reckon that Black Sheep know the deal better than anyone, because if you're from a pomping family you don't choose to become a Pomp, you choose not to. "Punter?"

"Yeah." I tap my phone with beer-thickened fingers. Is this thing broken? I wonder.

"Maybe it's someone else's gig," he says, hopefully, looking from me to the phone and back again.

I shake my head. "No. The schedule's up. Nothing about a Pomp being required here. Second time today."

"And you neglected to tell me this?"

"I thought this wasn't a work meeting."

"See what I mean?" Tim says, pointing at the space where the dead guy stands. "This is why we worry when Mr. D goes fishing."

I throw my gaze around the room. The last time this happened someone started shooting at me. Can't see that happening here.

"Something's not working," Tim says. "Shouldn't you . . . ?" He nods toward the dead guy.

"Yeah." I put down my beer and roll my shoulders. There's a satisfyingly loud crack. "I've a job that needs doing."

I get up, and an afternoon's drinking almost topples me. I grip the table, perhaps a little too desperately.

Tim reaches out a steadying hand. "You right?"

"Yep. Yep." I push him away. "I'm fine."

There is no way I should be doing this drunk. I could lose my job. I'm sure it's somewhere in my contract. But technically this isn't supposed to happen. There's a dead guy here, and no one to facilitate his next step. It's a crowded pub, and yet there's this empty space—empty to everyone but me. If it didn't piss me off so much it would be funny to watch. Anyone who gets close to the dead guy frowns then darts away.

If only that space was near the bar.

The dead guy's head jerks in my direction. His eyes widen and he blinks furiously: a look that would be almost coquettish if it wasn't so familiar.

"It's all right," I say.

It isn't, he's dead. But there's nothing that can be done about that. Whatever could have been done wasn't or failed. We're past that. Pomps don't deal with the dying but with what comes after. We're merely conduits, and gatekeepers. The dead pass through us, and we stop the Stirrers coming back. But this—this dead guy in the Paddo, and me—is too reactive. Someone should have been sent here by head office. He should be on the schedule. But he isn't. And that leaves a very bitter taste in my mouth; I do have some pride in my job. Death is the most natural thing in the world but only because we work so hard to make it look easy.

I look around. Just in case . . . Nope, no other Pomps in the building. Should be able to feel one if there is, but I *have* had a lot to drink.

"Sorry," the dead guy says, his voice carrying perfectly despite the noise.

"Nothing to be sorry about." I'm wearing the most calming expression I can muster. I know he's scared.

I reach out my hand, and he flits away like a nervous bird, and brushes a bloke's arm. The poor guy yelps and drops his beer. Glass shatters and the circle around us widens, though people don't realize what they're doing. I can feel eyes on me. This must look more than a little crazy. But the gazes never linger for long—looking at a spot where a dead person is standing can be almost as uncomfortable as bumping up against one. The average human brain makes its adjustments quickly and shifts its attention elsewhere.

The dead guy steps back toward me.

"What's your name?" I ask him, keeping my voice soft and low. His eyes are focused on my lips.

"Terry."

"You want to talk, Terry?" A name is good. Morrigan would describe it as being of extreme utility. It's a handle, a point of focus. Terry's eyes search my face.

"No. I—this isn't right. I've been wandering, and there's nothing. Just—" He blinks. Looks around. "What is this place? Shit, is this the Paddo?"

"You shouldn't be here, Terry," I say, and he's back, looking at me. There's more confidence and less confusion in his eyes.

"No shit. I haven't been back to Brisbane in years. I—do people really still listen to grunge?"

"What's wrong with grunge?"

Terry rolls his eyes. "Where to begin..."

I take another step toward him. "Look, it doesn't matter, Terry." This is inexcusable. Someone has majorly screwed up, and I'm certain I know who. But that's for later. I need to stay calm.

"Terry, you know where you need to be," I say gently, as gently as you can above the cover band's rendition of Nirvana's "Smells Like Teen Spirit."

He nods his head. "I can't seem to get there."

"Let me help you, Terry."

I reach out. This time he doesn't dart away. I touch him. And Terry's gone, passing through me, and into the Underworld. There's the familiar pain of a successful pomp, a slight ache that runs through me. I take a deep breath. Then, between blinks, all that space around me fills with people. I elbow my way toward my table none too gently; I reserve softness for the dead. I'm fuming with a white-hot rage, my body sore from the pomp.

Derek's in trouble, now. If he's messed up the rostering this badly, what else is he doing wrong? I'm filled with a righteous (and somewhat enjoyable) anger. I'd call him right now, but anger isn't the only thing I'm filled with and it's decided to remind me in no uncertain terms.

I make a dash for the toilets, stand at the urinal, and it's a sweet relief. I glance over at the mirror; the hair's looking good.

"You're in danger," a familiar voice whispers in my ear, and I jump. It's the dead girl. She smiles that mocking smile.

"Jesus! Where the hell did you … What do you mean, in danger?" I'm a while framing that question.

She shakes her head, her eyes a bit fuzzy. She blinks. "I'm not sure." Then there's some clarity in her gaze. "Still trying to remember. You're really taking this people wanting to kill you thing very well. Or maybe not … Hmm. How much have you had to drink?"

I'm pretty unsteady on my feet, and I'm still peeing. So, a lot.

"I...Would you mind turning the other way? I don't think *people* want to kill me, that was just some crazy guy with a gun."

The dead girl's face creases. "A crazy guy who just happened to take potshots at you?"

"Which is why he's crazy. I mean, why would anyone want to blow my brains out?"

Someone's walked into the toilet. The movement catches my eye. I turn, free hand clenched, a move I know is hardly intimidating, particularly while I'm pissing. I sway there a moment.

"Not him," she says.

"How do you know?" I demand. "You're hardly a reliable source of information, what with the dropping in and dropping out."

The poor interloper hesitates for a moment, looking at me, looking at the urinals, and feeling the presence of dead person pushing him anywhere but here. He heads straight to a stall and locks the door.

And I'm suddenly feeling a whole lot more sober. The dead girl stands far enough away from me that I can't pomp her. It's not like I'd touch her before washing my hands anyway.

"Are you really dead?" I zip up. The room's swaying a little, which can't be good.

She nods. "The real deal. And you need to get out of here, there's stuff I have to tell you, I think." She looks down at her hands, and there's something about the gesture that makes me ache. "It's much harder keeping this together than I expected. And the urgency, I'm trying to hold onto that...But I'm remembering." She looks up at me. "It's getting a little clearer. That's something, right?"

I wash my hands, studying her in the mirror. A dozen contradictory emotions dance across her face. All of them legitimate, and every one of them adding to her confusion. And here I am leaden with drink. This demands sensitivity. I want to help her but I'm not sure if I can. Maybe the best way, the most professional way, is by pomping her.

But I'm also angry. She's scaring me, and that's not supposed to be the way this works.

"Good," I blurt, "because I really want to know why someone was shooting at me."

The dead girl scowls. "Maybe I should just let you die."

I shrug, drunkenly belligerent. I'm not the dead one after all. "Maybe. Then at least we'd—"

That's when the beer, the I've-been-shot-at-and-lived-to-tell-the-tale beer, has its effect on me, and I'm running for the nearest stall, the one next to the poor guy I scared off the urinal. When I am done, after a series of loud and desperate sounding hurls, I feel utterly wretched. I look up at her, because she's followed me in. "Bad Chiko Roll," I explain, half-heartedly.

The dead girl grimaces at me. But her eyes are more focused. The mere act of talking, of a person's interest in her, has helped ground her.

She even smiles. Nothing like a spew as an icebreaker. "Do people even eat those anymore?"

What is it about the dead today? Everybody's talking back. "Yes, and they listen to grunge."

"What?" She rubs her chin thoughtfully. "Though that might explain it."

"It was a legitimate movement."

"The stress is on the *was*, though." She's looking more coherent, almost concrete.

"Name's Steven," I say, and I instinctively reach out toward her. It's my job after all. She darts back, a look of horror on her face.

"Watch that!"

"Sorry, it's just habit." My head's feeling clearer.

We stand crammed in the grotty stall for a moment, just staring at each other. There's a tightness in my throat, a ridiculous sense of potential in a ridiculous place. Whatever it is, it passes. She nods, taking another step back, so that she's almost out of the stall. She keeps an eye on my hands.

"Lissa," she says. "Lissa Jones."

Which sounds a hell of a lot better than Dead Girl.

I open my mouth to say something, anything, but she's gone. And again, it's nothing to do with me. She's just gone. I'm suffering an altogether unfamiliar hurt, and it's awful.

4

im is far too drunk to drive me home. But sober enough to get me a taxi with what appears to be some sort of magic gesture. It's as though he plucked the car out of the night.

Tim presses the packet of cigarettes into my hands. "Hide the evidence, eh. And look after yourself."

"You too."

He gives me the thumbs up. "'S all good!"

And I know that he'll be at work *sans* hangover tomorrow, which brings a slight wave of resentment to the top of my rolling-drunk thoughts because my day off isn't going to be nearly as pretty. I watch him pluck another taxi from the ether.

"Where to?" the driver asks me. I mumble directions. Tim's taxi is already off. His driver probably knew where to go before Tim had even opened his mouth.

The taxi ride home is just swell, though a couple of times I nearly hurl again: seems my stomach has found more than that Chiko Roll to challenge it. Both times the driver is just about ready to push me out the door. I swear, one time I feel his boot on my back. But we make it, and he's happy enough to take my money, and happier still when I wave away his vague, and extremely leisurely, attempts at giving me change.

The taxi pulls away and I stare at my place. It's all a bit of a blur really, except for the brace symbol marked above the door. It's glowing: there must be Stirrers about. Not my job, though, the night shift will be dealing with those.

As I unlock the front door Molly's greeting barks are gruff and accusatory. She may be the most patient border collie in the world, but even she has limits. I realize that I hadn't fed her before I left. I make up for it, nearly falling flat on my face as I scoop dog food into her bowl, then walk into the bathroom and splash my face. I hardly feel the water. The space around me seems packed in cotton wool. I poke my cheek and it's as though I'm touching something inanimate. For some reason that saddens me. There's a few of Robyn's things still in the bathroom cupboard. A small bottle of perfume, a toothbrush. Three years and I've not managed to throw them out.

Molly pushes her black and white snout against my leg; she's wolfed down dinner and needs to go outside. There's an impatient gleam to her eyes. I think she's just as sick of me mooching over Robyn as everyone else, and Molly never even knew her. I bought her after Robyn left. Yeah, rebound pet ownership—real healthy.

"Sorry, girl."

She's on my heels all the way through the house to the kitchen and the back door, rushing past me as I open it. The refrigerator hums behind me.

In the backyard the air is cool. It's a typical spring

evening and the city is still and quiet, though I know that's a lie because it's never really still or quiet. People are always sliding away to the Underworld, and things are always stirring. But I can imagine what it would be like to believe otherwise. I sit on the back step, smoking one of the cigarettes that Tim bought—yes, I'm *that* drunk— and wait for Molly to finish her business, thinking all the while about Lissa. I'd helped Terry easily enough. Why couldn't I help her? She's the most striking girl I've ever seen, but that shouldn't matter. I'm already feeling the remorse that no amount of alcohol can shield you from, because drinking is all about remorse.

Molly trots up next to me and I scratch her head. "What's wrong with me, eh?"

She's got no answer to offer. She's happy, though, to receive the scratching. I yawn at last, get up and leave the unquiet city outside.

I'm drunk and exhausted but I'm restless as all hell. I walk about my house, not really connecting with any of it. All the stuff I've bought. The useless shit, as Dad calls it. The posters, the DVDs, and CDs: some not even out of their wrappers. None of it plants me here. None of it means anything. I might as well be a ghost. I wonder if this disconnect is how it feels to be dead. I'll have to ask Morrigan—if anyone will know, it'll be him. Molly follows me for a little while but can see no sense in it, or just gets bored, and wanders off to her bed. I drop onto the couch in the living room, and sit on my cordless phone. The damn thing beeps at me.

I press the talk button and hear the familiar rapid blipping dial tone: there's at least one message on my voicemail.

I ring through to check. Two missed calls. The alcohol steps politely aside for a moment. One of the calls is from Morrigan: too late to call him back. Besides, if it had been really important, he would have tried my mobile.

There's a message, too. The phone crackles, which means either there are Stirrers about or we've hit a period of increased solar flare activity. Both mess with electrical signals.

"Steven," Dad says. "Hope you haven't been drinking." He doesn't sound too hopeful. "Thought I'd call to let you know you were right, it wasn't a coincidence. The police released the name of the gunman. Jim McKean."

McKean...

McKean...

The name's familiar. Dad fills in the blanks. "McKean's a Pomp... Was a Pomp. Sydney middle management; didn't show for work yesterday. I've heard he was doped out: on ice, that's what they call it these days, isn't it? Out of character, completely out of character."

Of course, McKean!

I remember him. A quiet guy. Always seemed nice, and a little bookish. We'd actually talked science fiction at a Christmas party a few years back. He was a real Heinlein nut, not that I'm saying anything, but...

"Morrigan's using his connections, digging into the why, but—whatever the reason—McKean is behind bars. You don't need to worry."

But I am. The guy came after me with a gun. Even with Molly the house seems too... empty.

"Give me that phone, Michael." It's Mom. "Steven, your father was less than speedy in passing on to me the details." Mom stresses the last word. "Your rather worthless father said you'd had a tough day. He neglected to tell me that you'd been shot at. You'll be having dinner with us tomorrow night. No excuses. Now, I hope Tim hasn't gotten you too drunk. We're all rather worried about you."

The message drops out.

I've a dinner invite for Wednesday, and I'll be there. Mom and Dad are excellent cooks. I might have inherited the pomping career but the culinary skills seemed to have skipped me. I might even have made enough peace with my stomach to be hungry by then.

I play the message over, twice, just to hear their voices. It grounds me a little. The dead aren't the only ones who like to feel that people care. I check my mobile but no missed calls, no texts, and the schedule hasn't changed.

I switch on the television, and flick through the channels.

Two of them are running stories about McKean. Shots of him being taken into custody, backlit by a frenetic clicking lightshow of camera flashes. There's something not right about him but I guess you could say that about anyone who decides that today is a good day to start firing a rifle into a crowd. No one was killed, thank Christ, but not all of that is luck: he wasn't gunning for anyone else. There's nothing in the story linking him to me. Nothing about me at all.

The sight of him draws a rising shudder of panic through me that even the weight of alcohol can't suppress. I guess it has affected me more than I care to admit.

I turn off the television and switch on my Notebook, hook into Facebook, and the Mortmax workgroup—Morrigan set that up—and there's Jim McKean in my network: looking his usual awkward self, and nothing like a killer. I check his profile. His life/death status is up as dead. Morrigan installed that morbid little gadget a year or so ago. Pomp humor is very much of the gallows sort.

Peculiar, as McKean *isn't* dead. But that slips from my mind in an instant, because there's Lissa's face in his friends list. I click on her profile photo.

She worked for Mortmax?

I bang my head with my palm. Of course she had. Lissa Jones. Melbourne agency. It's all here, and I must have met her before. Her green eyes mock me. Her status though, according to this, is living. Something's wrong with that gadget of Morrigan's.

I open Dad's profile. *Dead.*

Then Mum's. *Dead.*

I open my own profile. Status: *Dead.*

Then I'm opening all the Brisbane pages. And every single one of them, including Morrigan, is the same.

Something prickles up my spine.

I switch to Mr. D's profile. It has his usual picture, a crow on a tombstone. His is a dry and obvious sort of humor. But Regional Managers are like that. Death, after all, is the reason for their existence. His status: gone fishing.

Nothing peculiar there. Our RM loves to fish—most of the Orcus do. I've heard he has a boat docked at the piers of Hell, and that Charon's own boatmen run it. I've seen the photos of the things he's caught in the sea of the dead—the ammonites, the juvenile megalodon, the black-toothed white whale with old mariner still attached.

Regardless, the timing is odd. I get the feeling that there's something I'm not seeing, but there's a thick and somewhat alcohol-muddied wall between the truth and me.

I switch off the Notebook. Then look at my watch. There's no one I can reasonably call about this. So I call Dad.

"Do you know what time it is?"

I don't realize that I'd been holding my breath until he answers. Morrigan's gadget is wrong, thank Christ. "Sorry, Dad, but…" I mumble something drunkenly at him about the Facebook accounts.

Dad lets out a weary breath. "*That's* what this is about?"

"Yeah, it's, I—"

"We'll discuss this tomorrow, when you're sober."

"But Dad—"

"Get some sleep."

There's a long moment of silence. Dad sighs again. "OK, there's some sort of glitch on the server. If we'd kept to the old ways…well, I wouldn't be answering a call from you in the middle of the night. I tell you, Steve, it's been a hell of a week." Which is saying something, as it's only Tuesday night. "Just a wonderful one for Mr. D to take off. Morrigan's looking into it. Now, go…to… sleep." Dad sounds like he is already, which is good or I'd be in for a lecture.

"Sorry," I say.

"'S OK," he says. "I'm just glad you're not hurt. We'll talk about this tomorrow." He hangs up, and I'm left holding the phone.

Dad said I'm safe, earlier. I can't say that's how I see it.

It's a weird world. A weird and dangerous world. When you're a Pomp, even such a low level one as me, you get your face rubbed in it. Robyn couldn't handle it. I don't think she believed in half of what I did. I don't blame her for leaving, not one little bit, nor for the hole she left in my life. She didn't grow up with all this, hadn't seen some of the things I've seen, or witnessed some of the deaths I've attended. Still, until today I'd never been shot at.

I walk around the house checking the locks, and then double-checking the front and back door. Then I'm looking in cupboards, even under the bed. It's a drunken, shambling sort of scrutiny. And when I catch myself stumbling to the front door for the third time I snort.

"Ridiculous."

Molly, who's been watching all this from her mat with a bemused tilt to her head, stares up at me.

"Ridiculous," I say again, and scratch behind her ears.

She grins at me.

"Safe as houses, eh, Moll?" I stumble to the bedroom, and crash onto the bed, after flipping my shoes across the room where they land with two dull thwacks against the wardrobe mirror. My reflection shivers at me.

"Buffoon," I whisper at it.

The bed begins a wobbly spin, even as I'm slipping into sleep. I stare at the window to steady that roiling movement. It works, but I know I won't be awake for much longer.

One drawn out blink, and then another, and I'm sure Lissa's face is pressed against the window or through the window. Then it's just the moon, full and blue. "Luminous," I whisper, at the pale light.

The moon says something, but I can't read her lips.

The window rattles as a car mutters in an eight-cylindered tongue down the street. Exhaustion has its hooks in me, and I'm too far gone, and full, to find a pause from my fall into slumber.

No wakefulness. No dreams. Just dark, dark sleep: that's where I'm headed. And Lissa, the moon, and all the questions rushing around me like Mr. D's crows, cannot follow me there.

5

My status on Facebook isn't the only thing that's dead.

Someone has jimmied open my skull and poured highly flammable liquid migraine directly into my brainpan. I can taste stale vomit, a night's worth of spewing crusted to the roof of my mouth. I open my eye a crack and admit a jack-hammering Brisbane morning light that ignites all that potential pain at once. I shut my eye again. The room, windows closed, smells delightfully of sick and ashtray.

The phone rings, and I'm immediately regretting the decision to have a handset in my bedroom. The ringing is an ice pick swinging into my forehead.

I ignore it. Let it ring out. A second later my mobile starts up. Fucking ice pick all over again.

I open my eyes. The light is merciless as I scramble around hunting for my mobile, and it keeps ringing and ringing and ringing. This has to be some sort of cruel and unusual punishment. Sliding out of bed, I realize that I'm

still half in my jeans: the other pants leg has the pocket
with my phone in it.

I snatch out the mobile, consider hurling it against the
wall, then see the number and moan.

Mortmax. And whoever's calling has disengaged the
message service, which gives me more than a clue as to
who is responsible.

I flip the phone open. "Yes."

"Steven," Derek says, "we need you in the city. No later
than ten."

He hangs up.

Yes, king of bloody small talk. And do I have a thing or
two to talk about with him! Starting with Lissa, and ending with Terry. Derek's messed up a few too many times
in the last couple of days.

I look at the clock. 8:30.

Shit! I can't imagine this hangover leaving before late
afternoon. It has teeth and cruel hangovery hands that are
less than gently clenching my stomach, engendering an
argument over which end of me is most likely going to be
needing to evacuate the evils of the evening before. There
are good odds it could be both at once. It's a finger-in-all-
pies sort of hangover.

How do I get myself in these situations?

My phone chirps with a text. Tim. *Hope you're feeling
OK :-)*

Prick.

Just chipper, I text back. Even texting is painful and
nausea inducing.

I fish through cupboards, and drawers, until I find
something strong for the pain. I manage to keep it down.
Molly's waiting, eyes lit with a weary impatience, to be

let out the back door. Opening it only lets in more of that brutal morning light. I wince, leave the door open for the dog, and make the trek to the bathroom.

Oddly enough Molly follows me. I shrug at her. "Suit yourself."

There's blood in the bathroom. On the walls; a little on the mirror. I wrinkle my nose at it. Molly sniffs at the walls, doesn't bother licking them. This ectoplasmic blood is mildly toxic. The first time she encountered it, gobbling down what she obviously thought was a marvelous, if peculiar, free feed, she had diarrhea for two days. Now *that* was pleasant for the both of us. Whenever there's an increase in Stirrers this happens. These sorts of portents come with the job. I do my best to ignore the sanguine mess. Cleaning is for post hangover.

The shower, alternating hot and cold, helps a little. I even manage to think about Lissa, wondering where she is and how horrible that state of limbo must be. Her having been a Pomp at least explains some of the why of it. She's got the know-how. Though I don't understand how she's managing—but maybe she isn't, maybe she was pomped last night. I finish my shower with that disturbing thought, and reach for a towel. The movement sets my head off again. It's as though the shower never even happened, except I'm dripping wet.

This is hell, self-inflicted or not. I stand still for a while, taking slightly pathetic little breaths. Then get dressed, moving like an old, old man in a particularly didactic anti-alcohol advertisement.

Molly barks from the backyard. I stumble out, and she's there with her mini-football in her mouth, wanting a game. One look at me and she changes her mind, dropping it to the ground with an expression that breaks my heart.

"Sorry, girl," I say.

I step back from the door, into the kitchen and I consider breakfast, and then ruefully laugh that idea off. Besides, I've run out of time. I fill a bottle with tap water.

Molly isn't too happy to come back inside, but she does. I pat her on the head, tell her how sorry I am, that I'm such a lousy fella, and make a mental note to take her for a long walk tonight, no matter how awful I feel.

People go on about the quality of light in Brisbane. Whatever it is, there is far too much of it today. My sunglasses only cut it down by the barest fraction; the migraine ignites again. If I had a better excuse there's no way I'd be going in today. But I don't. I still have all my limbs, and I'm not dead.

Now, Derek and I have our differences, but there's one thing I'm sure we'd both agree on: if I don't make it to the office, I'm gone for sure. I look at my watch. 9:30.

Half an hour's cutting it fine, but I manage to catch the next train. It's crowded for this time on a Wednesday morning. Someone's mp3 is up so loud that we're all getting a dose of Queen's "We Will Rock You." That pounding rhythm is pretty much in time with my headache. I glare at the culprit but he isn't looking in my direction.

Derek's been hunting for a reason to fire me for a while now, and I've never been a favorite of the other states' administrators either. I do tend to get into a bit of trouble. I can't help it if people don't get my sense of humor. Really, how can that be my fault?

The only thing that has kept me in the job is that I'm good at it, and that Morrigan likes me. Morrigan's influence as Ankou can't be denied. Mr. D's close working relationship with Morrigan tends to piss off the state admins mightily—and Derek cops that because Morrigan is a person you don't want to cross. All of which pleases me no end, because Morrigan is virtually family.

Morrigan and Dad rose through the ranks together. Dad, a traditionalist; Morrigan, an innovator. Dad coordinates the cross-state linkages, pomps, and helps oversee Mortmax's non-death-related industries—the various holdings in supermarkets, petrol stations and other businesses. He used to run the scheduling too, but a couple of years ago the side businesses expanded to such a degree that he had to let that slide. Morrigan had been pushing to stop him pomping as well but Dad prefers to keep his hand in.

I'd like to think that I could have taken over the scheduling. But a desk job's dull. Derek, on the other hand, loves it. Too bad he's doing such a miserable job.

I glance at my watch. It's going to be close. Not showing up for a meeting is the fastest route to unemployment. Punctuality, under all manner of stress and duress, is an absolute necessity in the pomping trade. A hangover doesn't even begin to cut it as an excuse.

I'm pretty sure I can make it, even riding what seems to be the slowest train in existence, but whether or not I can avoid spewing over Derek's desk is another matter. But it would be a pathetic vomit at best: the last thing I ate was that Chiko Roll.

Anyway, getting into work is going to furnish me with some answers. There's just been too much weirdness in the last couple of days. Too many things are unsettling me. If I wasn't so miserable, they'd be unsettling me even more.

I get off at Roma Street Station, ride the escalator up and out onto George Street, taking small sips of unsatisfying water as I go.

I don't notice anything is wrong until I touch the front door to Number Four.

I push, and the door doesn't give. So I push harder.

Nothing but my knuckles cracking. The door doesn't even draw its usual drop of blood. That's the way it is with Pomps. You need blood to close certain doors, and blood to open them. But not today.

Number Four is locked up tight and toothless.

My first thought is that this is Derek, that he's getting his revenge. Except the two wide glass windows either side of the door are dark. Not only that, but the brace symbol above the door has been removed. That symbol, an upside down triangle split through the middle with a not quite straight vertical line, keeps away Stirrers. It has to be refreshed every month or so, redrawn with ink mixed with a living Pomp's blood. Now it's gone, and that's crazy.

The door should have opened. The lights should be on inside. But they're not. I peer through the window to the left of the door, or try to. It's totally dark beyond. My reflection stares back at me.

I touch the door again. There should be a buzz, a sort of hum running through me on contact, but there's nothing, no sense at all that this is a point of interface between the living world and the dead one. It's just a door. A locked metal door. I glance around, there's no one I know standing around ready to tell me this is all some sort of joke.

The door leads into the vestibule of the building. There's a desk at the front. Some chairs, a couple of prints, including Mr. D's favorite painting, Brueghel's "Triumph of Death." Beyond the desk is a hallway leading to old-fashioned elevator doors, lots of brass, glass and art nouveau designs. The elevator has twelve floors marked, but our building only has eight storeys here. The other four are in the Underworld. That linkage between the living world and the dead should have me buzzing. Hell, standing this close to Number Four should have *anyone* buzzing.

It's the reason we don't get a lot of hawkers.

I reach toward the door again, then hesitate. Because in that moment it…changes. The door suddenly possesses a sly but hungry patience: as though it's waiting for me to touch it this time. *Just put your hand up against me, eh.*

Instead, I press my face against the window to the right. Again, nothing but darkness. The hair rises on the back of my neck. Then something slams against the glass.

I get a brief sensation of eyes regarding me, and of blood. A soul screams through me. It passes, as though thrown, so fast that I don't even get a sense of who it is I've just pomped. I stumble back from the window. They may have moved fast, but they'd been holding on. Their passage a friction burn, I'm seared a little on the inside.

I don't tend to get the violent deaths but I've pomped enough to recognize one. Someone has just died, savagely and suddenly. Someone I know. Maybe Tanya behind the desk, or Clive from records. Brett was always down there, too—had a thing for Tanya. "Jesus."

And then there's another one. The second death is so quick on the back of the first that I moan with the fiery biting pain of it, then retch a little. Another violent exit, another desperate but futile clawing at survival.

"Get out of here, Steven." The voice is familiar.

My mouth moves, but nothing comes for a moment. I turn toward Lissa, fight my almost instinctive desire to pomp her. At least that would be normal. But the urge passes in a wave of relief. Here she is, at last. How can she do this to me, this rising excitement, even now? But she does.

"What?"

"You have to get to Central Station," she says, sliding around me, slipping out of hand's reach, then darting in to whisper. "You need to get as far away from here as possible."

I blink at her, expect her to disappear, but this time she doesn't. In fact she seems much more together than I have ever seen her—a layer of confusion has been sloughed away and replaced with a desperate clarity.

"Hurry. We don't have much time. Someone is killing Pomps." She smiles at that, then frowns, as though the first expression was inappropriate. "You're the first one I've managed to save. And I'm getting tired of repeating myself."

The door picks that moment to open. Just a crack. A cold wind blows through it, and it's not the usual breath of air conditioning. From within comes the distant rasping of the One Tree, the Moreton Bay fig that overhangs the Underworld. That sound, a great sighing of vast wooden limbs, dominates the office. Hearing it echo out here in the street is disturbing. Christ, it terrifies me. It's as though Hell has sidled up next to the living world and has pulled out a bloody knife. I hesitate a moment. I know I should be running but those two pomps in quick succession have scattered my thoughts. And this is meant to be a place of refuge. There's a gravity to that doorway, borne of habit and expectation.

Lissa swings in front of me. "Don't," she says. "You go through that door and you're dead."

And I know she's right. It's like a switch finally turns off in my brain.

I sprint from the doorway, glancing back only when I'm at the lights (fighting the urge to just run out into the traffic, but there's too much of it and it's moving too swiftly) to see if anyone, or any thing, has come through the door after me. I get the prickling feeling that someone's watching me.

I blink, and the door's shut again, and that sensation of scrutiny is gone. I take a deep breath.

"Roma Street Station's better," I say, trying to keep focused, even as my head throbs. This really is a bitch of a hangover.

"What?"

"Central's too obvious. If I was looking for someone trying to get out of the city I'd go to Central."

Lissa appears to consider this. "You're probably right."

I know I'm right. Well, I hope I am. I need to have some semblance of control, or I am going to lose it right here in the middle of the city.

We're on George Street, heading to Roma Street and the train station, stumbling through late-morning crowds: all the business and government types up this end of the city, heading out for their coffees, oblivious to what's going on. People are being killed. My people. It can't be happening. Part of me refuses to believe it, even now, but those violent, painful pomps tell me otherwise.

I could feel resentful, but that's going to serve no useful purpose. The further I get away from Number Four though, the better.

To the left are the council chambers, reaching up into the sky, looking like a Lego tower of Babel constructed by a not particularly talented giant infant who none the less had *big* ideas. Just to my right is Queen Street Mall where, only yesterday, I was running for my life. Who'd have thought it would become something of a habit? Behind me, the state government building looms shabbily, a testament to, or rather an indictment of, eighties' architecture.

Tim works in that building.

"Where are you going?"

I turn around heading toward Tim's building, hardly realizing I'm doing it.

Lissa's in my face, hands waving, sliding backward to keep out of my reach. "Are you stupid? This is the wrong way."

I stop and stare at Lissa. How do I even know I can trust her? But there's something there, surely. Something in her gaze that tells me I can.

"No, it isn't."

"I don't want you to die."

"I know," I snap. "That much I get." And I don't want to die either, not with her around.

Her face creases with irritation. "You're making the concept easier for me, though." She slides to my right. Turns her back on me. I'm almost relieved; the fire in that gaze would consume me. She passes into a patch of light and is almost completely devoured by it. But then she's out and staring at me.

"Well? Aren't you going to keep moving?"

We cross George Street, pass the stately sandstone edifice of the Treasury Casino. The street's not as crowded on this side, away from the shops. There are a few buses coming and going and people are heading toward the government building, or office towers; suits and skirts of the power variety. The Riverside Expressway is a block away, and a cool breeze blowing up from the river carries all that traffic noise toward me. Traffic, not the creaking of the One Tree.

I get to the glass doors which front the government building and stop. A couple of blocks down, the door to Number Four is waiting. My skin crawls—that sense of being watched again. Still, I hesitate. I reach into my pocket, pull out my phone.

No, I can't draw him into this. Not yet. I put the phone away.

I have to figure this out. On my own, or with the help of my kind. This isn't Tim's problem, he's a Black Sheep—government liaison or not—and my best friend, and there's no way I'm going to drag him into whatever this is. He made his choice not to be involved in the business years ago, and I'm going to honor that. Besides, I doubt there is anything he can do.

I turn around, walk back down the street in the direction of Roma Street Station, keeping to as much cover as I can. Lissa's presence makes me stand out in a crowd—to those who know how to look, anyway.

I think about that damn disconcerting door, and whoever it was I pomped. The pomps had been too fast for a visual, but the souls seemed familiar somehow. Perhaps Morrigan, or Derek? I can't imagine either of them dead.

The day's warm but I'm shivering in my suit.

Lissa looks at me. "It's going to be all right. Take some deep breaths. Try and calm yourself down, Steven."

"You really think this is going to be all right?" I growl. She looks away. "How the fuck is this going to end well?"

"You have to believe it will, or you might as well just sit down now, and do nothing. Wait for whoever it is to find you, if you want. Let me tell you now, they won't be gentle."

"I'll get home, and we can sort this out."

"No," she shakes her head stridently, "you don't want to go home. They'll be there. I went home, and it was the last mistake I made. I can't tell you how angry it makes me, to have died this way."

I look at her more closely; she's starting to fade a little. I need to bring her back. "Why didn't you tell me that you were a Pomp, Lissa? I found you on Facebook last night."

"I'm surprised it took you that long," she says.

"Well, what with the shooting, and the running, and your appearing and disappearing...I'm a Pomp, not a detective. And then I had a lot to drink." The hangover's circling again and, in the busy street, everything's starting to tilt into the surreal. Lissa gives me a look that could pass as sympathetic but for the edge to it. Her gaze holds me and, stupid as it is here and now, I'm thinking how beautiful she is. My kind of beautiful—and I'd never really been aware that I'd had a kind of beautiful before I met her. Why now?

"I'm sorry," she says, "but death is...confusing. Painful, scary, everything moves so fast. I was shifting from Pomp to Pomp. With the first one I was fine, not that it helped him—knife to the back, horrible. But by the time I got you—and I wasn't controlling who I ended up with—I was rather...scattered."

"But how did you shift from Pomp to Pomp in the first place? That's not possible is it?"

"Look, I was desperate, and dead, Steven. Who knows what's possible?"

"How long has this been going on?"

"I know about as much as you. Two days at least. You saw me those first times. I was confused. You grounded me." She swings her face close to mine. I could just…I mean I want to…Those lips. There's a charge shooting up my spine. An ache I thought I'd never feel again.

Enough.

"That's my job. You know how it is," I say, and step away. She doesn't. How could she? Lissa is so far out of my league. I'm actually feeling a little lousy about not recognizing her from the start, because I *did* know her. Not personally, but enough that I realize that I recognize her. There aren't that many Pomps working in Australia. "You work in Melbourne."

"Um, I *used* to work in Melbourne," she says slowly. "No one does, now. They're all dead. There's a whole Night of the Long Knives thing going on."

I must be looking at her blankly because she slows it down even more. "You know, the Night of the Long Knives? Hitler gets an out-with-the-old-and-in-with-the-new attitude and kills his Brownshirts' leaders—"

I clear my throat. "I know about Nazis. I've got the History Channel, watch it all the time. You think this is an inside job? It doesn't make any sense."

Lissa regards me with those striking green eyes of hers, and I'm feeling stupid. "Think about it, Steven."

How can I think about anything when she's looking at me that way?

"Anything else doesn't make sense," she says. "Who-ever's doing this has to understand our communication system, our computers. We don't outsource any of that."

We stop at the corner of George and Ann, waiting for the lights to change. Big trucks and maxi-taxis roar by, dragging curtains of dust and diesel fumes. I don't hear the phone, just feel it vibrating in my pocket. Number Four, the LCD says. I show it to Lissa. She looks from the little screen to me, and back again.

"You better answer it."

I don't know what I'm going to hear, don't know if I want to hear it. I lift the phone to my ear. "Yes?"

"Steven?"

Finally, someone I know. "Morrigan, thank Christ." In the background, above Morrigan's voice, the One Tree creaks. Morrigan is definitely in Number Four.

Words pour out of me. "I tried to get into work. The door was locked, wouldn't shift, and then the door was something else." I sound like a child, reporting to their head teacher. Lissa watches me and my face burns, though there's no judgment in her expression.

"It's lockdown in here," Morrigan says. "Only we haven't done the locking. I don't know who it is. There's three of them. Stirrers from the feel of it, but not like any I've encountered before. For one, they're using weapons. They've not yet made it into the main offices. You're lucky you couldn't get inside, believe me. Everyone in the vesti-bule is dead."

"Do you want me to come back?" Something shatters. A gun fires. Even down the phone the sounds have me flinching.

"No, that would be . . . unwise." Morrigan's voice lowers

to a whisper. "We're holed up here. I'm trying to get some word out. Just keep away. Derek's here. If we can keep them out of the main office, I can still keep track of people."

I hesitate. "I'm not far away . . . I could—"

"You'll do no such thing," he snaps. "You keep away, Steven. Keep moving. You did good running. They'd have just gotten you too. We're losing Pomps."

"I know, Lissa told me."

He's silent for a moment. Then, "Lissa—Lissa Jones is with you?"

"Not exactly."

"Oh." I can hear the sadness in his voice. Morrigan knows everyone. He may be based in Brisbane, but he has a lot of influence in the other states, too. You don't get to the top without knowing the people beneath you. "You listen to her, Steven. This is worse than I thought. If Lissa's gone, Melbourne's gone, too, probably Sydney as well. She'll help you. I need you to stay out of this. Tell her, I'm sorry."

"Maybe Tim—"

"No, keep him out of it. The last thing we want is the government involved. If they trample over this the whole country's going to circle the drain. He's your cousin, Steven, but he's not one of us. He made his decision."

"OK, no Tim."

"Good lad. Steven, I should have seen it coming."

"Seen what?"

"I'd found references in some books, though I never believed—"

The phone dies, there's nothing down the end. I smack it with the palm of my hand.

"That's not going to do anything," Lissa says.

"Makes me feel better." I jut out my lower lip, and scowl. Just how petulant can I be? My face reddens again but Lissa's ignoring the show, considering the problem like I should be. After all, I'm the living one here.

"Is there some drift?" she asks.

I shake my head. "No, the signal's strong." I show her the phone. "The under and upper worlds are in sync. They're almost rubbing up against each other."

"Maybe that's why all this is happening. All this death. All these murdered Pomps."

"It's not murder," I say. "It's assassination."

And then I have a terrible thought.

Something so obvious that the realization hits me hard and cold.

"Gotta call Mom and Dad."

"Too late, Steve," says a voice at my ear.

It's Dad, and Mom is with him.

"Been too late for at least half an hour," he says.

6

This is the moment I've dreaded all my life. I'd always imagined it differently. But here it is, as it is for civilians: unexpected, sudden and utterly terrible.

Dad's in his usual attire—pants, and a light tan sports jacket. All of it crumpled. He's even wearing his favorite fedora, hiding his thinning hair. Pomps are well dressed in the main. Most of the time we're in a suit, black, of course; comes from going to so many funerals. But Dad could get away with wearing a pink Hawaiian shirt to a funeral. Charisma, I guess. He dresses sloppy, but it's charming sloppy. I've never really understood it but people tell me it's there. Everybody loves my dad.

"It's not your fault, Steve," Dad says. His face is lined, but those lines were drawn by smiles. It's a generous face, though he's already losing that—the emotions are slipping away to the One Tree. He frowns. "Did you have a big night last night? You sounded like it on the phone."

I shrug: avoid eye contact. Standard guilty son response. "I may have...indulged." Parents, even dead ones, know how to push the right buttons.

"Look at me, boy. That's better. Son of mine, I worry about you." And he does, it's in his face, even if it is fading. It shames me a little.

I want to hold him. I want to hold Mom. But I can't. The moment I do, they will go. "Dad...What happened? How?"

He coughs. The spirit clings to these old habits. "It was fast, didn't even suspect, until it was over. We hadn't even finished breakfast. Just don't go over to our place. Promise me that."

I nod my head, feeling sick to the stomach.

"Same happened to me," Lissa says, and Dad turns toward her.

"This is Lissa," I say.

"Ah, Melbourne isn't it? The Joneses?" Dad asks, and then he catches me looking at him. "Never forget a face."

"Particularly a young woman's," Mom says. She's as I remember her, in a sensible woolen jumper and pants, both mauve, both as neat as Dad's are crumpled. She's wearing (technically projecting) her favorite brooch: a piece of Wedgwood. There's a clarity and a calmness about her that she'd never had in life. That's over for her now, only the One Tree waits. There's still enough life left, though, to bring up these age-old arguments.

Lissa turns a remarkable beetroot red.

"Now, that's not exactly fair," Dad says, hands raised placatingly. "The Joneses are an old pomping family. Hardly any Black Sheep, too, I might add."

"Not *that* old," Mom says. She looks at Lissa. "I was

very sorry about your loss last year. Both parents, and so quickly."

"It's all right," Lissa says. "We of all people know that."

"Still—"

"Leave off, Annie," Dad says. "She obviously doesn't want to talk about it."

"I'm trying to be compassionate here, and you start on this. You're just uncomfortable talking about your feelings. And look at what that did to your son."

"Please," I say wearily, though I really don't want an end to this. Mom and Dad can argue for as long as they want if it means I can still have them here. "This isn't the time or place."

But there's no time, and only one place for them, and we all know it.

"Sorry," Dad says.

Mom nods. "Yes, he's sorry."

Yet again, I'm waiting for the lights to change, on the corner of George and Ann Streets, the edge of the CBD. I can't move. Dead people who no one else can see, though their presence must be raising some hackles, surround me. I don't care. I don't want to share this space with anyone. There's a huge black dog barking madly across the road, its eyes firmly fixed on my posse and me. It strains on its leash, the dog's owner shaking her head with embarrassment, doing her best to stop it pulling her across the road.

The living are stepping around us as though I'm stinking of urine and praising some cruel deity at the top of my voice, a vengeful one, obviously.

The lights have changed a half-dozen times at least, but I'm not ready.

I'm dazed.

Various cousins and aunts and uncles, well their spirits at any rate, keep dropping by. Uncle Blake dressed in his golf clothes shocks me with how calm he is, dead or not. There's none of the bluster, the fire that made a lot of the de Selby Christmas parties so interesting. He just seems resigned. Aunty May grabs my arm, perhaps in shock at her death, and is pomped at once. There can't be that many Pomps left in Brisbane. The conversations are mainly like this.

"Steve, oh, they're—"

"Did you?"

"Boyo, be careful."

"Who's that? Oh—the Jones girl." (Am I the only one who doesn't know this girl and her family?)

"Love, be careful."

It's my younger cousins that hurt me the most. Too young, all of them. Too young. They sigh and moan as they pass through me.

My Aunt Gloria looks at me sadly. "Just call Tim, will you? Promise me that. Let him know that Blake and I love him and that we always will."

I think about what Morrigan told me. Maybe calling Tim isn't such a good idea. But I can't keep this from him. "He knows that already, Aunty G. He knows how much you love him."

She gives me a look—the family look—a mixture of stern disapproval and dismay that only someone who truly loves you is capable of, and that engenders a kind of cold, chemical, panicky reaction in my stomach.

"I'll call him. Once I sort this out." That last bit has become something of a refrain. But I don't think I'm ever going to sort this out. Then she pomps through me, and is gone.

The lights change but I hover on the corner. All of this is really starting to sink in. I'm in serious trouble, half the Pomps I know are dead, and most of those are family. Now my entire living family consists of poor Tim and an aunt in the UK.

"Are you all right?" I ask Mom, and she's looking at me with the eyes of a dead person. There's love there, but it's a love separated from life. I'm regretting that I haven't been around to see them outside of work in a while, and now I've promised to not see what is left.

She blinks, looks at Dad, then back at me. "It didn't hurt, if that's what you're asking."

"Absolutely," Dad says. "Whoever did it was a professional. Quick and painless."

Of course it hurt, but they're trying to spare me that. I try and respect their pretense and play along, but I can't. Quick death is always painful, always dislocating.

"Mom, I need to—"

"You don't *need* to know at all. You *want* to." Her voice hardens. "Steven, you know the deal, we all do. I'm not happy with this, but it's happened."

"But why? Why has it happened?"

"If either of us had any idea, we'd be telling you," Dad says. "But we don't. You're going to have to find out, and even that may not save you. I had no inkling of this in the office, and I thought I knew everything."

I think about the phones, the rise in Stirrers. Something had been coming. Maybe I'd even felt it before I first saw Lissa. It's easy to see that with hindsight. But that isn't going to help now. I will get to the bottom of this. If this is death most definite then I'm determined to understand it. I just—I just wish I felt a little more capable.

Mom and Dad smile at me. Part of me is missing them already, and another part of me is so damn mad that I could kill someone. But there's no one, or thing, I can direct my anger at. Not yet.

"We'll come with you for as long as we can," Dad says. "But..."

"I understand," I say, though I wish I didn't.

There's more dead coming through. Pomps and regular punters, drawn to me because the number of living Pomps is shrinking. I'm giddy with it and feeling sick at the same time. I've never had this many people to deal with.

Pomping hurts. Each pomp is like a spider web pulling through my flesh. The silk is fine, but every strand is crowded with tiny hooks that snag and drag until they're through. It's more of a discomfort than a hurt, but with enough of them things begin to ache. I'm raw with the souls I've pomped.

I've heard stories about the world wars, about the Pomps there, how it nearly killed them. So many dead rushing through. I lost a lot of great-uncles, most to the meat grinder of the front, but some to the job itself. I don't want that to be me.

The lights change. Time to get moving.

I'm moving down Roma Street, up and over the overpass, heading toward the Transit Centre, the underbelly of which is Roma Street Station.

"You know I love you," I say to my parents. I'd said it nearly a dozen times in the walk between Ann Street and the overpass. I knew I didn't have much time; they couldn't stay with me forever.

"Course we do," they say in unison, and like that, in the blinking of an eye, they're gone.

The last contact I get is their passage through me. Such a swift pomp. I'm never going to see them again. I try to hold on, to keep their souls with me, but there's nothing I can get a grip on. All it does is draw out the hurt.

The grief is almost paralysing when it hits.

I'm right out in the open, not yet at the escalators sinking down into the station. I stop and hunch over, because this is agony. I'm not numbed by their absence, I'm hurting. A coughing sob shudders through me. I'm going to lose it.

Just because I know what goes on in the afterlife doesn't mean I'm not missing my parents. I need time.

But there isn't any.

"Hey. Hey," Lissa says.

"You're still here?"

I look at her, and even that hurts me. She's beautiful, and I won't get a chance to talk to her in the flesh. My mourning tugs me this way and that. Have to slap myself. My cheek stings.

Doesn't help.

Lissa looks at me as though I am mad. There's pity in her expression as well, and that makes me more than a little angry: mostly with myself.

She isn't gone yet. I'm not quite alone.

I walk into the station.

"Hey!"

I spin on my heel, cringing. When's the bullet coming?

"Your ticket!" The guard at the gate frowns at me, looking through Lissa, though I know how uncomfortable that must make him. It doesn't help that she then swings a tight circle around him. His face twitches in synchrony with her movements. At any other time it would be amusing to watch.

"Yeah, right. Sorry." I dig my pass out of my wallet.

He takes it from me. Nods. "Next time think about what you're doing." He pushes it back into my hand.

I nod, too, smile stupidly, and walk through the gate into the underpass that leads to the platforms.

"You have to be more careful than that," Lissa says. "You have to stay focused. Something like that may get you killed."

"I'm doing the best I can."

She's clearly not happy with my answer. But it's all I've got.

I know where I have to go. The only place that I might possibly find some answers.

It might also kill me. That's on the cards anyway. In fact, I imagine that's where this will all end up. I'm a Pomp after all. Death is what it's all about. Death is what it's always about.

So I keep moving.

Are you sure this is a good idea? I mean the Hill…"

I'm sitting in the train heading west along the Ipswich line, out of the city, my forehead resting against the cold glass of the window. People sniffle and cough all around me. The carriage is heavy with the odors of sickness: sweat and menthol throat lollies duke it out. It's flu season all right, I can feel something coming on myself—or maybe it's the last remnants of the hangover, combined with the ache of all those pomps.

I pat my suit jacket. "At least I'm dressed for a cemetery. Do you have any better suggestions?"

Lissa shrugs. I know she wishes that she did. So do I.

"The Hill's the only place I might get some answers," I say. Problem is, the answers I'm after are just as likely to kill me as save me.

I try Tim's work number. Can't get through. His mobile switches straight to voicemail.

How do I tell him? I need to warn him. I need to tell

him that his mother and father are dead. His voicemail spiel ends and I'm silent after the beep, working my mouth, trying to find words.

Nothing comes. The silence stretches on. Finally: "Tim, I don't know what you know. But I'm in trouble, you too, maybe. You have to be careful. Shit, maybe you already know all this. Call me when you can."

I hang up.

Lissa stomps up and down the aisle. People shudder with her passage, burying themselves in their reading matter or turning up their mp3s. She's oblivious to it, or maybe she is taking a deep pleasure in the other passengers' discomfort, the dreadful chill of death sliding past life. I don't know. Our carriage is emptying out fast, though. I find her movement hypnotic. Her presence is tenuous and vital all at once. I've never seen a dead person like this. Nor a live one, if I'm honest.

She catches me looking at her. The grin she offers is a heat rushing through me. My cheeks burn and for a moment my mind isn't centered on life or death. I'd thank her for that, if this was going anywhere but Hell.

I've fallen in love with someone I cannot have. Someone who isn't really a someone anymore. How bloody typical. But even this misery is better than the ones that crowd around me, grim and cruel, on that train. At least it's bittersweet rather than just bitter.

The train rolls into Auchenflower. The Hill's presence is already a persistent tingle in my lips like the premonition of a cold sore. Every place has a Hill, where the land of the living and the dead intersect. In Brisbane it's Toowong Cemetery. I know the place well. Used to picnic there with the family. Lost my virginity on its grassy slopes when I was seventeen. Mary Gallagher. Didn't last. None of my relationships ever had. I'm thinking of Mary as the train stops at the station. I don't even know what happened to her. Married, I think, maybe has a couple of kids. Robyn was just the last in a long list of failures.

I get off the train, Lissa with me, and I'm sure everyone in the carriage behind me breathes a sigh of relief. The train pulls away, leaving a few people on the platform. All of them walk in the opposite direction to me. I'd find it funny, but the nearby Wesley Hospital distracts me. My perception shifts. There's an odor as unsavory as an open sewer coming from there. Something's going on in the hospital's morgue.

Lissa drifts that way. Face furrowed.

"You sense it too?"

"It's not good." She coughs as though clearing her throat. "Something smells well and truly rotten, wouldn't you say?"

"Stirrers, I think." I wonder if they're like the ones Morrigan described, different.

"Nothing you can do about that now."

Yes, but I don't like it. The air around there is bad and a kind of miasmal disquiet has settled into the building's foundations: an unliving and spreading rot. *Someone hasn't been doing their job*, I think. *Who's left to do it? Who's going to sort this kind of stuff out?* These things can get quickly out of control and then you're rushing toward a full-blown Regional Apocalypse. Think Stirrers and death in abundance. Civilizations tend to topple in the wake of them.

I try not to think about it. Lissa's right, there's no time. I head in the opposite direction; take the underpass beneath the station and away from the hospital. If I get a chance I'll come back. I push the hospital to the back of my mind, where it settles uneasily. Nothing good can come of this day.

My head is pounding again. Then a caffeine craving hits me all at once. It's a deep, soul-gnawing pit in my stomach. I'm tempted to swing into Toowong, casually order a coffee—a nice long black—and sit on the corner of High Street and Sherwood Road and watch the bus drivers try and hit pedestrians; tempted till it's a throbbing ache. Now, I'm hurting. The last time I remember talking to my living, breathing mom was over coffee. Both of us had been real busy, like I said—flu season.

We keep moving through inner-city suburbia, up and down the undulating landscape of Brisbane, swapping the disquiet of the hospital for the jittering energy of the Hill. We reach Toowong Cemetery in pretty good time, though I have to catch my breath. Squat, fat Mount Coot-tha rises up before us like the great dorsal fin of a whale. My eyes burn as though there is suddenly too much fluid within them. Something else is straining to inhabit my vision.

This close to the Hill, Pomps get flashes of the Underworld. I can hear the great tree creaking. I can even see it. This is why Mount Coot-tha and the cemetery were once called One Tree Hill. For a moment this other view stops me—the tree, a Moreton Bay fig, is spectacular, all sky-swallowing limbs and vast root buttresses. Then Mount Coot-tha's silhouette returns, marked only by blinking rows of transmission towers.

A traffic chopper is flying low over the Western Freeway like some predatory bird hunting snarls and head-ons. As we climb the undulations that lead to the hill there's a hint of the city to the east, gleaming red in the afternoon sun. We're out in the 'burbs, the beginning of a vast carpet of houses that stretches almost to the granite belt in the west. Hundreds of thousands of homes. But here, it's old city, Brisbane's CBD isn't too far away. It's close to sunset and I'm still not sure what it is I'm doing. I circle around the base of the Hill, keeping clear of the open areas, and staying as close as I can to the trees amongst the tombstones. The Hill has multiple nodes: connection points with Number Four. The Mayne crypt is one, but that's too obvious, with its ostentatious white spire and curlicues, and it's big and toward the top of the Hill—we'd be too easy to spot. I'm heading to a quieter node, near the place Tim and I used to sneak off to, to smoke.

"Listen," Lissa says. She spins around me, gesturing at the lengthening shadows. I'd almost forgotten she was there. We haven't said a word since we edged into the cemetery. "I'm serious, listen."

"I'm listening," I say.

She shakes her head. "Not to me. To this, the cemetery."

And then I'm *really* listening. I've never known a place to be so quiet. Where are the crows? Where are the chattering, noisy myna birds? There's not a sound, not an insect clicking or buzzing. Even my footsteps in the dry grass seem muted.

"Maybe this wasn't such a good idea," Lissa says, right into my left ear.

I jump. "I never said it was a good idea, but it's the only one we have."

"The only one that *you* have."

"What's your idea?"

"Head for the hills, not the Hill."

"I promise, I'm being careful."

"Is that what you call it?" She darts away from me. Runs up the hill and back again. In this light, she's a blue-stained smear of movement. She's back by my side in a breath.

"Didn't even break a sweat," she says.

"See anything?"

"Nothing. But that doesn't mean they're not closing in."

"You're making me paranoid."

She swings her face close to mine, her eyes wide. "Good."

I find the right tombstone halfway up the hill, a David Milde, RIP 1896. It's been a while since I've done this, but the spot recognizes me. The stone shudders, becomes something more than a mere memorial.

"Watch yourself," Lissa says.

I glance at her. This close to a node, her form is losing some of its clarity. "Maybe you should too."

She raises a hand toward her face. "Oh."

The node would take her to the Underworld, if it could. But I'm in control here. I wait until Lissa steps back, and then I reach over and settle my fingers on the rough stone, wincing at the electric shock that strikes my fingers on contact. My teeth clamp shut, and I taste blood.

The cemetery is gone. I'm in Number Four. And it's not pleasant.

The air is alive with exclamations: bullet hard. The last thoughts of the dying, before the mind and body scatter.

There are other Pomps here. Not just Morrigan and Derek.

The first thing I feel are their deaths.

Each one smacks against me, and I try to hold onto them, and work through these errant memories. But it's no good. There's nothing there. Nothing of use anyway, merely pain, the unsuspecting howls of the executed. Jesus, I've been lucky to get even this far. For a moment I envy those gone, that it's over for them, that they're not left flailing in the dark. I concentrate, move through the muddy haze of dying minds and then: There are upturned desks, reams of paper scattered around them like the shattered stones of a stormed castle. Mainframes have toppled. And there's blood, every-fucking-where. My heart's doing 160 BPM easy. I almost drop out of the node then.

There's a man bent over, hacking up blood onto his yellow tie. He's wheezing, "Fuck. Fuck. This is. Oh—"

Blood crashes in my vision as a bullet makes a crater in his chest. He lifts his head, and there's a moment of recognition, just a moment. The bastard even manages a scowl.

"Derek," I say. Poor old officious Derek.

But he's dead; he falls almost gracefully onto the floor. There are no answers here. I have to get out.

Then a head peers over the desk. Morrigan looks over at me, his eyes wide with terror. "Steven, what on earth?"

"I needed to find out what was happening," I mumble.

"Jesus, Steven, get away from the Hill!"

"Who's doing this? Can I—"

"There's nothing you can do. We're being slaughtered. They hit us hard, more people than we first thought, and at the same time as I called you." He pats his arm, there's a bloody wound there. Shrapnel scars his cheek. "Steven, you need to get moving. Get away from the Hill and keep away from Number Four."

"I need to get moving? What about you? I can get you out."

Morrigan scowls at me, the facial equivalent of the stone you'd throw at Lassie to get her to run away.

"There's a Schism—maybe one of the other regions, wanting to muscle into our space. I don't know, but they're good." He fires a pistol over his desk. Someone fires back; woodchips explode from the table he's hiding behind. "I can't get to Mr. D. He's closed himself off. Don't trust anyone, Steven. Leave your phone on. I'll call you if I can."

Still, I hesitate.

"Steven, you will go *now*! GO!"

I break contact with the tombstone and reality whoomphs around me. I shake my stinging fingers, my heart pounding in my chest, blood streaming from my nose. Everything's moving too quickly. I drop to my haunches, gulp in air, try and slow my breathing down.

"Steven? Steven?" Lissa's voice pulls me out of it. I blink and look up at her.

"We have to get out of here," I say. "Number Four's gone, or soon will be. Morrigan's wounded. He told me to run, that he'd try to get in touch with me. I can't see him making it. Lissa, there was blood everywhere." I peer around the tombstone, careful not to touch it again. There's nothing, just Lissa and her ghost light. "Morrigan thinks it might be one of the other regions trying to take over."

Lissa glares at the tombstone, as though this was its idea. "That's unheard of. Why would anyone want to shut a region down, Steven? Because that's essentially what a take-over would do. Regional Managers can be ruthless, but that would be stupid, it's too much extra work for no gain. And what about the Stirrers?"

"Maybe something's changed. Maybe the Stirrers are just taking advantage of the whole thing."

"No, things don't change that much. You don't understand the system at all if you think otherwise. There's no advantage to a Regional Manager if they take another region. And then there's the increased Stirrer activity. That's been happening for weeks. They're in on it, somehow. Mr. D would know."

I shake my head. "Morrigan's been trying hard to contact him. No luck. Maybe he's in the dark as much as we are."

"Now you're scaring me," Lissa says.

"I'm scaring both of us. We have to get out of here."

Lissa nods.

"And quietly," I say.

"I'm dead." Lissa gives me a dark look. "I can't make any noise."

"I was just trying to remind myself."

We're as silent as a pair of ghosts as we come down the hill. Easy enough, I suppose, when half of the couple is a ghost. And we're moving pretty quickly, which is why I almost stumble upon them, and why they don't see me.

And this is the first time my fear turns to something else. *No fucking way!*

My parents are weaving around the tombstones ahead.

Not my parents, just their flesh. They're not moving like Mom and Dad, and that's the oddest part of seeing them. Mom and Dad, *my* mom and dad, but they're all wrong. The creatures that inhabit them haven't got the hang of the real estate yet. Dad holds a rifle, Mom is speaking into a phone.

"Stirrers," Lissa says and I roll my eyes at her. Of course they're Stirrers—zombies, I suppose, in the common vernacular. The second part of our jobs as Pomps, the things we're supposed to stop stirring. These aren't your "Grr, brains" zombies. Nah, that shit doesn't happen. These are more perambulatory vessels. My parents aren't infected or blood crazy; Stirrers inhabit them.

It's the only way that Stirrers can exist in our world. They were long ago banished from the land of the living, but they want back in any way they can. I've heard that if they tip the balance—inhabit enough bodies, get more than a toehold—they might just be able to return in their real form, whatever that is. If that ever happens, we're all screwed.

These aren't my parents. They're just the place of death. My parents have gone over into the Underworld.

I'm taking it pretty well. My blood is only partially boiling, I'm only clenching my fists until they hurt, not until they draw blood. I groan as another soul passes through me, another Pomp. Real pain. Someone is hurling souls at me.

Normally we're directed to a specific location to physically sight and sometimes touch a spirit. But now, maybe because there are so few Pomps left, or because most of the dead today have been Pomps, they're actually hitting me wherever I am. These are really violent deaths, and they're coming hard and fast.

Those spider webs are starting to grow more hooks. It's like having a cold, and a constant need to blow your nose—at the start the tissues are soft, but by the end they're more like razors wrapped in sandpaper—except that the razor burn runs through my whole body.

On top of that I can now sense the Stirrers. And if I can feel them...

"Shit," Lissa says.

I do a double-take. I look at Lissa—and then to Lissa. "That's—"

"Somebody has to pay for this." She covers her face with her hands, but the rage and the hurt radiates from her.

Stirrer Lissa strides down the hill, away from the tall white spire of the Mayne crypt, talking on a phone. And she's walking toward me.

"The Hill is compromised," I say at last.

"No shit, Sherlock," Lissa says, and I'm already backing away. There's a distant clattering sound, like someone hurling ball bearings at a concrete wall.

Great, we're being shot at. It's my dad with that rifle. He fires again. I wait for the bullet to hit me, but it doesn't come. His aim is out, still not used to the body, I suppose. A tombstone a few meters away cracks, exhaling shards of dirty stone.

"Run," Lissa yells, and once again, I'm sprinting.

8

Two blocks away from the cemetery, after a dash through suburbia—streets filled with jacarandas dripping with blooms, and with enough cars parked on the road that we have some cover—we come across a bus shelter.

Miracle of miracles! There's a bus pulling in, on its way toward the city, but I don't care where it's going, I just need to be heading somewhere that isn't here. I'm on it. It's the first time in my life that a bus is exactly where and when I want it. With what little sense of mind I have left, I realize I still have my pass and I flash it at the driver. He looks at it disinterestedly, and then I'm walking to the back of the bus, past passengers all of whom assiduously avoid eye contact. Ah, the commuter eye-shuffle. I must look a little crazy. I certainly feel it.

I'm breathing heavily. Sweat slicks my back, and is soaking through my jacket. It's only the middle of spring but the air's still and hot. For the first time in about an hour I'm aware of my body, and it's telling me I'm tired, and hung-over. The adrenaline's not potent enough to keep that from me forever. Sadly, I feel like I could do with a beer.

Lissa looks as fresh as the first time I saw her, if you discount the bluish pallor. You're never fitter than when you're dead.

Finally we've time to talk with no rifles firing.

"So why are you back there? And how?" I ask beneath my breath, but it still comes out too loud. People turn and watch.

"That's not me!" Lissa is furious, and I can understand. I wouldn't want someone wandering around in my body, either. But I'm also wondering why she's so worried. Worry's a living reaction; it's not like she needs that body. She is acting most unlike a dead person, but then she has from the start. "That's not me," she says again. "Don't you *dare* think of that as me."

I raise my hands. We're tripping up on semantics here. "Your *body*...Why was your *body* back there?"

Lissa looks out the window. "I—I don't know. Whoever's doing this is using Number Four and shipping Stirrer-possessed Pomps around via the upper offices. And they're using my body. Shit, shit, shit."

I really want to hold her and tell her that this is going to be OK, but I can't do either, because I really don't believe it, and the Lissa I might possibly be able to hold without pomping is behind us somewhere, and she would kill me without hesitation.

This relationship is complicated.

"The upper offices? Can you really do that?" I think about Number Four, and those labyrinthine upper floors.

"You can if you know what you're doing. It's dangerous if you're not an RM, but people do it from time to time—saves on airfares. I've heard that you can enter any one of Mortmax's offices through them. It's probably how the Stirrers got into the Brisbane office. They could have come from anywhere."

"We'll work this out," I say.

She glares at me. "How, Steve? Just how the hell are we going to work this out? I'm dead. My body's walking about the Hill, inhabited by a bloody Stirrer. It's not enough that I've been killed—whoever is doing this is rubbing my face in it. You were right, as much as I didn't like it, the Hill's the only place we had a chance of finding out what's going on."

"Which was exactly why it was being guarded," I say. "They knew we had to get there. And my parents were there, too. This isn't just about you."

Lissa shakes her head. "Who deals with Stirrers? It's freaking insane! You can't deal with Stirrers. They've nothing to offer but hatred and hunger."

Apparently someone has, and quite successfully. I don't understand it any better than Lissa does. The idea chills me and I'm even more afraid about this whole thing. But at least it explains why Jim McKean was shooting at me. I couldn't work out how I might have pissed him off. There are others with whom it almost wouldn't have surprised me (Derek being one of them) but Jim hadn't made any sense.

"We just need to keep moving," I say.

"No point in running." The voice startles me, coming from behind. It's all rather too pleased with itself. I jerk my head around.

There's a dead guy sitting on the rear seat. He looks at me, and then at Lissa. When he sees her the wind comes out of him. "Sorry, darl," he says, "they got me too, just out of Tenterfield."

That's it. I'm dead. I don't see how I stand a chance.

The guy with us is Eric "Flatty" Tremaine, state manager of the Melbourne office, which puts him almost as far up the ladder as Morrigan. He's a friend of Derek's—maybe his only friend—and another paid-up member of the Steven de Selby Hate Club.

I notice the way he's looking at Lissa, and the way that she's looking back. There's definitely a history there. I catch myself; I'm not going to survive this if all I'm really thinking about is Lissa and her previous relationships. But it does no good. Jealousy, wearing Eric Tremaine's smarmy face, has brought matches and it's lighting them up inside of me.

"So what's going on, Flatty?" I ask, and for the first time Eric seems truly aware of me, even though my presence must have drawn him here. He gives me a wide, almost manic grin, and slaps his knee.

"Steven de Selby. Wonderful, so you've managed to stay alive. I wouldn't have put money on it. You never really struck me as the sharpest knife in the drawer."

"Enough of that," Lissa says. "Play nice."

"Who's behind this?" I demand. I don't have time for point scoring, even if I am still hunting for some sort of witty comeback.

Eric shrugs. "I don't know. All I can say for sure is that they're very good at their jobs, and they know a lot about ours." He glances significantly at Lissa. "Why the fuck are you hanging with this loser?"

"You tried to call Mr. D?" I ask, ignoring the insult. After all, he *has* just died.

"Of course I have." Eric nodded. "Line was busy, which makes sense for a couple of reasons."

"Yeah, everybody would be trying to call," I say. Though, to be honest, I really hadn't thought of it. Thinking about Mom and Dad had been occupying my mind more—that, and the running. Besides, Mr. D is...difficult. I take a deep breath. "Maybe I should try him. Can't be too many Pomps left."

Tremaine makes an ineffectual grab at my arm—his hand passes through my flesh and he's nearly dragged through me with it. His face strains as he struggles to stay in this world, and part of me can't help laughing at such a basic mistake. I have to respect his strength of will, though, because he pushes against the pomp, his form solidifying.

"No! You don't want to do that!" he says, once he's managed to stabilize his soul. "I tried to call him just out of Tenterfield. The buggers got me there on the New England Highway. They're obviously using the phones to find us. Please don't tell me you've got yours on."

"Oh." The blood's draining from my face. I switch off my phone, and then slide it into my pocket.

Eric gives Lissa an "I told you so" look. His gaze, when it returns to me, is condescension stirred with pity. He doesn't expect me to live much longer, either.

"You're going to have to talk to Mr. D, but not now," he says. "I suspect he's out of the loop somewhat. He has to be, I can't believe that he'd let this happen."

"Someone has," Lissa says.

"Yes, and I have my theories, but they're just theories.

Steve, you're going to have to talk to him face to face. Draw him out of wherever he's hiding, or being held."

"You think he's being held?"

"He's hardly on a fishing trip now, is he?" Tremaine says archly. "He's too intimately connected to all of us. Every death must be filling him with pain and anger. For something like this to succeed you'd need to remove the RM as quickly as possible, before you start trying to kill Pomps. You know how Mr. D is. He knows when one of us dies, and he's always there. Let me tell you, he wasn't there for me. This has to be an inside job."

He lets that sink in.

"Then how am I going to be able to talk to him?"

"There are ways that can't be stopped. If you know what you're doing." He looks at me.

I take a deep breath. Maybe I should just pomp the prick. I'm a little threatened by the thought of one-on-one time with Mr. D. I've only ever met him a few times, and they were with my dad.

"Mr. D's not that bad, really," Lissa says, and I realize that she is almost touching my hand with her own. At the closest point her form is wavering. It must be uncomfortable for her, but she holds the position. I'm the one who pulls away in the end. Tremaine gives her a look, and I smile like the cat who got the cream.

"If you say so. I've just never had much to do with him."

"Regardless, you're going to—and soon," Tremaine says with all the nonchalance that a recently dead person can muster. "Maybe too soon." He points out the rear window.

There's my dad's body, driving his red Toyota Echo,

not too well, but well enough to be gaining on the bus. But this is the least of my worries because Mom's body is on the passenger side, and she's scowling in a most un-Mom like way and pointing a rifle at me.

"Shit!" I drop to the floor behind the seat as the rear window explodes.

9

There is a carpet of gleaming glass before me. I'm sure I'm breathing the smaller fragments of it into my lungs. It doesn't help that I'm almost hyperventilating. Another shot blasts a hole in the back seat next to my head. I'm feeling like a cartoon character. I know the double-take I give that burning hole, stuffing everywhere, must look almost comical. I'm surprised I haven't shat myself, but of course there's still plenty of time for that ...

The bus driver brakes: all that commutery tonnage comes crashing to a halt and we've got a whole domino effect, of which I'm painfully a part, passengers tumbling and screaming. Then the red Echo slams into the back of the bus. I'm thrown forward onto the broken glass from the window. It's safety glass, but those little beads still hurt when you fall on them.

Metal screams and I'm yelping as the back seat deforms inward. The rear side windows shatter. There's glass and seat stuffing everywhere.

The Echo's horn is droning in an endless cycle like a

wounded beast, and there's the sharp, stinging odor of fuel. I shake my head. I try to slow my crashing breaths. I want to rub my eyes, but there's no telling what I'd be grinding into them.

I reckon I've got about thirty seconds, maybe a minute, before they're out of that car. It's going to take much more than a collision with a bus to stop them. There's bits of glass in my hands but no deep cuts; it hurts like a bastard, though, which is actually a good thing since it distracts me from the headache regrouping in my skull.

"Are you all right?" Lissa asks.

"Can anyone in that bland suit be all right?" Tremaine says.

I'd be better if he shut up. I've never been a fan of Tremaine, but then again, he's never been much of a fan of me or my family, either. He sees us Queensland Pomps as a bunch of slackers and, sure, I may have gotten drunk at a couple of training sessions, but the guy's about as boring as they come.

"You and your taste." Lissa shakes her head.

Tremaine gives her a smug smile. "Darling, it *was* yours for a while."

"We all have to regret something, Eric."

I glance at these two—Lissa scowling and Eric giving her the sleaziest, most self-satisfied smile I've seen outside of a porno. Bastard. *Oh God, Lissa and Flatty Tremaine!*

I'm jealous: bloody burning with it. But there's no time for this. I scan the bus; people are slowly recovering from the shock of the collision. I was the only one who had a moment's warning, and I'm still as shaky as all hell. There's a few nosebleeds, but that seems to be the worst of it. I have to get out of here fast, or someone is going to die.

It may not be me, but it's sure as hell going to be my fault. I run for the front door of the bus.

"Have to get out," I say.

The driver's on the radio, calling it in. No one seems to know a rifle was involved. Everyone is shaken but not as disturbed as they should be. The driver waves at me irritably. "No, you're staying on the bus until I say so. Council policy."

Fair enough, but not today. I reach over, turn the release switch. The door sighs open.

He grabs my arm; I tug my arm free, and bolt for the exit.

"What? You! Get back—" I hear him slamming down on the switch.

I'm almost through and the door closes on my leg. It's a firm grip and I'm hanging, suspended by the door. I yank my leg like some sort of trapped and clumsy animal, and something gives because I'm dropping onto the road, the ground knocking the breath from me.

"Smooth," Tremaine says.

"Screw you," I manage, which is stupid because I shouldn't be wasting any of the breath in my lungs. Blobs dance in my vision.

"And ever so charming."

I give him the finger. Tremaine raises an eyebrow. Lissa's watching the bus.

"Get up," she says. "Get up, get up."

Winded, I lie there on the side of the road. Even with the adrenaline coursing through me that's about all I can manage. I stare blankly at the looming city with its skyline of genuflecting cranes. I'm on the verge of slipping into manic, gasping chuckles. The sky is lit up by the city, everything's calm...and I've been shot at—twice—by my parents.

"Get up," Lissa says. "Now."

At last, after what really can't have been more than a few seconds, breath finds my lungs.

"I'm trying." I get very unsteadily to my feet. Which is when the bus driver comes crashing through the door and tackles me.

I'm back down on the road. More cuts, more bruises.

"Get the fuck back in the bus!" he growls, his arms wrapped around my legs.

"No, I can't!" I scramble, kicking and twisting and flailing, to my feet.

We circle each other. He's taking this personally, his face beet-red, his hands clenched into fists. The driver is a big man. I'm not, just tall and thin. He also looks like he might practice some particularly nasty form of martial art that specializes in snapping tall, thin people in two.

"I don't want to have to fight you," I say, mainly because I don't want to have to fight him.

"Then get back in the bus." The way he says it suggests there's no gentle way of getting back into the bus.

He advances, his eyes wild, obviously in shock, or just extremely, extremely pissed off. I lunge to the right, then sprint around the side of the bus. He crashes after me, swearing at the top of his lungs. There's not much room to move—we're hemmed in by traffic, though none of it is moving that quickly, on account of the accident and the show we're putting on. We get around twice; I've got the edge on him, speed-wise, which is kind of meaningless because all I'm going to do is end up running into his back.

There are cars pulling up everywhere. Some industrious

and extremely helpful guy has stopped and is directing traffic, and there's a woman over at the crumpled, smoking Echo. She sees me and starts waving at me to come over, maybe to help. I yell at her to get away. Someone is moving in the car, and I suspect that someone is going to have the rifle. Every passing second improves his or her hand–eye coordination.

The bus driver's boots crunch on the gravel behind me. "Get back here, you prick!" the bus driver yells. I glance around to see how close he is. He catches a mouthful of smoke and bends over, coughing. The air is positively toxic. For a moment I worry that he might just drop dead. But at least he's not running after me anymore.

"This is all going so wonderfully," Tremaine says, startling me. I ignore him.

I pull my sunglasses over my eyes and sprint-sneak over to the helpful guy's car, a green hatchback. I feel like an absolute bastard. The keys are in the ignition, which is a relief. I start up the car, and shoot down Coro Drive, fishtailing around the bus, and nearly smash into oncoming traffic. I straighten the hatchback at the last minute, not knowing where in Christ I'm going.

In my rear-vision mirror the bus driver is roaring away at me between coughs, the helpful guy with him. He's not looking that helpful now, and I don't blame him. I feel awful, like I've mugged a nun.

"Was that wise?" Tremaine is grinning at me, now also in the rear view mirror. I've never seen a dead guy looking so full of himself.

"Shut the fuck up."

"It's so nice to see that you can keep your cool in a crisis."

Tremaine's lucky he's dead already. "Well, only one of us is still alive," I snarl.

Low blow, but true. Tremaine is a prick, and being cruel to him is the least of my crimes today.

"What the hell else was he supposed to do?" Lissa asks him.

They flit around each other in the back seat of the car, two aggressive and luminous blurs.

"Not breaking the law might have been a good beginning," Tremaine says prissily.

Yeah, I could have fled the scene on foot. Not having the police chasing me as well as Stirrers would have been a good idea. But the Stirrers would have caught up with me for sure. I needed to get out of there fast, even if that meant stealing the Good Samaritan's car. I glance back at Tremaine. "Next time we'll follow your plan. Which was... Hey, didn't we already ascertain that you were dead?"

"You're *deadest*." Tremaine clenches a fist in my face. "That's what you are. Which really doesn't surprise me, you bloody hick Queenslanders."

"Come a little closer, and I'll fucking pomp you, dead man."

"Oh, shut up," Lissa says. "Both of you shut up."

Four blocks later, and heading back into Paddington away from the city, I ditch the car (leaving whatever money I have on me in the glove box for the owner's trouble) hoping that there are no CCTV cameras around. There's nothing to connect me to it. I should be safe, particularly when I shave off my beard, which I am going to be doing very soon. Clean-shaven, I'll look like a different person; certainly not the kind of guy who would steal a car, anyway.

OK, so that's the story I'm running with, because I have to believe *something*.

I walk another four blocks looking for the right bus. I must be a sight: bloody hands, torn pants and edgy as all hell, glancing up and down the streets, ducking for cover at the slightest noise. Any second I expect a bullet to come driving into my brain or worse, into my back, driving me to the ground where I'll writhe like road-kill. If I'm going to be killed I want it to be as quick and pain-less as possible.

Finally, the bus I'm after is trundling down the street. Why does public transport travel at such glacial speeds when people are trying to kill you? I flag it to a stop, flash my pass and get on board. The driver barely gives me a second glance.

"Where are you going?" Lissa asks.

"My question exactly." Tremaine's voice drills into my skull.

"Home," I say, keeping my voice low and spinning toward the dead couple. "Is that all right with you two?"

Lissa slaps her forehead disdainfully, and looks at me like I'm an idiot. "Surely you wouldn't be so stupid as to—"

"Exactly. Surely I wouldn't be," I say. "There's a back way—well, it's actually someone's yard. They're not going to expect me to go home, anyway. They're going to expect me to go to Mr. D."

"He has a point," Tremaine says, which immediately makes me suspect my own logic. "Besides, you can bring Mr. D to you."

"I don't like it." Lissa frowns.

"Any more than you don't like being dead?" Tremaine

winks at me. He's certainly taking a bipartisan approach to pissing people off.

"Hey," I say. "That's below the belt."

Tremaine shakes his head, even manages a laugh. "Boy, you've got it bad."

Lissa is looking at me, with that mocking expression I'm getting to know so well. I feel about two inches tall. "He does, doesn't he?"

"Yes, he does, and he's not going to get far with that. And if he thinks so then he's as big an idiot as any of the Queensland crew."

"Stop talking about me as though I'm not here." I glare at Tremaine. "Just tell me how I bring Mr. D to me."

"All right, it's difficult, and location specific, but not . . . Oh—"

And then he's gone. But not smoothly. Eric struggles in a way that I've not encountered before. As though he's trying to take me, too. I grit my teeth, feel dizzy, shout, "Not yet, you bastard! Not yet."

Half the bus is staring at me, or trying to ignore me, but I can't afford to give that too much consideration. Finally he releases. I feel it as a sort of shocked sadness, as though he can't quite believe it. I have to admit, the man had stamina.

Lissa groans. I look over at her, she's getting hazy. Fading out.

Eric's passage through me must have opened the door a little, or left a sort of wake. It's threatening to take her, too.

"Keep your distance," I say, teeth clenched. I close my eyes and try to find some sort of center to the chaos of Eric's passing. It hurts to delve so deep into the process, like shoving your fingers in the guts of a machine while it's ticking over. I find something.

Yes. There's a calm space there. The door closes, the wake subsides. Now, that wasn't pleasant. Not one little bit.

I open my eyes a crack, Lissa's still here, looking more substantial than she did a moment ago. I'm beginning to wonder why she's sticking around. What exactly it is that's holding her here? She reaches toward me, and then pulls back at the last second.

It taxes her, or whatever it is that is left of her. My body is trying to draw Lissa in, and no matter how much I don't want it to, I can't switch it off. I don't even want to consider the effort it must be taking for her to resist the pomp. She grimaces and sits a seat away from me. The two nearest seats are empty.

"Your nose," she says. "It's bleeding."

I grab a tissue from my pants pocket and wipe my face. Blood, and plenty of it. "Shit. Eric even pomps roughly. You OK?"

Lissa nods. "I'm OK. I'll be joining him soon enough."

"Both of us," I say. "I've lost my one chance of getting in touch with Mr. D."

"Not at all. I know how to bring Mr. D to you," Lissa says. "It's not very pleasant, and will be rather painful."

Of course it will. Messing around with death offers that as a given.

"I need to go home first." And I do. Dangerous as it is, I have to. "I can't keep wearing this suit, and I can't be walking around with this beard." I lift my bloody paws. "And these need seeing to. There's no way I'd be any safer at a hospital."

I remember Wesley Hospital and shudder.

Lissa gives me one of her disapproving stares. "I don't think you should."

"I've got no other choice."

And whether she thinks it's a good idea or not, she has nothing to say about that.

10

The back door hasn't been broken down or even tampered with, as far as I can tell, which is a good sign. And the brace symbol above the door is whole. Another good sign, literally, though it's glowing even brighter now, but that's to do with the increased Stirrer activity. I take a deep breath and open the door.

There's another reason I had to come home, and she almost knocks me off my feet. That's how pleased she is to see me, though not half as happy as I am to see her. I crouch down and give Molly a hug, scratch behind her ears, and apologize for her horrible treatment. She's forgiving.

"Lovely dog," Lissa says.

Molly is sniffing at my heels. She glances up at Lissa, isn't fussed by her being dead. Seems if she's good enough for me, she's fine with Molly. I get Moll to sit then throw her a treat. "She's my best girl, my Molly Millions girl," I say, and rub her behind the ears again. She grins her big, border collie grin.

Lissa snorts. "Molly Millions, hah. You *are* a geek."

"So, I like *Neuromancer*. Who doesn't?"

"But, Molly Millions..."

I glare at her, then smile down at Molly. "I just had to make sure she was OK," I say.

And I'm thinking of the time when I brought her home, the tiny bundle of fluff that she was then. Puppies, particularly bright ones, can be trouble but she never was. She grins up at me again, and I grab another treat from the bucket by the fridge. She catches it in one smooth motion, then crunches it between her teeth.

We walk through my place and Molly sticks to my side. I know it's because she can sense how unsettled I am. I can tell no one has been here—there are no unfamiliar presences, and there's certainly no stench of Stirrers. And Molly isn't acting too weird. I stop in the living room.

There's a photo of Dad and Morrigan on my mantelpiece.

Those two have been pomping as long as anyone at Mortmax, other than Mr. D. Both had graduated from Brisbane Grammar and both had had something of a reputation as hellraisers in their day. The stories I had heard from each about the other, and *always* without implicating themselves, were told with relish, and were usually accompanied with a lot of eye rolling from Mom.

Morrigan is family in the best sense: family you choose. I feel a twinge of worry for him. But that's all I allow myself, I can't wallow in grief and fear. There are walls building inside of me. I don't know how sturdy they are, but I'm unwilling to push them too hard. At least I know that there's an afterlife.

Dad and Morrigan both came from a long line of

Pomps; they could trace their line back to the Black Death, but Dad's focus had always been family. Not so Morrigan, death had been his life, and he'd risen in the ranks faster than any other Pomp in the business. He knew more about the processes than anyone except, of course, Mr. D.

But where Mr. D was aloof and, let's face it, creepy as all hell, Morrigan was extremely hands-on. He'd set up the automatic payroll, all from Mortmax Industries' accounts. Before then Mr. D had paid Pomps with checks, and those bastards always took a week to clear, partly because Mr. D's handwriting was so bad, but mostly because banks like to take their time with other people's money. Morrigan had also set up the phone network. Sparrows had been used prior to that. We still used them on occasion but only in trials and ceremonial events, and mainly to humor Mr. D who is decidedly old school. None of us enjoyed the sparrows that much, because they were bad humored at the best of times, and the process involved a little pain—a short message for a drop of blood, a longer one for an opened vein. Blood and pomping go hand in hand, from the portents to the paint used in bracc symbols. And without blood you couldn't successfully stall a Stirrer. But the sparrows were different. They insisted on taking it for themselves, and they were pretty savage about it. Like I said, old school.

Above all, Morrigan had actually done something that no other member of the organization had ever achieved: turned Mortmax into a profitable business. There's no money in pomping, and it was the side businesses, the companies that Mortmax owned that made the money—a couple of fast-food chains, a large share in a mining collective. Once Morrigan had started working that side of the business our pay packets had all increased rather dramatically, which is how I can afford to live the way I do. It's not that extravagant, but I can certainly afford to pay my mortgage and eat takeaway once—well six, maybe seven, times—a week.

Dad never really approved of the changes, though he was happy to take the pay rise. He used to say that pomping was for Pomps and business was for arseholes. I think he was quite shocked by how good he was at the business side of things. Mom often said he was merely proving his axiom.

"Great music," Lissa says, and I lift my gaze toward her in the corner of my living room, checking out my neat racks of CDs. "The Clash, Dick Nasty, Okkervil River. Shit, you've got all the Kinks' albums, and Bowie's. Don't you ever get your music as downloads?"

"Yeah, I'm eclectic," I say as she follows me into my bedroom. "And I don't like downloads, I want my CD art and liner notes."

"I see, so you're not quite geeky enough to do everything as downloads, and not quite cool enough to buy vinyl."

Lissa is already digging around the bedroom. "And it's a relief to see a little mess. Walking through the rest of your place I was beginning to worry that I was hanging out with a serial killer. A serial killer obsessed with peculiar bands, and science-fiction DVDs. A geek serial killer."

"Thank you," I say. "You really know how to charm a fella."

Lissa grins and shrugs.

I grab a backpack and start throwing clothes from my

floor into it. A cap, T-shirts, socks, underpants and jeans. Most of them are clean. There's a bottle of water on my bedside table and I throw that in, too.

"What I like about you," Lissa says, peering under my bed, "is that you don't leave your porn stash lying around. Clothes, yes, but not the porn. Can't tell you the number of dates I've—"

"This isn't a date. Could you get out of there...please?" Her face is buried in my cupboard, and I'm trying hard not to admire her from behind. *She's dead. She's dead, you idiot. And people are trying to kill you. Now look the other way, dickhead.*

Yeah, my inner monolog is pretty brusque. Sometimes it's like a crotchety Jiminy Cricket; you know, a conscience that doesn't whistle or sing, and is all bent up with arthritis and bitter at the youth of today. My inner monolog would write letters to the council and the local paper, complaining about apostrophe use. Heaven help me if I ever live to anything approaching a ripe old age. I'll be a right pain in the arse.

I try to ignore it most of the time.

Lissa keeps checking through my stuff. "Aha! I knew you kept them somewhere, how polite."

"I'm a real gentleman," I say. Though my face is burning, I'm also wondering if Tremaine kept his stash lying around, and why I've never thrown mine out, because I can't remember the last time I looked at it, other than yesterday. "Could you stop perusing my porn...please?"

"A real gentleman who likes *Busty Trollops*, eh?"

"That isn't mine." I push into the closet and Lissa steps out of my way. I reach past the DVDs and grab a thick roll of fifty-dollar notes.

"Hmm, you leave that much cash lying around? What, you expected to run into trouble?"

I shrug, but maybe I had, or maybe I just like the idea, and the somewhat philanthropic notion, that anyone who breaks into my house and makes it past the porn will get a lovely surprise. "Glad I did, though. Now, what else do I need?"

"For one, you're going to need a knife—a sharp knife, sharper than the one you use on the job. A scalpel would be perfect. And you're also going to need a pen, with the thickest nib you can find."

"How about a craft knife? Got new blades and everything."

Lissa raises an eyebrow. "What do you need a craft knife for?"

I shrug. "Crafty things." I'm not going to start explaining my scrapbooking. Even I'm a bit embarrassed about that.

"Crafty things, hah! And this place is so neat, admittedly not the bedroom—but who has a neat bedroom? Even your dog looks neat. Just who are you, Mr. de Selby?"

"What are you talking about?"

She shrugs. I smirk back at her.

I'm packed—clothes, craft knife, pen with a thick nib (yeah, scrapbooking again), even some brace paint, which is my blood mixed with a couple of small tins of something I bought at a hardware store. After seeing those Stirrers on the Hill, I suspect I might need it.

I risk a shower, Molly standing at the door, a grinning sentinel. The pressure's crap, and the hot and cold are sensitive, but I've mastered it over the years to the point that showers with regular pressure seem odd to me. Within a minute I'm enjoying the heat. Washing away a little of the terror. I even clean the morning's blood from the glass. It's an empty gesture but it makes me feel a little better.

I have a pair of tweezers in the bathroom cabinet, and under the steamy shower I pick the beads of glass out of my palms. There isn't a lot of it, thank God, but it hurts. The blood washes away down the drain.

I don't know how long I'm standing there beneath the water but I'm back to thinking about my family, and that starts to put me in a spin.

"Nice tatt." I look up, and Lissa's there leering at me. "Never got one myself."

"Yeah, I live the cliché." Most Pomps have tattoos. Mine is on my left biceps, a cherub with Modigliani eyes It's bodiless, with wings folded beneath the head.

It's a cherub, but it's a menacing, snarling cherub. Actually it's downright creepy looking. I know it's wanky; I had it done when I turned nineteen, had far too much money and way too much to drink. The bemused tattooist wouldn't have let me do it except, well, Tim was there. Actually I think the whole thing was his idea. And he can be so persuasive. Thing is, I don't remember him ever getting a tattoo.

That was before I decided on the path of single-income home debt, and I was heavily into Modigliani. And I liked the irony of it, drunk as I was. Despite what you see on Victorian era tombstones, cherubs have had nothing to do with pomping in centuries.

Most Pomps go for the hourglass, with all the sand at the bottom, or butterflies. Depends on how old you are, I reckon. We like our symbolism. Morrigan has a small twenty cent coin-sized skull tattooed on his forearm, and a flock of sparrows on his back, which extend to sleeves over his biceps. But he can do things with his that I'm incapable of—they're genuine inklings. I've seen them break the cage of his flesh and go flying around the room.

Mom and Dad had been horrified at my ink. Going against the trend, neither of them had even a hint of iconography in their house, let alone on their skin. They'd always been a bit suspicious of my own interests in that area. Morrigan had talked them out of disowning me. After all, he had tatts too, so it couldn't be too bad.

Thing is, Lissa isn't looking at my tatt. I feel my face flush.

"A little privacy please," I say.

"But we've already bonded over your porn collection. And Molly's sitting there."

"Out," I say. "Both of you."

"But you look so happy to see me. Well, I hope that's because of me." And she's gone. Oh dear, part of me misses her, even if it's rapidly deflating. She is dead after all. Molly turns tail, too, and I get the feeling that she's laughing at me.

I rinse off the soap and begin the process of shaving off my beard. I only cut myself twice which means that my hands aren't shaking as much as they were. Once done, I dry myself down and dress, quickly and somewhat timidly, feeling decidedly self-conscious. Once dressed I take a few deep breaths and work on my hair. My hands sting, but they're glass-free.

No one's come crashing through the front door. I'm careful not to pick up my phone. Maybe coming home was reckless, but I had to recharge. I needed this—I'm hungry, and I'd kill for a cup of tea. I boil the kettle on my gas stove, cupping my hands over the flame.

It's gotten cold. I hate the cold, and I've put on a duffel coat that Lissa says makes me look like a thief. I'm tired; I can't be bothered explaining that the coat was my father's. He gave it to me when I was little. It used to be twice my size, then—height and width. The first time I could wear it without tripping over its hem was one of the happiest of my life. While I have this coat, I've still got something of my dad.

I set two cups down and ask Lissa if she takes milk or sugar. It's an automatic gesture. She shakes her head.

"I'm not a tea drinker," she says, and we both laugh. I open the pantry door, take out a Mars Bar, and start gulping down its various essential nutrients. I realize the last thing I ate was a Chiko Roll. I may actually manage to kill myself with my diet before someone gets me with a gun.

"One thing I can't stand is noisy eaters," Lissa says. "If you're going to inhale that thing, at least do it quietly."

"Anything else you don't like?"

"I never really liked my job."

I'm impressed by her segueing. "Well, quit."

Lissa glares at me. "Aren't we Mr. Glib."

I'm feeling a little better. The kettle's boiling, I pour the water into my cup. Mom loved her tea. The thought that I'll never have a cup with her again takes the breath from me. I'm not sure I want it anymore. I put it back down and step away.

Lissa's giving me a worried look, now. Is this the best that I can get? Concern from a dead girl? Someone who was lost to me before I even got to know her, someone who should be receiving that concern from me. What's wrong with me? And here I am having a cup of tea.

"You're scaring me a little here," Lissa says.

"Mom," I say, gesturing at my cup.

Lissa frowns. "Well, she wouldn't want you to stop drinking tea, would she?"

I shake my head. I need milk for the tea. I drink my coffee black, but I take milk with my tea. Mom was very particular about that, even with tea bags—boil, then steep, then milk, but no sugar. Don't get me started on that. I open my fridge.

"Shit."

There's a bomb in there. A mobile phone, wrapped in a tangle of wires that is buried in a lump of explosive like a cyber tick on a C-4 plastique dog. And the phone's LCD is flashing.

Lissa screams, "Run!"

I'm already doing it.

"Molly," I yell, as I grab my bag in a reflex action that may just get me killed. I hurtle out the back door, down the steps and into the backyard. "Moll—"

I'm consumed by brilliance. A wave of heat comes swift on its tail. I'm lifted up and thrown into the bamboo that lines the back fence. Behind me the house is ablaze. A few moments later, the gas tanks beneath the house detonate. Molly, where's Molly? I throw my arm over my face and weep. My house, the one I've been paying off for the last six years, is all gone. Fragments of my CD collection are part of the smoldering rain falling on my backyard.

I crawl back through the bamboo. It's digging into me, there are shards of wood that are actually stuck in my flesh. I wrench myself out of the thicket, dragging my bag. Something whines.

"Oh, Molly."

She's broken. Her back is twisted at an angle that makes me sick with the sight of it. She tries to rise, even manages it for a moment. She moans and slumps back to the ground. There's blood all through her fur.

I'm running to her side, and she looks at me with her beautiful eyes, and there's terror and pain there. *This isn't fair. It isn't fair.* She doesn't understand what's happening. She tries to rise again. "It's OK, girl," I say, and I rest my hand on her head, and her breathing steadies a little. It's the only comfort I can offer her. "Molly."

I don't know what to touch. I don't know how to hold her, what's not going to hurt her anymore. She's shivering, and I stroke her head. "Molly, good girl."

What's left of my house burns, flaring up when something particularly flammable catches alight. My face is hot, and I stroke my dog's head. *Shit. Shit. Shit.*

Molly takes one more shuddery breath, and is still. And she isn't my Molly anymore. Something passes through me, gentler than a human, but it hurts regardless.

I look up and Lissa's watching me, her eyes wide.

"I was going to get Tim to pick her up," I whisper, as though I have to justify this. Christ, what if Tim had opened the fridge?

"Oh, Steve. I'm so sorry."

"It's OK," I say. "It's OK." But it isn't.

Molly is dead. There's only her ruined body, and even now it's growing cold, and it doesn't look like her anymore, because with Molly it was always about the way she was thinking. The way she moved. She really was a clever dog. She didn't deserve this. She put up with so much. She never got enough walks. Molly's gone, and I can't make it up to her.

Lissa's gaze stops me. Her eyes, green as a hailstorm now, are serious, and they're focused on me. For a moment they're all I see. Lissa saves me with that stare. I don't know how to explain it. It's as though she's always been a part of my life, as though she knows exactly what to say or do to comfort me.

I'm in an alternate universe, though, and one far crueler. One where Lissa and I never connected when we were alive. Never had a chance to tumble into love, and all its possibilities. Her gaze saves me, but it also makes me bitter because I'm never going to get that chance. She's dead, and my parents are dead, and Molly's dead.

And that fills me with something hard, cold and resolute.

"We have to get out of here," I say.

"Yeah, we do."

One last look at Molly and I jump the fence behind the burning bamboo into the neighbor's backyard. The sound of sirens is building, filling the suburbs as they rush toward my home. People are heading toward my house but I'm running in the opposite direction, and it has to look suspicious. My house is going to be on the news tonight. My face is going to be there, too, and beard or no beard, the people on the bus are going to remember that face, and the guy whose car I stole. But I try not to think about that. And while I need it, desperately need it, I have no space for strategy, except this.

I have to stay alive now.

Someone has to pay for what has been done to me and mine.

11

We're halfway down the block when the pale blue sedan pulls up alongside us. Its headlights flash. I flinch, wondering whether or not this is it. There's nowhere to run, just the road to my right, and tall fences to my left. No one pays this car much attention besides me but that could well change if someone starts firing rounds out of it. The passenger-side door opens.

"Get in," Tim says.

My jaw drops.

"There's no time to explain, just get in!"

"Can you trust this guy?" Lissa demands.

I'm already in the car, shutting the door behind me. Tim races down the road. I can sense Lissa's displeasure emanating from the back seat of the car.

"This isn't your car," I say. The car smells of cigarettes. Tim has the radio on and we have a background of inconsequential jokey disc jockey chatter. It's somehow calming where I would usually find it irritating. Bad radio hints at normalcy, and this is seriously bad radio.

"Do you think I'd be stupid enough to drive my own car?" Tim looks terrified, and wounded, like a man who has lost his parents. I recognize the look I had seen in my own face earlier. He takes a deep breath, slowing the car down to the speed limit.

"Didn't think about that," I say. "I haven't really been thinking about anything."

"Shit. Steve, what the fuck's going on?" Tim lights up a smoke, waiting. Suburbia streaks by. My house is the only one that's exploded, but everything looks wrong, feels wrong. The lens of losing everything has slipped over my eyes and I wonder if I'll ever see the world in the old way again.

Tim keeps swinging his gaze from the road to my face and back again, as though it or I have answers. I'd put my money on the road. "I don't know. I don't know. How did you ..."

"I got a call. I don't know who from, just a male voice, it was all very confusing. They said you were in danger, and that I needed to get to your place right away." Tim smiles, it's a weak, thin thing, but a smile all the same. "They also said not to drive my car, that people might be looking for it. I borrowed this. It's a neighbor's. When I got to your house it was in flames. I saw you leap the fence."

He sighs. "Why didn't you call me again? That message you left, what the fuck was that?"

"I didn't want you to get dragged into—"

"Jesus, I'm always going to be part of this. You Pomps, you snooty bastards. I'm a Black Sheep, but that doesn't mean I can't be some help. Shit, my parents are dead. They were murdered, so were yours."

I turn to Lissa. "Why didn't I ... ?"

She shakes her head. "The day you had, Steve. It's lucky you're not dead."

"I'm sorry," I say to Tim. "I really am."

"Yeah. At least you're OK."

As if this can even remotely be called OK. None of us are.

"Who's in the back there?" Tim asks.

"It's a dead girl. She's been following me around."

I hear a loud humph, at that from the back. "Following, well, I—"

"You two have a thing going?"

I shrug. "She's dead, Tim."

"She's also right here," Lissa says. "Like, hello!"

I frown at her. Then turn back to Tim. "Someone's killing Pomps. She's a Pomp, she knows how to trick up death a bit. She warned me."

"Mom's dead," Tim says. "Dad, too. The family. She couldn't have warned them."

"I was just lucky, I suppose. Just lucky," I say, and I know that's not quite right but I can't think of anything else to say.

Tim jabs a finger in my face. "The next time you call me, fucking be a little more specific, eh." He glances toward the road, just in time to swerve out of the way of a fire engine, its lights blazing. "Maybe I could have done something."

"It was already too late then," I say. "If there'd been anything I could have . . . Christ, Tim, you weren't the only one to lose family."

Tim slows the car.

"They're all gone. Your mom said that she loves you. Tim, you and Sally, and the kids, you have to—"

"I'm not going anywhere," Tim says. "Sally, the kids, they're already on a flight to London."

"Aunt Teagan?"

"Yeah. Steve, we have to get you out of here. I'm safe, they're not going for Black Sheep. I've checked the register. Not a single fatality in six weeks. You're the only one in danger here. Not me, certainly not the dead girl."

"Lissa," I say. "That's her name."

He looks at me, shakes his head. "You've never made it easy on yourself. The ones you fall for."

My cheeks are burning, so there's no point in denial. Tim pretends to ignore it.

"I'm sure Lissa doesn't want you dead. It's crazy that you don't run."

I raise my hands in the air. "I know, but I'm staying. I need to get to the bottom of this. Maybe after this is done, whatever it is that needs to be done. If I live long enough. But if I stop now, and think..." My eyes start to well up. There's a dark wave of loss towering over me, but I can't acknowledge that now. I wipe the tears away with my thumb.

A couple more fire engines race past us. "Jesus, Steve, you've put on a show," Tim says.

"I can't have you driving me around," I say. "Even in this car. It's too dangerous. I'm a target. Every moment you're with me puts you in danger. I don't care what the guy on the phone said. I need you to stay out of this."

"Fuck that."

"Tim. I can't be responsible for your death. I just can't. You've got kids. A wife. You have to think of them, mate."

Tim's shoulders tense. "That's bullshit," he says. "Here

we fucking go again, just because I'm a Black Sheep. Because I didn't become a Pomp."

"No, it isn't, and you know it. Shit, if you were a Pomp, you'd probably be dead by now." I take a deep breath. "You need to be safe. Promise me you will."

Tim glares at me. There's an anger there that I'd never seen before, and it hurts me to see it. Then the more methodical part of his brain starts reining in his rage. "OK," he says at last. "Where do you want me to take you?"

I give him an address, not very far away. We're there in a couple of minutes. No one follows us: the streets are almost empty. Tim pulls the car to the side of the road.

"Thank you," I say. "If you can, get out of town. I think this is going to get worse before it gets better—if it ever gets better. Stay at a friend's place for a few days."

Tim nods, though I know he's just going to go home and try and deal with what's going on. "Be safe, you bastard," he says, then turns and speaks to the back seat. "Take care of him. He's all the family I have left, even if he is a Pomp." I don't have the heart to tell him that Lissa's already out and standing on the side of the road.

"You be safe, too." I get out of the car.

Tim glances at me, and all I see are the wounds that he's carrying, the hurts that I recognize because they are the same as my own. It almost brings me to my knees. He slips the car into gear and shoots off down the street.

"Interesting guy," Lissa says. "Now, tell me, why are we here?"

"My car's round the back." I point at the nearby garage. "It's supposed to be fixed." I jingle my keys. "We're going to be on the road in no time."

We're just turning into the mechanic's—the place is closed for the night, just the cars waiting to be picked up—when there's an almighty explosion. A wave of heat strikes me. I smell what's left of the hair on my arms.

"Don't tell me," Lissa says.

"Yeah."

Bits of my car fall from the sky. A dark shape streaks out of the flame toward me. It's a crow—a big one—and its wings are aflame. It races toward my head, a shrieking, flapping comet. An omen if I've ever seen one. I cringe and duck, throwing my hands up before my face. But it's already gone.

I swing around to Lissa, her pale blue face lit by the fire coming from my car, her mouth open. She looks as horrified as I feel.

"What the hell does that mean?" Lissa asks.

"It means that wherever we're going, we're walking for a bit." I look around at all that flame, and the dark sky filling up with smoke. My environmental footprint has broadened considerably this evening. "Maybe we should start running again."

Things can't get any worse, except I'm certain that they will. It's the first new law of the universe according to Steven de Selby's life: things *always* get worse—and then they explode.

12

So I'm dead," Mike says to me and blinks, his eyes wide.

The newly dead blink a lot.

It's more from the memory of the flesh than any brilliance in the afterlife. There's no walking into the light or any of that nonsense, their eyes are just adjusting to a new way of seeing the world. It's a doors of perception sort of thing.

I have an inkling of what that feels like now, because my world has had its doors and its walls blown open, one after the other with all the ruthlessness of a carpet bomber. I'm feeling a little more than angry. Which isn't the kind of thing you want to bring to the job, it's wildly unprofessional. If this is even a profession anymore.

"Yeah, Mike." I glance around, not sure if anyone is following us. "I'm sorry to say it but, yeah, you're dead."

"Well, this wasn't what I was expecting." He's a bit hesitant. I can't get near him, maybe I'm not helping that much. I'm not really in the mood.

Mike is the fourth dead person who's found me since my car exploded, and that was only an hour ago. Two others were Pomps, the third a punter like Mike. I hadn't seen the Pomps since last year's Christmas party; one of them had gotten a little amorous with the bar staff. Poor bastard—that stuff sticks to you—even dead he couldn't look me in the eye. With them gone I'm probably the only Pomp in the city. Maybe the only Pomp in Australia. And every dead Pomp means more work for me, more of that dreadful pain.

"I'm sorry," I say again to Mike, and I really am.

"Don't be. I'm OK with it," Mike says, shrugging. He's not a Pomp, just a punter, a regular dead guy. "It was hurting at the end. This is much better. I'm really OK with it."

"Good." I'm not OK with death, but I'm trying to cling to my flesh and bones. Shit, I catch myself, I'm being so unprofessional.

"So who is she?" Mike points a thumb at Lissa.

"I'm dead too, Mike," Lissa says, even manages a smile.

Mike nods. Lissa lets this sink in. He blinks, looks her up and down. He obviously likes what he sees. Once again I feel a little tug of jealousy. "You cool with it?" Mike asks.

Lissa sighs. "What you gonna do, eh?"

Mike laughs. "Yeah."

I reach out a hand, pat his wrist and he's gone. I grunt with the pain of it, hunched over. Then I cough.

Every one of these is getting worse, and there's only ever going to be more of them. Souls always take the path of least resistance. As the number of Pomps fall, the souls of the dead are going to go to the closest Pomps they can find, and they're going to come in hard and fast. Sure, some will use Stirrers but if I had a choice of a nice well-lit hallway or a cave dripping with venom, I know which one I'd pick. Doesn't mean I like it.

"I'm doing your job for you," Lissa says, as I straighten with the slow and unsteady movements of the punch-drunk. It seems a long way up to my full height. And there's blood in my spit: a lot of it. My mouth is ruddy with the stuff.

"What the hell do you mean by that?"

"Some punters need talking down. That guy didn't even need it and you still couldn't manage to be professional."

I raise my hands. "Whoa, you're being much too hard. For Christ's sake, I don't even know if there's a job now."

Lissa flits around me. "As long as they keep coming to you, you do your job." Her eyes are wide and set to ignite. "You didn't want this? Well, neither did I, boy. But we chose this, none the less, when we chose to do what our parents did. Without us, without you, things are going to get bad and fast. So do your job."

"Yeah, well, easy enough when you're not experiencing each pomp." I can feel the sneer spreading across my face. "I'm bruised on the inside. My job is going to get me killed." One way or the other it will, I'm certain of that now.

"Maybe, maybe not," Lissa says. "But you've got to keep moving, and you've got to keep sucking it up. Death doesn't end."

"What the hell do you think I'm doing?" I demand, while not moving at all. My hands are on my hips, and

I've a growl stitched across my face, my jaw bunched up so tight it hurts.

"Stopping, wandering aimlessly, a little bit of both." Lissa counts out on her fingers. "Oh, and I could throw in some misdirecting of anger."

She's right of course, but I'm not going to admit it.

I'm walking toward the river—there, that's a destination, everything in Brisbane leads to the river, eventually—through the pedestrian and cyclist underpass near Land Street, concrete all round. The traffic of Coronation Drive rumbles above. Cyclists race past me, all clicking gears and ratcheting wheels, thunking over the seams in the concrete, each thunk jolting me into a higher level of stress.

All these people are in a hurry to be somewhere. Going home, they're the last wave of the working day, the sunset well and truly done with. Until yesterday I was one of these restless commuters, my phone always on, hoping that it wouldn't ring with a change of schedule.

"You know, I had a home once," I whisper. "Had four walls, a dog and a bloody fine CD collection. Shit, I didn't care about the CDs or the house, but Molly. Molly."

"We've all lost things, people we care about," Lissa says. "I've got feelings, too. It's all I have. If you give in to your losses you may as well give up."

I walk around in front of her. She stops, and we hold each other's gaze. "What was your place like?" I ask.

"It was nice, near the beach, not far from a tram line. Oh, and the restaurants." She stops. "Bit of a pigsty, though. Never really got into the whole house-frau thing."

"No one's perfect."

Lissa smiles. "Would have driven you mad."

"I'm sure." I want to say that I would do anything to be driven mad by her. But now's not the time.

I pull my duffel coat around me. The evening's grown a gnawing chill. A wind is funneling through the underpass, lifting rubbish, and it swirls around us like this is all some sort of garbage masque. For a moment it passes through Lissa's form, spiraling up almost to her head. She blanches, shifts forward, and the rubbish topples behind her, leaving a trail of chip packets, cigarette butts and leaves.

"Well, that's never happened before." There's something delightful about her face in that moment, something starkly honest that hurts me more than any pomp. I want to touch her cheek. I ache for that contact, but all we have are words.

"Look, I'm sorry about before," I say, startling a jogger, one of the few I've passed not listening to an mp3. He looks at me oddly, but keeps running.

"So am I," Lissa says. Suddenly a part of me wants to take another jab at her, because maybe it would be easier if she hated me. After all, I'm going to lose her. But I clamp my jaw shut.

I reach the river end of the underpass. There's a seat there and I slump down into it and stare at the water, the city's lights swimming like lost things in the restless dark.

"I think that little fellow wants you," Lissa says.

I look up. There's a tiny sparrow perched on the ledge behind me. I look at it more closely. It's an inkling. One of Morrigan's. Its outline is an almost ornate squiggle of ink.

The little bird regards me with bright eyes, its head

tilted, then hops closer. It coughs once, strikes its beak against the ledge and coughs again. I put out my hand, flinching slightly as the sparrow jumps quickly onto my finger. Its squiggly chest expands and shrinks in time with its breathing, and all the while its eyes are trained on me, unreadable and intelligent.

There is a tiny roll of paper clipped to its leg. I reach for it, and the sparrow pecks down hard on my arm, drawing blood. An inky tongue darts out.

"Shit." I'd forgotten about that, mobile phones are a sight easier than this stuff. The sparrow needs to know that it has the right person, and there's also a price. Blood's the easiest way. Satisfied that I am the correct recipient, the tiny roll of paper falls from its leg into my open palm.

The sparrow looks at Lissa and starts chirping angrily, fiercely enough that it's almost a bark, surprisingly loud from such a small creature. Lissa glares at it and the sparrow gives one final growl of a chirp, launches itself into the air, and is gone into the night.

"I don't think it was too happy to see me," Lissa says. "In fact, I know it wasn't."

"Why?"

"Because I've outstayed my welcome, I shouldn't be here. The world wants me to go."

"I don't want you to go."

Lissa crosses her arms. "Steven, you haven't been acting like it."

"I—"

"Just look at the note, would you?"

I unfold the paper. Morrigan's handwriting is distinctive: all flourishes and yet completely legible, even when it's covered with bloody fingerprints.

Still alive, Steven. You're not the only one. Don's in
Albion, Sam is too. Get there if you're able. Your best
chance is together.
    Be careful.
    M

I read it aloud. Lissa frowns as she looks from the note to
me. She shakes her head. "Steven, this doesn't feel right.
It could be a trap."

"Everything feels like a trap, though, doesn't it? Every
street's a potential ambush. If we keep this up, whoever
our opponent is will have won." I heft up my backpack.
"Morrigan's alive. I have to cling to some sort of hope."

Lissa's lips tighten, she's not happy at all. "But there's
hope and then there's insanity, Steve."

I look her squarely in the eyes. "I've got a bit of both, I
reckon. And anyway, besides you and the contents of this
pack, it's all I've got."

I'm also much happier following Morrigan than trying to get Mr. D's attention. Lissa has explained the ritual,
and why the craft knife is necessary. Anything else has to
be worth trying first. Lissa knows that. It's hanging there
in front of us, this secondary truth. Drawing Death the old
way scares the shit out of me, and I can understand why
most Pomps would be unfamiliar with the process. There's
too much pain. It's one thing to have people wanting you
dead, another entirely to take yourself to that place.

Now all I've got to do is get to Albion. It's a north-
ern suburb, about twenty minutes away. Once I'm there
I'm sure I can find Sam and Don. Pomps can sense each
other—it's an innate thing, hard to describe, but you know
when they're near and, if you know them well enough,

you can tell just who is about. I haven't sensed any Pomps since the Hill and I'm a little hungry for it. There's a loneliness within me that is completely unfamiliar.

I realize that all my life there have been Pomps around and now there seems to be nothing but the polluting presence of Stirrers. I need my own kind with a desperation that is almost painful.

And I'm terrified that they'll be dead or gone by the time I get there.

13

I can't believe I'm asking this, but, are you going to steal another car?" Lissa asks.

I have to laugh. The thought had crossed my mind. "I might be mad but I'm not stupid." Besides, actually finding an unlocked car with its keys in the ignition in this part of the city looks like it would be impossible. I'd like to think I could hot-wire a car after breaking into it, but I can't.

I run up the steep stone staircase, two steps at a time, that leads from the river onto the jacaranda-lined traffic of Coronation Drive, and jog to the nearest bus stop, Lissa pacing me all the way. Behind me, a CityCat glides down the river toward the Regatta pier. I stare after the big blue catamaran's flashing lights as a bus comes to a halt. I clamber aboard, and show my pass like I'm just going to Albion for a curry or a pizza. How I wish I was, and with Lissa, too. But the truth is I'm probably going to Albion to die.

"Got a clear run at last," the bus driver says. "Some idiot messed up a bus, then stole a car." I doubt he'd be so friendly if he knew I was the one responsible, which then makes me distinctly uncomfortable with the idea of traveling in a bus. Bad memories surface. Perhaps I should have stuck it out and found a car.

"Yeah, some people, right?" I say.

I sit in the middle of the bus nearest the exit. The driver's already put the bus into gear and is nudging into the traffic on Coronation Drive. From this angle I have a view of the west and I can see a thin trail of smoke darker than the night coming from the direction of the garage. All that's left of my car is blowing in the wind.

The bus rumbles toward the city then takes the Hale Street exit, peeling away from the skyscrapers to the right of us, heading toward the inner-city bypass and Albion. It's also how you get to Royal Brisbane Hospital, and the airport. I'm familiar with the hospital, most particularly the morgue, but it's been a long time since I've been to the airport, and that was only to pick up friends and family. There was a time I'd dreamed of traveling, just never got around to it. Wish I had. I catch myself at that thought—I've indulged in more than enough self-pity. I look at Lissa.

"What?" she asks.

"So tell me about Lissa Jones," I whisper. No one seems to notice that I'm talking to thin air.

Lissa rolls her eyes. "Gorgeous, single, thirty-something."

"Something being?"

"Thirty, and only just. It was my birthday yesterday."

"You could have told me earlier."

She snorts. "What, so you could buy me a cake?"

"Well, happy birthday, Miss Jones." I dig the bottle of

water out of my backpack and take what I reckon is a suitably celebratory swig.

"Never wanted to be a Pomp," Lissa says.

"Really? I know you said it, but I thought you were joking."

Lissa raises an eyebrow. "Joking, eh? Because the last day has been such a barrel of laughs."

"Sorry." There's a bit of silence, and it's only going to deepen unless I dive in. "For me it was always something I was going to be." And it was. My parents had never said anything outright banning me from considering anything else, but they'd never really encouraged me to explore my options, either.

Lissa chuckles. "I studied event management," she says, and her smile widens. "I certainly learned a lot about staging a good funeral."

"Your parents used to take you to them?"

"Didn't yours?"

I laugh. "I actually used to think that wakes were just something that people attended every day. I had a black suit from about the age of four."

"Bet you looked cute."

"Yeah, and none of that past tense, thank you." I smile, though there's part of me still demanding that I stop flirting with a dead girl. I know I'm being unprofessional, and she knows I know but, then again, after what has happened to my profession, it hardly seems to matter anymore. "I remember Dad stopping a stir in Annerley. The body was actually twitching, and Dad went up to the coffin and slapped the corpse on the face. Stalled it then and there. People were looking at him as though he was mad, and I was just grinning, proud as punch.

"Dad did most of the hospital gigs, the staff knew him. Doctors and nurses, particularly the nurses, they see all the weird stuff. They understand why our job is so important. So they were always polite around him, respectful. I liked that."

Lissa smiles. "Dad's boy, eh? I didn't want the job. I didn't want to spend my life going to funerals and morgues. But the job picks you, and it sticks in the blood. Anyway, in my family it does, whether you want it or not."

I'm not sure if she's making fun of my family's rather high Black Sheep to Pomp ratio—Aunt Teagan, my late Uncle Mike, Tim—so I just nod, and go along with it. "It makes sense, though, could you imagine pomping cold? Shit, that would really screw you up."

It was different in the old days, there was something of a cultural scaffold. If you started to see weird shit, everyone knew what it was. Well, it's not like that anymore. Without family guidance those first few pomps would be nightmarish. I wonder how things are going to work now, who's going to pass on all this information to the next generation. Surely not me.

"I was stubborn, though," Lissa says. "Finished my degree."

"Good on you," I say.

Lissa glares at me. "Anyone ever told you you're a patronizing shit?"

"Yeah, but I'm serious. I only got through the first year of my BA—if you can count four fails and four passes as getting through."

Lissa shakes her head.

"Neither do I."

"You can always go back." I love her for saying that,

talking as though there might be some sort of long-term future.

"Nah, I'm scarred for life." The sun's been down a while now and the city's luminous, a brooding yet brilliant presence to our right. "Which isn't going to be too much longer, anyway."

"Don't say that," Lissa says. "You can't think that way. You mustn't."

"Well, it's true. You spend your life around death like we do, pomping and stalling Stirrers, and it tends to make you numb. Hell, it numbs you a lot. You know it does. I have plenty of free time, and what do I do with it? I accumulate things. Not ideas, just things, as though they're ideas. Shit, half the reason I gave up at uni was that I decided it was easier *not* to think.

"And when you decide it's easier not thinking then you're only a short step away from deciding it's easier feeling nothing. I can't remember the last time I cried before today."

"I remember my last tears," Lissa says. "Like I said, I never wanted to do this job. I cried whenever I thought about that too much."

"See, I envy you your pain," I say.

"Don't." Her eyes hold mine in that electric gaze of hers.

"But at least you strived for something, even if you failed at it. That's incredibly heroic, as far as I'm concerned," I say.

I tried my hand at non-Pomp work, the regular trades as we call them. I gave up the mobile and the pay packet, and it just didn't fit. Honestly, though, I really didn't try that hard. What I did learn was that I wasn't really a people person—I'm too much of a smart arse for one thing.

Anyway, you get hooked on the pomping, the odd hours, the danger. It's certainly more exciting than working in retail: it didn't matter if your clientele weren't always cheery as there was no follow-up, you didn't have dead people coming to see if their order had arrived, there weren't any secret shoppers, and you never had to clean up the mess (a blessed relief in some cases).

For me, pomping was the perfect job. There was no real responsibility, and it was good money. I had few friends, other than family, and a few people whose blogs I read. There I was, walking and talking through life, not having much impact, not taking too many hits either.

The problem with that is that it doesn't work. The universe is always going to kick you, and time's waiting to take things away. If my job hadn't made that obvious, well, I'd deserved what had happened to me.

In my case it had taken everything at once. And put in front of me the sort of woman I might have found if I'd actually been in there, living.

I realize that I've been staring into her eyes.

"Don't fall in love with me," Lissa says.

Too late. It's far too late for that.

"You've got tickets on yourself," I say softly. "Fall in love with you? As if!"

I look up. The bus driver's staring at me. Half the people in the bus are. I didn't realize I'd been talking so loudly. Talking to myself, as far as they can tell.

"I'm serious." Lissa turns her head, stares out of the window.

"Too serious," I say, not sure that she is even listening. We sit in silence for the next few minutes until we're a stop away from the heart of Albion. I jab the red stop signal like it's some sort of eject button. The bus pulls in, the doors open and I'm out on the street, in a different world. Restaurants are packed to the rafters with diners. The place is bustling.

That's not where Don and Sam are, though.

"Aha," I point west. "I can already feel them."

We wander down the street, a steep curve, the traffic rushing by, desperate for whatever the night has on offer.

There are some nice parts of Albion. On the whole it's a ritzy part of Brisbane, but no one's told this bit of the suburb. The restaurants are behind us now, and we're descending from the urbane part of suburbia to the sub. It's no war zone but there's a burnt wreck of a bikie club a few blocks down, and a couple of brothels nearby. You can smell petrol fumes and dust. The city's skyline is in front of us, high-rises and skyscrapers bunched together, lighting the sky. You can't see Mount Coot-tha from here but I can feel One Tree Hill, just like I can feel Don and Sam. They must be able to do the same.

They're holed up in an old Queenslander which would have been nice, once, with its broad, covered verandah all the way around, big windows and double doors open invitingly to catch afternoon breezes. Not anymore, though. You *could* describe it as some sort of renovator's delight—if they had a wrecking ball.

"Absolutely delightful place," Lissa says. We both have a little chuckle at that.

The corrugated roof dips in one corner of the front verandah like a perpetually drooping eye, as though the house had once suffered some sort of seizure. Some of the wooden stumps the building's sitting on have collapsed. It's a dinosaur sinking into itself.

"Still looking at about half a million for it I reckon."

"Real estate, everything's about bloody real estate," Lissa says. "That's the problem with the world today."

"Well, it's a prime location."

Lissa grimaces. "If you want easy access to pimps and car washes."

"The train station is just up the road, don't forget that."

"And what a delightful walk that is."

I make my way gingerly up the front steps. One in every three is missing. The front porch has seen better days, too, and that's being generous. The wood's so rotten that even the termites have moved on to richer pastures, and whatever paint remains on the boards is peeling and gray, and smells a little fungal.

As I reach for the door, something pomps through me, another death from God knows where. Not again. There's more of that far too frequent pain, and I'm bent over as the door opens a crack. I'm too sore to run, so I push it and find myself staring down the barrel of a rifle. I know the face at the other end of the gun, and there's not much welcome in it.

"Hey," I say. "Am I glad to see you."

"Stay right there," Don growls.

"Don't be stupid, Don," Sam says from the corner of the room. I can just see her there. She's holding a pistol and not looking happy. "It's Steve."

"How'd you find us?" Don demands.

"Morrigan," I say. "He's alive."

"Of course he is," Don says, his face hardening. "He's the bastard who betrayed us all."

14

Don has old-school Labor Party blood running through his veins. Broad shouldered, with a big jaw that the gravity of overindulgence has weakened somewhat, he looks like he should be cutting deals with a schooner of VB in one hand and a bikini-clad babe in the other. He has the dirtiest sounding laugh I've ever heard. The truth is he's a gentleman, and utterly charming, but two failed marriages might suggest otherwise. After a couple of beers, he slips into moments of increasing and somewhat embarrassing frankness. "They were bitches, absolute bitches."

And after another couple, "Nah, I was a right bugger." And then, "Don't you ever get married, Steven. And if you do, you love her, if that's the way you butter your bread. You *do* like women, don't you? Not that it matters. It's all just heat in the dark, eh? Eh?"

Yeah, charming when he wants to be. Which isn't now. To suggest Morrigan is behind all this is ridiculous. Even I'm not that paranoid.

Don looks ludicrous with a rifle, even when the bloody thing is pointed at my head. Maybe it's the crumpled suit or the beer gut and his ruddy face. But he's serious, and he hasn't lowered the gun yet. No matter how silly he looks, he can kill me with the twitch of a finger.

He stinks of stale sweat and there's a bloody smear down his white shirt. There's a hard edge to his face, and I recognize it because I'm sure I look that way, too. It's part bewilderment, part terror and a lot of exhaustion. We three have probably been doing most of Australia's pomping between us for the last twelve hours.

Sam, on the other hand—even in her cords and skivvy, with a hand-knitted scarf wrapped around her neck, and a beret that only a certain type of person can pull off— looks like she was born to hold a pistol. Sam is what Mom would call Young Old, which really meant she didn't like her. I couldn't say what her age is, maybe late fifties or early sixties. Her pale skin is smooth, except her hands— you can tell she has never shied away from hard work. She grips her pistol with absolute assurance.

Interestingly, it's aimed at Don.

We've gone all *Reservoir Dogs* in Albion, and I almost ask if I can have a gun, too, just to even things up a bit. I'm also wondering if I can trust anyone. Don certainly doesn't trust me.

"Jesus, Don, put the bloody thing down." Sam jabs her pistol in his face. This could all go bad very quickly. "There are enough people trying to kill us without you helping them."

"You put yours down first," Don says sullenly. I open my mouth to say something, then glance back at Lissa who shakes her head at me. She's still outside, and out of sight of Don and Sam. There's no need to complicate this stand-off any further. I close my mouth again, partly to stop my heart from falling out of it. It seems I'm getting more familiar than I've ever wanted with the actuality of guns—and it's not getting any more pleasant.

"On the count of three," Sam says.

Don lowers his rifle immediately. He's not much of a conformist. "You're right," he says. "I know, Sam. It just got under my skin a bit . . . the whole damn situation."

"I have a tendency to get under people's skins," I say.

"So do ticks," Lissa whispers, but I'm the only one who hears her, and I don't even bother flashing her a scowl.

Don chuckles. "That's what I've always liked about you." He reaches a hand out to me, and pulls me into a sweaty bear hug. At the human contact I struggle to hold back tears. "Sorry, Stevo. Christ, I've just had a bad kind of day."

"We all have," I say as he pulls away.

Sam runs over to me and her hug is even more crushing. She smells a lot nicer though, mainly lavender and a hint, just a hint, mind, of some good quality weed.

"I'm so glad you're all right," she says.

If you can call this all right, then you're way more optimistic than me, I think. Still, I hug her tight, and this time I can't quite hold back the tears.

"It's all right," she says. The bloody Pomp mantra: It's all right.

Does she think Morrigan's responsible? Surely not.

"You want a cup of tea?" Don asks, looking a little embarrassed. He nods toward a Thermos in the corner of the room sitting somewhat incongruously next to a sledge-hammer, a new one, its handle coated in plastic.

"Tea?" I say, wondering at the hammer.

Don smiles ruefully. "I'd get you a beer but, well, I haven't had time to run to the bottle shop."

Too busy worrying about Morrigan, I think.

"Tea would be great," I say.

"I'll have one, too," Sam says, then blinks, staring out the open door. "Lissa? Oh, I'm sorry."

Does *everybody* know this girl? So I wasn't a member of the Pomp Social Club, but Jesus, how did I never meet her?

"Don't worry, Miss Edwards," Lissa says. "It was quick. I've had time to adjust."

"Miss Edwards?" I'd always known her as Sam, and this throws me.

"Some people are more polite than others. In your case, most people," Sam says to me. "You were lucky she found you."

I nod my head. "Lissa's the reason I'm still alive."

"No surprises there," Don says. "You couldn't piss your way out of a urinal."

Well, isn't this the Steve de Selby support group. I'm about to say something narky but I notice that Don's hands are shaking, enough that I think he may soon spill the tea. I take the cup gently from his grip.

"No arguments from me," I say, even if I'm grinding my teeth slightly. "How did you two make it?"

"They got a little over-enthusiastic," Don says. "I was finishing at a wake—no stir, oddly enough—when some bastard just starts shooting. They missed, and I could see something wasn't quite right. Turns out he was a damn Stirrer. That in itself was peculiar, because I should have felt him. Then I realized he was a Pomp...well, used to be. I recognized him, but didn't know his name, though I've since seen a few I do. I blooded up and touched him, too quick to get some answers, and then all I had was a still body and a rifle. Then I got the hell out of there, once I'd made sure." His fingers brush at his blood-smeared shirt.

It has to be touch, and it has to be blood to stop them. Death is intimate, and bound in life. And blood and death are entwined. Think about all those ancient tales that mix them up, like vampire myths. Stirrers don't feed on blood, but life, and a Pomp's lifeblood is the only way to shut the gate.

Death is up close and personal and we're all staring into its face. Which is why pomping can hurt, though death is less traumatic than life. If every pomp was as painful as childbirth, the world would be crowded with dead people desperate to cross over to the Underworld. And they'd damn well want to be paying us more.

"I got lucky, too," Sam says. "I saw the Stirrer before it saw me, stalled it, took its pistol and got in touch with Don."

"We were both lucky," Don says.

Sam wraps an arm around his waist. I look at Lissa, she smiles at me. I didn't know that these two were a couple: one of the many things on the list of stuff that I don't know about my friends, family and colleagues. Don bends down and gives Sam a kiss.

"I'm sorry about your parents, Steve," Don says. "But there was nothing you could have done."

I don't know how to respond to that. *Was* there something I could have done? I run the options through in my mind. I was just as much in the dark as anyone.

Don changes the subject fast. "So you said that

Morrigan's alive?" He looks over at Sam as though to say, I told you so.

"Doesn't prove anything," Sam says. Aha! So Sam doesn't agree with Don!

"Last time I saw him, via the Hill, he was in Number Four, and he was wounded," I say. "Then an hour or so ago, a sparrow got a note through to me. I suppose he had a fair idea where I might be. Sparrows are good hunters."

"A sparrow. One of those inklings of his?"

I nod. "Yeah."

Don and Sam exchange looks. "He sent you here?" Don asked.

"Not here, exactly, just the general direction." I don't know where he's going with this, but I'm starting to not like it.

"We haven't spoken to Morrigan."

"Do either of you have your mobiles on?" Lissa asked.

Sam pales. She pulls her phone out of her handbag, it's a hot-pink number. She flips it open. "Shit."

"Turn it off," I say.

It starts ringing, and Sam jumps. We all do. She hurls it at the ground and stomps on it with her purple Doc Martens until it stops ringing and is nothing but bits of plastic and circuitry. But still it looks sinister somehow, and puissant, because we know it's too late.

Other than Morrigan, we're probably the last three Pomps in Brisbane, the lucky ones, and now we're clumped together. If Morrigan is behind all this... "We have to get out of here, right now."

And then a dead guy appears in the middle of the room. We're standing in a rough circle. He's tugged this way and that by our individual presences.

He blinks at us. "Um, where am I?"

We all look at each other.

"Queensland," I offer.

He shakes his head, and looks about the squalid room. "Shit, eh? Queensland. What's this? Am I . . . ?"

"Yes," we all say.

"Well, what does it all mean?" He scans the three of us, as though looking for a point of egress. He's about to make a break for it. But I'm not anxious to pomp him, my insides are feeling tender enough. Don gestures furiously at me to do it, but I'm pretending I don't notice him.

"I don't know what it means. But it's all right," Don says. He winces and then gently touches the dead guy on the back. The fellow's gone.

"We're all playing our A game today," he says, looking from me to Sam and back again. When we say nothing, he shrugs. "I'll check the back."

I feel like an absolute shit, but I'm so glad I didn't have to make that pomp.

Don's at the back door, peering out, his rifle held clumsily in one hand. He stiffens, closes the door softly and backs away down the long hallway to the living room. "There's someone out there." Don's pale as a sheet. "Couldn't see them, but I could feel them."

Now that he's said it, I can too. It's similar to the darkness that I had felt around the Wesley Hospital. The air is slick with an unpleasant psychic miasma. It's catching in the back of my throat like smoke. Don is looking worse and I'm not surprised: he took that last pomp.

"Time to use the exit plan, I think," he says, glancing over at Sam.

She nods and lifts up the sledgehammer from the corner of the room. She looks like some weird combination of Viking god—blonde plaits hanging from beneath her beret—and hippy grandma.

Sam passes it to me and I grunt, the thing's heavy. Its plastic grip crinkles in my hands. I look at her, confused. How is *this* part of the exit plan?

"Steve, would you mind smashing a hole in the floor?"

"Not at all."

She points to the middle of the room. "About there would be good." Then she runs to the window, peers out and fires her pistol into the dark.

It's surprisingly easy to make a hole in the wooden floorboards—they're rotten—though every time I strike the floor, the whole house shakes and I wonder if I'm going to bring it down around our heads. Once the hole is big enough, even for Don, I step aside for the others.

Don drops down first, grunting as he hits the ground. Sam motions for me to go. I hesitate and she grimaces.

"Steve, I've got the gun. You go, and now."

I'm down and running at a crouch. Someone fires, and I'm not sure if it's them or us. I look back and watch Sam drop neatly through the hole. Her pistol flashes. Lissa's with me, and I don't think she could look more worried than she does. She darts away into the dark and is back in a heartbeat.

"There's three of them. Stirrers."

The moment she says it, their presence floods me. A foulness stings the back of my throat. "At least three," I whisper.

The house is musty and muddy underneath, and I'm getting mouthfuls of spider web. No spiders yet. I follow Don through a scrubby little garden and onto the road.

We don't stop running for three blocks, until we reach Don's brown transit van. Don's bent over, and having a spew. It's the perfunctory vomit of a heavy drinker. I wonder if I'm heading that way, too, since I've been hitting the drink pretty hard of late. Well, that's the least of my worries. Don straightens, wipes his mouth, and jabs his rifle butt at the van.

"In the back," he says to me, as Sam catches up to us.

I slide open the side door and scramble onto the hard bench seat inside. Sam's behind the wheel, Don beside her, and we're off with a squeal of tires. Sam takes the first corner so tightly that I'm thrown out of my seat and hit the corrugated metal floor with a grunt.

"Put your seatbelt on," Sam says. I clamber back into my seat and pull the seatbelt across my waist.

A car horn honks at us as we shoot past, and Sam gives it the finger.

"Keep out of the fast lane, ya dickhead!" Don yells.

Lissa's laughing. "Old people these days."

"You watch who you're calling old," Don says, "or I'll come back there."

Sam concentrates on the road.

"I hate driving in the dark." Don reaches over and flicks on the headlights.

"Don't you say a word," Sam growls.

We take another corner like we're a bunch of drunken hoons on a Friday night, and even with the seatbelt on I nearly slide off the bench again. Sam knows how to drive fast, but this van is hardly handling like it's on rails.

"So you really think Morrigan's involved in this?" I ask Don, as much to distract myself from Sam's driving as for my pressing need to know. The Morrigan argument seems absurd—I saw him wounded and I've known him for as long as I can remember. He talked me out of the nightmare of my break-up with Robyn, he's sat at the table for Christmas dinner. He's walked Molly—possibly more often than I did.

"He's about the only one who could pull it off. The man knows everything, runs everything. And we let him," Don says. "It's probably not a good idea to trust anyone at the moment."

Yeah, which is exactly the right thing to say to someone stuck in the back of a van while the two people up front both have guns. Then again, if they had wanted me dead I suspect that I'd be a corpse by now.

"One thing is certain," Don says, "we need to split up. Morrigan—or whoever's hunting us—wants us to stick together."

"Here?" Sam says.

Don nods. "Yeah, here will do." He smiles back at me. "Milton, not a bad suburb to dump you in. At least it's near the brewery."

Sam swings us off the road, and slams to a halt. Another car beeps its horn as it flies past, but Sam ignores it. "Sorry, Steve. I know you don't want to hear this, but Don's right. Together we're a bigger target."

Of course she was going to side with Don. They're lovers. "Are you two going to split up as well?" I ask, a little petulantly.

Sam nods her head, and I've never seen her look so sad. "That was the plan all along. We just wanted to see each other, before—"

"Before we sort this thing out," Don breaks in, "and make the bastards, whoever the fuck they are, pay." Don's

out of the van and is sliding the door open. "Keep breathing. I'm going to try and get in touch with Mr. D. I don't
think he knows about this."

"If he does," I say, "then none of it matters, we're all
dead."

Don nods. "That we're still breathing makes me believe
he doesn't. Mr. D has much more elegant tools at his dis-
posal than guns."

Which is absolutely true. Death stops hearts, and stills
brains with a breath. He could have killed every single
Pomp with a thought. After all, he is disease, he is misad-
venture, and he is just stupid bad luck, almost all of which
I've encountered in the last thirty-six hours.

"Speaking of which…" He digs around under the front
passenger seat. "Aha!" Don passes something to me. A
pistol. "Be careful with that, it's loaded."

I look at it like it's a scorpion. Sam rattles off some
details about the weapon, which bounce just as rapidly off
my skull. All I know is that it's a gun. You point it and
squeeze the trigger.

"… You got that?" Sam asks.

"Yeah, um, yeah. Of course."

"We have to go." Don shakes my hand roughly and I
wince. There might still be a piece of glass in there. Then
he pats me on the shoulder. "You'll be fine."

"Good luck," I say, and wave at Sam. The faux smile
she gives me is matched for false cheerfulness by the one
I'm wearing. We're chimps surrounded by lions, grinning
madly and pretending that the big cats are not circling ever
closer, and that it's not all going to end in slashing claws
and marrow sucked from broken bones.

"We'll be all right," Sam says. "You take care, and keep

that Lissa with you." She glances over at Lissa. "And, you, look after this guy. He's one of the good ones."

"I will," we both say.

Don's already back in the van. I step out and slide the door shut.

Sam's off, crunching the gears and over-revving the engine, leaving me coughing on the edge of the road in a pall of black smoke.

15

Think she needs to get that gearbox seen to," Lissa says. When I don't reply she looks at me more closely. "Are you OK?"

"I think so." Twin bars of tension run up my neck. I roll my head to the right and the crack's loud enough to make me jolt. I'm edgy all right. If this keeps up I'll be jumping at my own shadow, which might be sensible.

"Just you and me again, kiddo," Lissa says.

"There's worse company." My voice cracks a little. "Much worse. You've—I don't know what I'd—"

"Don't," she says, taking a step away from me, and I know what she means. There's no future for us. There can't be. That's not how this works. No matter what else has happened, she's dead, and I'm alive. The divide is definite.

But it's bullshit isn't it, because she's still with me. I'm not keeping her here. In fact my presence should be doing the reverse. She's a dead girl, and she shouldn't be here, but she is. That has to count for something.

"I hope they make it," I say, all the while wishing that Lissa had made it too. Though if she had, I'd probably be dead.

It's hardly a comforting thought, but there aren't any of those that I can find anyway.

We get a little further away from the road, closer to the rail overpass at Milton. A black car hurtles past, one of those aggressively grille-fronted Chevrolets that must burn through about five liters a kilometer. Its engines howl like some sort of banshee. I cringe, and drop to the ground. The bad feeling—mojo, whatever—coming from the car is palpable and all I can hope is that, at the speed they're going, they don't feel me. And they mustn't, or at least they don't stop. Maybe I'm not seen as a threat.

"Stirrers," I say, "a lot of them." I don't mention that one of them looked very much like Lissa.

Another car follows in its wake, likewise crowded, and this one driven by the reanimated corpse of Tim's father, my Uncle Blake. He's in his golf clothes, and would look ridiculous if his face wasn't so cruel, his eyes set on the road ahead. Once they've passed, I get to my feet and watch them rush up and down the undulations that make up this part of Milton Road.

In just a few moments they've run two sets of lights, nearly taking out a taxi in the process, and are already passing the twenty-four-hour McDonald's and service station, shooting up the hill past the Fourex brewery, leaving mayhem in their wake. Cars are piled up at both intersections, their horns blaring, shattered windscreens glittering.

"Their driving's almost as bad as Sam's," I say. Lissa drifts between the road and me. She looks tired and tenuous, her skin lit with the mortuary-blue pallor of the dead, and I wonder how much longer I'll have her with me. Not too much, I reckon. I ram that thought down, push it as deep as I can.

"Sam was flying, wasn't she?" Lissa says.

"Don't you mean, 'Miss Edwards'?"

Lissa's eyes flare, but she doesn't take the bait. "She and Don should be at least a couple of suburbs away by now."

I hope Lissa's right, but it's out of my control. "We need to keep moving," I say. Then, in the cold and the hard inner-city light, I'm suddenly dizzy. I stagger with the weight of everything; all those pomps. The ground spins most unhelpfully.

"You right?" Lissa's hand stretches out toward me but she doesn't touch, of course.

I take a deep breath, find some sort of center, and steady myself. Shit, I need food, anything. A Mars Bar is not enough to keep you moving for twelve hours, and I'd been running, hung-over, and on empty all day. Could I have picked a worse night to get so damn drunk?

"Yeah." I've started shivering, I am most definitely not all right. "I need to sleep." Exhaustion kneecaps me with an unfamiliar brutality. I almost convince myself that I could stumble down to the service station, or the McDonald's—both are open—but it's too soon on the tail of the passing Stirrers. Besides, those few hundred meters seem much, much further now. I need some rest, and a bit more time.

I look at my watch. It's 2:30. Dawn is a long way off. I walk under the train overpass, find a spot hidden and away from the road and try to ignore the smells of the various things that have lived and died, and leaked down here. Then I curl up under my coat, with my head on my bag, which makes a less than serviceable pillow.

"If I don't wake up," I say, smiling weakly, "well, see you in Hell."

"If you don't wake up, I don't know how I'm going to get there," Lissa says.

"You're resourceful, you'll find a way."

I slip—no, crash—arms flailing, into the terrible dark that I have no doubt will fill my dreams for the rest of whatever short fraction of life I have left. There's only sleep and running for me now. I'm too tired for self-pity, though, so that's one blessing at least.

I wake to the sibilant bass rhythms of passing traffic, with the bad taste of rough sleep in my mouth, and a host of bleak memories in my head. This is the first day that my parents weren't alive to see the dawn. I stamp down on that wounding thought as quick as I can.

My watch says nine, and the light streaking into my sleeping pit agrees with it. On the other hand, my body feels like it's still 2:30 am and I've been on a bender. I stretch. Bones crack in my neck and there's drool caked on my coat collar. How delightful.

"That was hardly restful," Lissa says.

"For you or for me?"

"I wouldn't call this resting in peace, would you?"

She points at the space around me, and there is blood everywhere. Portents. Stirrers. I'm not surprised but it's unsettling to see all that gore drawn here from the Underworld. It's a warning and a prophecy. Well, I've seen blood before, even if it's usually in the bathroom, or my own, curling down my fist, potent and ready to stall a Stirrer.

"I slept. That's one thing, no matter how poorly. How's my hair?"

"You really want to know?"

"You're chirpy."

"What can I say? I am—I *was*—a morning person."

"Well, you'll be pleased to know I was once a person who hated morning people."

"What changed your mind?" Her face draws in close to mine, well, as close as she can comfortably get without me pomping her. I'm treated to the scrutiny of her wonderful eyes. My cheeks burn.

My stomach growls. There's nothing like a stomach gurgle to change the subject—and this one is thunderous, a sonic boom of hunger. I rub my stomach. "I really need to eat."

Lissa gestures at all the blood. "Even with all this?"

I nod. "I can't help it. I *have* to eat."

Which is how we end up at a dodgy cafe in Milton, eating a greasy breakfast with black coffee. It's busy, but then again it's Thursday morning. The whole place smells like fat—cooking fat, cooling fat and partially digested fat being breathed out in conversation. That's the odor of the twenty-first century. I grin and bite down on my muffin.

The city's covered with a smoky haze. There have been grass fires around the airport. Spring's always dry and smoky in Brisbane—storm season's a good month off—and my sinuses are ringing. Everything about me is sore and weary, and even the sugar and coffee isn't doing much to help that. But it's something. Just like my snatches of nightmare-haunted sleep were something.

My head's buried in the *Courier-Mail*, partly because

my face is on the cover. It's not a great picture, and I'm bearded in it, but it's enough. The article within is brief and speculative in nature. It doesn't look too good, though. I've been around too many explosions of late and too many people connected to me have died. I'm wanted for questioning. There's no mention of Don, Sam, Tim or Morrigan and there are suggestions that this is all part of some crime war. They've got the war bit right at least.

I give up with the paper. I need to think about something else for a moment, before the crushing weight of it all comes back.

"Could be worse," Lissa says. She's sitting opposite me.

"How?"

"You could be reading that in jail."

"Thanks."

"And you're really not that photogenic, are you."

"What the hell do you mean by that?"

"I mean, you're much, much better looking in the flesh."

"You're far too kind."

"Where did they get that photo anyway?" She peers at it.

"Facebook."

"Well, then, it really could have been worse. You've never dressed up like a Nazi obviously, or they'd have chosen that for sure."

I stare at some kids playing in the courtyard of the cafe, working out their weird kid rules, which generally seem to be about making someone cry while the rest look on, or shuffle off to their parents.

"You want to have children?" Lissa asks.

"Not really. OK, maybe, but look at me. I'm sleeping under bridges...I'm twenty-seven years old, with only a small chance of living more than a few hours. Not exactly great parent material." I shake my head, and my neck cracks painfully, again. I feel sixty-five today. "Did you ever want to have kids?"

Lissa shifts into the daylight, maybe so that I can't see her face.

"I don't know, maybe, I never felt settled enough. Wasn't much of a nester."

"Robyn—my ex—wanted kids," I say. "She just didn't want them with me."

"Then it was lucky you broke up." She doesn't come out of the light.

I wonder how Don and Sam are going. I haven't felt them pomp through me, so I hold onto the slim hope that they're alive. I mean, *I* am, and those two are infinitely more capable. They managed to rustle up a hideaway and some alone time. All I'd done was arrive in time to see my house, and then my car, explode.

After breakfast, I stand in the car park, looking at all those cars, wondering if that's the answer. I certainly need to get moving. A little further up Milton Road squats the bulk of the Fourex brewery. The whole suburb smells of malt and smoke, like a poor-quality whiskey, and though it was only yesterday that I had the mother of all hangovers, I surprise myself by actually desiring a beer.

I consider mentioning this to Lissa then think better of it. I'm sure she already thinks I have a problem.

"You've got a visitor," Lissa says.

The sparrow has been looking at me for some time, I feel. It gives an exasperated chirp. So Morrigan has found me again. I'm a bit nervous about that, thanks to Don. But I bluff it.

"Hey," I say. "Sorry, little fella." I have to remind myself that being patronizing doesn't improve an inkling's mood. I've never seen a sparrow glare before.

I reach out my hand and it jumps up, pecks my index finger hard, much harder than is necessary, drawing blood. It'd be a hell of a lot more pleasant if the buggers just needed a handful of seed.

The sparrow drops its message, then gives my arm another savage peck and strikes out at the air with its wings. I curse after it, then my jaw drops as two crows snatch the bird out of the sky and tear it in half before it can even shriek. It forms a small puddle of ink and brown feathers on the ground. Then, with a black and furious crashing of wings, the crows are gone. It looks like human Pomps aren't the only ones doing it tough.

The message is brief.

Phone.
M.

I hesitate, then look at Lissa, who shrugs. "What have you got to lose?"

We both know the answer to that. But there is so much more to gain, even if it's just clarifying who my real enemy is.

I switch on my phone, holding it like it's a bomb.

It rings immediately. I jump, swear under my breath, then pick up.

"Steven," Morrigan says.

I can hear a background rumble of traffic. "Where the

fuck are you?" I ask. He's not the only one who can skip over small talk.

"Look, we don't have time," he says. "The phones, they can trace them. And the sparrows, well, I'm running out of tattoos. Something's attacking them as well."

"Crows," I say. "It's crows. I just saw them then."

"If someone's using Mr. D's avian Pomps, they're more powerful than I'd thought. This just keeps getting worse."

"Yeah, it does," I say. "How do I know you're not in on it?"

There's a long silence down the other end of the line. "The truth is you don't. But how long have you known me?"

I don't answer that one.

Finally Morrigan breaks the silence. "Steven, you have to trust me. I'm telling you, Mr. D has a rival. They need to kill all the Pomps, then they can start up their own outfit. There's going to be absolute chaos. Because while that's going on, there's no one to stop the Stirrers. In fact, I believe whoever is behind this is actually dealing with the Stirrers."

I could have told him that.

"Which is why we need to get together. If enough bodies stir, the balance will tip. We're talking end of days, Regional Apocalypse. It's not far off."

That chills me. The idea had already crossed my mind, but I hadn't really wanted to consider it. I may not have the greatest knowledge of Pomp history, but I know about this. Every one of the thirteen regions has experienced one or two of these down the ages. Death piled upon death. Stirrers outnumbering the living. It's a vast and deadly reaving. And there hasn't been a Regional Apocalypse in a long time.

Sure, there's been some bloody, terrible crap that's gone on in this country, all of which could be considered that way—genocides and wars—but this would be an end to life. *All* life. Stirrers don't stop at people. They don't even start at them, it makes sense to start at the bottom. Everything from microbes up would go. And it wouldn't be like a motion picture zombie apocalypse, or remotely close to an alien invasion—they're a walk in the park compared to a Regional Apocalypse. Stirrers don't bite their victims, they don't need to touch an unprotected person, they don't even need to be that close to them after a certain threshold point is reached. They're like a black hole of despair, and once they've taken enough joy and light, their victim is gone and there's another Stirrer getting about, snatching even more energy from the world.

"I don't know if I believe you. Maybe you're trying to draw me out." I feel terrible because I might as well be saying this to Dad. Before last night and Don's comments I would have trusted him with my life.

Morrigan sighs. "Who are you going to believe? Look, how can I be certain that you're not in on this somehow? Steven, you need to trust me."

Well, if he's actually the perpetrator he'd know.

"We're running out of time," Morrigan says. "Meet me at Mount Coot-tha, the cafe there. One o'clock." He hangs up on me.

I look at my watch. It's 11:30 already. I explain what's just gone on to Lissa.

"I don't like it," she says, which is beginning to sound like something of a running joke.

"Neither do I. But he's right. If enough bodies stir, things *will* tip, and there'll be nothing left within weeks." And I'm not being melodramatic. Where Pomps are conduits to the Underworld, Stirrers are gaping wounds—they're the psychic equivalent of blowing out the window in a pressurized plane, only instead of air, you've got life energy torn out of this world and sucked into the Underworld. One or two Stirrers is bad enough, but that would be only the beginning if we didn't stop them.

I remember seeing my first Stirrer when I was five, shambling away from my father, its limbs juddering as it struggled to control the alien body which it then inhabited. I remember the horror of it—the weird weight of its presence as though everything was tugged toward it—Dad squeezing my hand and winking at me, before pulling out his knife and slicing his thumb open; a quick, violent cutting.

He walked over to the newly woken thing and touched it, and all movement stopped. It was the first time I'd ever found a corpse—all that stillness, all that dead weight on the ground—comforting.

"Not so bad was it?" Dad had said.

The first one gave me nightmares. After that...well, you can get used to anything.

Stirrers are drawn to the living and repelled by Pomps. Well, they used to be, they've been attracted to them lately, which suggests they've realized that they've got nothing to fear.

But what it means is, whether I trust Morrigan or not, I have to get to Mount Coot-tha.

16

ount Coot-tha is broad and low, really little
more than a hill, but it dominates the city of
Brisbane. Inner-city suburbs wash up against
it like an urban tide line but the mountain itself is dry and
scrubby, peaked with great radio towers, skeletal and jutting in the day and winking with lights in the evening.

I have two options.

I consider climbing the mountain, approaching the
lookout and the cafe from the back way, up the path that
leads from a small park called J. C. Slaughter Falls, but
decide against it. If it's a trap, that way will be guarded,
though our competition has shown a marked disregard for
subtlety. Besides, I'm exhausted; the pathway is too steep,
and the name is far too bleakly portentous for my liking.

So I take another bus, in my sunglasses, my cap
jammed firmly on my head, with Lissa sitting next to me
not at all happy with my decision. I don't blame her, I'm
not too happy with it either.

I arrive at 12:58, check the return bus timetable then

head up to the lookout cafe. Morrigan is hyper-punctual, as usual. He is sitting at a table sipping a flat white and looking at his watch. The cafe is crowded with tourists. I slip off my glasses and cap, glad my coat is in my bag. The evenings are cold but, even here on the top of Mount Coot-tha, midday is too warm for anything more than jeans and a T-shirt. My shirt's damp and clinging to me already.

Seeing Morrigan actually centers me a little. In fact, I'm surprised by how relieved I feel. Here's something I know, despite Don and Sam's suspicions. Here's a much-needed bit of continuity. I'm desperate for anything that might bring me back to some sort of normalcy. Morrigan's gotten me out of trouble before. I can't help myself—I grin at him.

He doesn't grin back, just nods, and even that slight tip of the head is a comfort. Morrigan isn't one to smile that often though we've been friends for a long time. His face and limbs always move as though contained and controlled, and never more than now. There's a rigidity to him that is at once comforting and scary. Morrigan has always been a bit of an arse kicker, expecting everybody to lift to his level. A lot of people have resented him for this trait; some have even resigned over the years because of it.

Morrigan and I share very few traits, if any. I've never met a more disciplined man. He jogs every morning and lifts serious weights, though he has the lean, muscly build of a runner. His gaze is usually as direct as Eastwood's Man With No Name, only harder.

But for all that I have never seen him look so old, or so fragile. The last couple of days have wounded him, but there's no surprise there. The job is Morrigan's life in a way that it has never been mine. I doubt if Morrigan has ever made a friend outside of the pomping trade. This must be tearing him apart, almost literally if he's experienced as many pomps as I have recently. The front of his shirt is streaked with dark patches that can only be blood.

But he's alive. Can't say that about many of my friends these days.

"You're late," Morrigan says, looking up at me and wincing with the movement. And all at once I am unsettled and back on the defensive.

"Not according to my watch," I say, and stare at him with as much suspicion as I can muster.

"Enough of this bullshit. You don't trust me. I don't blame you." Morrigan coughs and wipes his lips with a handkerchief. Blood dots the material. He looks in pretty bad shape, his face colorless, his hands shaking as they bring his cup to his lips. "Yeah, I was winged," he says, in response to my expression. "I've got a cracked rib at the very least, and every time I lose a sparrow, I lose more than a sparrow."

He pulls up a sleeve. Bloody outlines of sparrows track up his arm. The neat Escheresque pattern of birds is ruined. One of the sparrows has lost an eye and dark blood scabs the wound.

I whistle, remembering the brutal efficiency of the crows. "How did you escape?"

"Luck, I suppose. They hit Number Four hard and fast. We're not a military organization." He nods to the bulge at my hip. "We're not killers. Jesus, Steven. I'm so sorry. Your parents. If only I'd seen this coming. But I didn't. The only one who could have was Mr. D, and he's gone."

Tears come—well, try to—and I staunch them. Now's

not the time for crying. We have a Regional Apocalypse to stop. "You've got nothing to be sorry about," I say. "And there's no time. What's going on?"

"A Schism."

"A what?"

"I didn't believe they were real. There are records but only a few. When a Schism is successful, there's not a single Pomp left to record anything. As far as I can tell, once they got Mr. D, they left Queensland until last. We were deemed the least threatening of the states that make up the region, I suppose.

"Look at us—two days and there's only you, me, Don and Sam left. And the other regions would stay quiet about it. These things can spread."

"So you're saying someone has their eye on Mr. D's window office?" Lissa says, and I can tell from her tone that she has a fair idea who is to blame, and that he's sitting directly in front of me.

"Good afternoon, Lissa," Morrigan lifts his gaze to her, shielding his eyes from the sun. I realize that Lissa has chosen the spot where she's standing in order to make it difficult for him to see her. It's not helping me, either, her body doesn't really cut out the sunshine, rather it is filled with it. She's not the wan beauty I'm used to but a luminous, translucent figure that stings the eyes.

"Miss Jones, thank you." Her arms are folded. Well, I think they are. Her voice suggests it at the very least. "You don't deserve such familiarity."

Morrigan shrugs. "Miss Jones, if that's what you want."

"I don't want to be dead. I don't want to see my body parading about, inhabited by a Stirrer."

"Oh," Morrigan says. "I'm sorry, I can't even begin to understand how that must feel."

"It doesn't feel good."

"Feelings are all you have, Miss Jones. And you're right, it is my fault. If only I had been more focused."

No one says anything and the silence is long and awkward, until a coffee arrives.

"I took the liberty of ordering you a long black—asked them to bring it over when you arrived," Morrigan says.

I thank him and sip at it, then grimace. The coffee's burnt and bitter, but it's still coffee. "So what do we do?"

"We need to get to the morgues. We need to get to the funeral homes. We have to stop the stirring. If we can contain it here we might stand a chance."

Morrigan's phone rings. He jumps, then flicks it open. "Yes ... No ... If you must, but there isn't much time ... All right."

He hangs up. Lissa and I are both looking at him suspiciously.

"Don," he says. "I spoke to him, too. He took some convincing, but he's swinging around to Princess Alexandra Hospital. Sam's on her way to Ipswich. I'm going to use the Hill and get to the North—Cairns and Rockhampton. If we want Queensland to keep going we need to do this."

"What about the rest of the country?" I ask.

"I'm trying to arrange some support from other RMs, Suzanne Whitman in the U.S. for one, but there's a hell of a lot of trouble getting calls out. It's not easy, but I don't think anyone wants a Regional Apocalypse. That doesn't matter—I want you to do Wesley Hospital."

A prickle runs up my spine. The place had tasted terrible yesterday. It's not going to be any better now.

"You'll be a target," Lissa says to me.

"Weren't you listening, Miss Jones? We're already targets." Then Morrigan grabs my arm. "Be careful."

"I always am," I say, and almost believe it.

We part company, I don't know how he's going to make it down to the Hill. It's probably better that I don't. I look at my watch: five minutes until the next bus.

"I still don't trust him," Lissa says.

"That's your call."

"I want you alive. I want to see you through this. It's all I've got left."

"You don't know the man."

"Neither do you."

That hurts a little. I think of all the parties, the time he got me out of jail for some stupid misdemeanor involving beer and a fountain in South Bank. "Yes, I do."

I'm walking toward the bus stop when another voice stops me.

"Mr. de Selby, I need you to come with me."

"Shit," Lissa says.

Shit indeed.

"There doesn't need to be any trouble," the police officer says.

17

He's a young guy, no older than me, and tall, though hunched down, maybe self-conscious like me about his height, or maybe because he has a bad back. But I don't care either way because he is an officer of the law, and here I am on Mount Coot-tha, my house a smoking pile of wood, having stolen a car (well, borrowed a car, and only for a little while) and my own car having exploded. Oh, and I'm *not* happy to see him, that *is* a gun in my pocket. Shit, I'd forgotten about that. I consider my options.

"Just why do you need me to come with you?" Maybe I can talk my way out of this.

"I think you know why."

Honesty seems the best policy. At least the one most likely to end without bloodshed.

"I have a gun in my pocket," I blurt out. His face immediately tenses. "I'm going to lie down on the ground. You can take it from me, I'm not going to put up a fight."

"Just pass it to me," the officer says. "Handle first. Slowly."

I do what he says, I'm in enough trouble already. It's all I can do to stop my hand from shaking.

"Do you want to handcuff me or something?"

"Do I need to?" He's got a no-bullshit sort of expression. I shake my head.

Well, this is about the worst thing that could have happened. At least I don't have to wait for a bus. Every cloud, right?

I'm bundled into the back of the police sedan. It smells like pine disinfectant. The seat is immaculately clean, though someone has still managed to scrawl phalluses deeply into the headrest.

The car starts up.

"Hell of a day, eh," he says, passing me back the gun. I hold it uncertainly. This is not how I expected it to go down. "I put the safety on your pistol, Mr. de Selby, I'm amazed you didn't blow off your foot. Do you even know how to shoot that thing?"

"I—"

He doesn't seem to care that much, just keeps rolling on. "Don sent me. I'm Alex."

"Don sent you? Thank Christ! You know Don? You know about Pomps?"

"Half the force does, mate." He glances back at me through the wire. "So who's the bastard trying to kill my old man?" I didn't know that Don had a son. Another Black Sheep.

Lissa laughs. "Oh, he's Don's boy! Heard he was cute. Now the rumors have been confirmed." I look at her in disbelief and she winks at me lasciviously.

"You're not out of the woods though," Alex says. Glancing at him through the rear-view mirror, I can see a lot of Don in him. The lantern jaw, the brilliant blue eyes. He's the sort of person who should be going through all this, and probably would have gotten to the bottom of it by now. Me? All I have is a passing acquaintance with mortality and a crush on a dead girl. "Stealing that car wasn't the brightest thing you could have done."

"Someone was trying to kill me."

"Yeah, like I said, not the brightest thing, but ballsy, all right. Find out who's behind this and we can make it go away. Right now, though, you're on your own, and pretty much regarded as Brisbane's, if not Australia's, biggest sociopath."

"I stole the car, yes," I say, "but that's it. I didn't have anything to do with the rest."

"I know that, Dad's told me. It's going to take time for people to cotton onto what's happening. And none of it's been helped by most of the bodies disappearing. Regardless, there's nothing we can do about this. This is your domain, and totally beyond our jurisdiction."

"But people have died. They're after your dad, too."

"Yeah, I know, which is why I'm going to help you—though this is entirely unofficial."

"I don't have much time," I say.

"I know," he says. "So where can I take you?"

I tell him, and five minutes later we're there. I get out and thank him.

Alex grins. "Don't worry about it. Just remember to keep the safety on that pistol—until you need to use it."

I watch the car pull away. "First break of the day," I say. "And it only took until 2 pm."

"Yeah," Lissa says, as we walk through the hospital grounds, heading straight for the morgue. It almost feels like coming home. "But what are we heading into?"

We both have a fair idea. The Wesley's feeling even worse than it did yesterday. Bile's rising in my stomach. My body's already reacting to this place and the creatures it contains.

And it gets worse as we get closer.

A park borders Wesley Hospital on one side, the train station on another. Coronation Drive is nearby, I can see the tall jacarandas that line the river. The Wesley is a private hospital but a big one, with new works always being constructed. Cranes and scaffolding generally cover at least one side of the building.

It should feel like a place of healing, not this sick-inducing death trap.

"Thank God," says an orderly, a fellow I recognize. His eyes are wide and wild. I can smell his fear. "Where have you lot been?"

"Busy, John. Busy." I don't have time to go into the details.

"At least we have these," John says. He lifts his sleeve, there's the bracing symbol tattooed on his arm. It's a good idea. Most orderlies working the morgues and mortuaries have them. You only need to see one Stirrer, and feel its impact on you, to change your mind.

"How many?" I ask.

"Seven."

I swallow uncomfortably. I've never seen that many Stirrers together in my life. This is bad, really, really bad. It's one thing to hear Morrigan talking about Regional

Apocalypse, it's another, much more visceral experience, to face it alone.

"We've got them tied down. But someone is going to hear the screaming. You've got to—"

"I know what I've got to do," I say, a little shortly. I don't really want to do it, but I have no choice.

Dealing with seven Stirrers strapped to gurneys is not something I'm looking forward to. The first thing I encounter are their screams. Another orderly comes at us. "You need to do something!"

"That's what I'm here for," I say.

I walk into the room. Lissa follows me in, though she keeps her distance from the gurneys. A Stirrer could draw her straight through to the Underworld. I don't want her here with me—it's too dangerous—but, Christ, I'm glad she is.

Their presence (or absence) is choking. It's like stepping into a room with no air. It's freezing in here and condensation has turned to ice on everything, a sort of death frost. The Stirrers are flailing on the gurneys, held down tight, but not tight enough for my liking. I look at Lissa. She shrugs. She hasn't seen anything like this either.

I've heard about the world wars, how these things were common at the front where there was so much death gathered in one place. But this is inner-suburban Brisbane.

I sigh. Take out my knife and slice open a fingertip. Once the blood is flowing I reach out toward the first one.

"Can't stop us," it whispers, and then the others are taking up its cry, their voices not quite right. More gurgle than chant.

"This isn't good," Lissa says.

I look at her. "Tell me something I don't know."

"Just thought I'd say it."

"Can't stop us," the Stirrers chime in.

Yes I can.

I press my bloody finger to each Stirrer's hand. They still for good.

But the last one, a bulky fellow, snaps a hand free of its constraints. His fingers clench around my wrist. Bones creak and I wince. I yank my hand free and swing my blood-slicked fist at his face.

"Can't stop us!" he howls, then is gone, my bloody touch stalling him. I get out of that room as quick as I can.

That took more blood than it should have. The Stirrers are getting stronger.

I glance at John. "These won't stir again, and I'll return if I'm alive." I don't tell him how unlikely a proposition that may be when charted against the days—no, the hours—ahead. "But there will be more. I rather suspect that everyone who dies will be...reinhabited."

I incline my head at his tattoo. "You might want to brace as many rooms as possible with this." I give him a tin of paint. There's a few drops of my blood in it and it should provide some limited protection for the hospital at least.

John frowns, as he pockets the paint tin. "And where will you be?"

"If I can come back, I will. I'm just not sure that it's an option."

I'm still a bit shaky as we walk out of the hospital. Stalling takes a lot out of you. One or two is bad enough, but seven is off the chart. Morrigan was right, we're nearing some sort of tipping point. The Stirrers can sense something is wrong. I can imagine the queues of Stirrer souls just crowding around waiting to get into newly dead bodies. Humans have become prime real estate in a way that hasn't happened since the darkest days.

A basketball center's to the right of us, on the other side of the train line. There must be a couple of games going, I can hear the screech of shoes, the indignant shriek of whistles.

"We need to get the system up and running again," I say to Lissa.

She shakes her head. "Sorry, *you* need to get the system up and running."

"Well, running might be a good idea," says a familiar voice. Don's ghost is standing by Lissa. They circle each other.

"Where's Sam? Is she alive?" I demand.

Don shakes his head. "I don't know."

"I'm sorry, Don. Really, really sorry," Lissa says.

Don fixes her with a stare. "You know how it is."

His form flickers. He blinks.

"What the hell happened?" I ask.

Don grimaces. "I feel stupid." His irritation is without much edge, though. He's already sliding away into the land of the dead, though he manages to fix me with a stare. "It's Morrigan."

"I knew it," Lissa says. "All that polite bullshit. All that sympathy. What an absolute dickhead."

"The bastard tried to pomp me, too. But I managed to—" he glances at Lissa. "Christ, how do you keep this up?"

"It gets easier."

Don shakes his head like he doesn't believe her. "Morrigan's decided he doesn't need to hide now. And there's something you need to know: every time a Pomp dies, he becomes more powerful. Whatever presence or energy they have, well, he gets it. That's something he let slip."

Which means he must be pretty powerful now if there's only him and Sam and me left.

"But I was speaking to Morrigan this morning, at Mount Coot-tha," I say, feeling the blood drain from my face. Then I do what anyone would do in that situation—start with denial. "It can't be him. He didn't look powerful at all. He told me—"

"Well, he's a fine actor. Must be, to have pulled all this off. Steve, the bastard shot me," Don snaps. "How much more of a definitive delineation of betrayal do you need? We have to get you out of here, out of the city. Morrigan's holding off on killing you now."

"I met Alex," I say. We're running out of the car park and onto the road, then around under the train tracks and into the basketball court's car park. My head is spinning. I really thought I could trust Morrigan. It had been a good feeling, having a central point in all of this, the idea that someone was guiding the ship again, and now

Don grins. "My Alex, a good boy. Total Black Sheep. I love the kid. Was going to go to the footy with him on Sunday. Broncos match. Hate the Broncos, but the boy's dead keen." Don shook his head. "I couldn't believe it, about Morrigan, I mean. I started trusting him when you made it alive down off Mount Coot-tha. I think that was the plan all along. No offense, Steven, but Morrigan reckons he can kill you off when he likes, when the rest of us are done with. But he doesn't count—"

Don's gone with a soft sound like the ringing of a tiny bell, a sparrow cutting through him, pomping him, its wings whirring. I'm still blinking at the sight of Don sliding out of non-corporeal existence, trying to understand why Morrigan might be keeping me alive. The bird flits past me.

It's one of Morrigan's sparrows. The inkling twists sharply in the air and hurtles toward Lissa.

I'm running at her, trying to get in between her and the sparrow. If it gets there first then I'm alone. I just make it, the sparrow hits my chest hard enough to hurt. It thumps off and onto the ground, and I stomp down. Little sparrow bones crunch beneath my boot. And then it sinks away into a tiny puddle of ink and feathers.

Hope that hurt you, Morrigan.

And then there are more of them. And more.

Someone slows in their car beside me, and then picks up speed. I don't blame them, I must look insane thrashing and swinging at the little birds. I dance around as one sparrow, then another and another and another, descends. They're all around us. I can't do anything about it.

But something else can. Crows crash from the sky, like the eagles in *Lord of the Rings*. If someone had started yelling *"The crows are coming! The crows are coming!"* I would have cheered. The black birds are cawing and crying, snatching sparrows out of the air with their dark beaks in a maelstrom of wings above and around us.

Then the crows are gone and the only remnants of the melee are inky puddles.

"That was…interesting," Lissa says.

"Wasn't it just," I say.

We look at each other. There's another player in the

game. The sparrows are Morrigan's; the crows, they belong to Mr. D. So maybe he's not as in the dark as we believe.

I'd seen Morrigan form an inkling once, at a party. He was charming then as usual. We were talking about tatts, comparing our ink. My cherub had gotten a few appreciative comments, newly cut. Then Morrigan, one never to be outdone, had said, "That's a fine tattoo, boy, but can you do this?"

He'd pulled up his sleeve to the first Escheresque tangle of sparrows that ran from his sinewy biceps and over his back. He whistled then, a shrill, short note, and a bird pulled free of his flesh. "Inklings are quite simple once you get the hang of it."

The sparrow flew around the room, picking up snacks and bringing them back to him.

It had appeared effortless, until I saw him later, coming out of the bathroom. He'd been a bit shaky on his feet. I could smell the sweat on him, even over his cologne. I didn't want him to have a stroke, still, I'd respected his pride and just quietly helped him to a chair. If only I had known what it would come to . . . Well, I would have kicked the legs out from under him.

That had been one sparrow, now we had seen tens of them. And he was using them to pomp the dead. Don was right, Morrigan's powers had increased incredibly.

18

So what do we do?" I ask, staring at the ink-stained ground. "I can't see how I can keep you safe."

"First we're going to need cover," Lissa says, and heads back toward the hospital car park. I follow, hurrying to keep pace.

"You're going to have to bind me to you and this realm," Lissa says.

"I'm unfamiliar with the process. I've heard of bindings, but never seen it done."

"There's a reason for that. OK, a couple of them, the first being that it's old. You wouldn't have come across it unless you're particularly interested in the history of pomping. And there really isn't much written about Pomps. It takes quite a bit of research." Lissa smiles, a little too mockingly for my liking. "And, no offense, you don't exactly strike me as the studious type."

I take immediate offense at that. "Morrigan never exactly encouraged it."

Lissa nods. "Well, we know why now. Anyway, people

don't talk about this stuff, in the specific. You have to really dig. The process is...It's a little confronting." She flashes me another smile. "But if we don't do it, I'm worried that Morrigan will pomp me, and you need me." She's so right, but I rail against that a little. She can see it in my face, and her laugh is both affectionate and mocking. "Don't you try and suggest otherwise, laddy."

We're under the cover of the car park. "OK, so how do I do it? How do I bind you? It sounds pretty kinky, you know."

Lissa reddens, just a little, and I get the feeling that she's more embarrassed for me than anything else. "Well, it sort of is."

"What do you mean?"

"Most of these types of ceremonies involve blood, but in this case that's not enough, because you're not pomping, you're binding." Her eyes seem to be having trouble meeting mine. "You're going to need semen. Your own semen."

"Here?" I turn in a quick circle. There's no one about, but this is a car park. Of course I'm sure there's been plenty of that here, but not mine. "I'm supposed to—"

"This is no time to be squeamish, or prudish," Lissa says impatiently. "There might be a whole flock of bloody sparrows on their way."

"Pressured is the word that comes to mind, actually."

"Performance anxiety, eh? Well, I'm dead, it'll be our little secret. Besides, I've already seen you naked."

"Well, there's naked and then there's naked." I am utterly exposed out here, and it's cold. The odds of me being able to ejaculate are pretty grim. Lissa leers at me. That doesn't help.

She rubs her hands together. "Well? Pants down, prong up."

"Could you look away?"

"I'll look away," she says. "Just think about some of those busty trollops and you'll be OK."

Wicked woman!

There's got to be cameras around here somewhere. I imagine the image as I, um—present—another addition to the caseload against me.

"Hurry up," Lissa hisses at me. "I can hear a car coming."

OK, deep breaths: a half dozen of them. I know that I have to do this, that there's nothing else to be done, but I'm feeling very peculiar about it. In fact, I'm feeling very dirty-old-mannish. Friction isn't enough. Nor is strength of will.

It has to be done. It has to be done.

And it is. And at the moment of ejaculation, a quick hard orgasm, I see Lissa's face.

I open my eyes, and I'm looking into Lissa's face. Oh. My. God.

"You were supposed to look the other way," I grumble, my face burning.

"Good work," she says, ignoring me, though she seems a bit flushed, too.

I've got the semen in a handkerchief. I'm not sure if I've ever been more embarrassed in my life.

"Can I have a look at your, um, handiwork?"

I comply, careful to keep my distance.

She frowns, looks like she's doing maths in her head. I'm not exactly sure how the dead perceive the world but she couldn't possibly be counting the little swimmers. "That should be enough."

"It better be."

The car drives slowly past. I give it a wave. Nothing to see here, now.

19

Crouching down like some maniacal Gollumesque creature, I scrape with a stone the Four Binding Elements (as Lissa called them), basically four triangles, each containing a circle on the cement of the footpath. Lissa stands in the middle of my esoteric squiggling.

"You need a drop of your doings for the center of each circle," Lissa says.

I mark each one, then step back.

"Now, look at me. We need eye contact, and total concentration."

I take a deep breath and gaze at her. It's not gazing, it's grazing, I hunger for her stare. I could look into those eyes forever, they are a fire in my chest and in my stomach. Lissa holds my gaze. I don't know how long we stand that way; it's intense but pleasurable, how my orgasm should have been. The air around us pushes in. I feel the weight of all that sky, and I am bound in a kind of leaden warmth. And then it bursts. The pressure is gone in an instant. And it's just me and Lissa, and the car park. The air is cold. I let out a breath.

Lissa stumbles back from the circle of triangles, her eyes wide. She looks at me, her lips moving soundlessly. Whatever moment we shared has passed. She smiles. "Well, you've bound me. I cannot be pomped on this plane, except by an RM, and we haven't seen too many of those about lately, have we? It won't last forever, but for the next few days it should do."

A few days are probably all I have, anyway, though I keep that thought to myself. I've already shared far too much with Lissa in the last half-hour.

She winks. "Naughty, isn't it?"

"Easier than I thought," I say.

"Well, I *was* thinking that about you," Lissa says.

"So what do we do now, have a cigarette?" I'm shaking a bit, my face is still burning with the intimacy of the ceremony.

"If only...but what we have to do is get you out of Brisbane. We need time to think. To get Morrigan on the backfoot."

"I'm not so sure. Tremaine said we should contact Mr. D."

"Let me tell you about Eric Tremaine. He's a bit of a tosser but, of course, you know all about that." She chortles. "I don't know if you can totally trust anything he has to say. Me, on the other hand..."

Tremaine must have really had it in for me. Sure, I'd let down the tires on his car at a convention last year, but it had just been a bit of fun. Maybe that was one of the reasons; other people had found it a lot of fun too. After all, it was how Tremaine had gotten the nickname, Flatty.

.

"One of my reasons for breaking up with him was that he was too negative."

"It's hard to be upbeat when you've just been killed," I offer. I can't believe I'm coming to the guy's defense.

Lissa glares at me. "You're telling *me* that?"

Yeah, that's me, Mr. Sensitive. "I'm sorry," I say.

"I still agree with Don," Lissa says. "You need to get out of here. Out of Brisbane altogether. And out of mobile range. This is Queensland, there's got to be lots of places like that. Morrigan knows he can't let the Stirrers grow in serious numbers. He wants to be the new RM, and if he's going to become part of the Orcus, he needs to keep the Stirrers in check. Leave it up to him. I think you have to take yourself out of the picture for a while."

"I know a few places that—"

"No, they have to be places you don't know, towns that Morrigan isn't going to look."

She's right. And Queensland *is* perfect for that. I could jab my finger at a map of the state with my eyes closed and find a hundred of them. Once you get out of the south-east corner or away from the coast, most of the country is hot and dry and empty.

People get lost there all the time. Often they're never seen again.

I find some cover after sunset, and try and rest while Lissa keeps guard. I wake from bad dreams to the dark.

"I have to call Tim," I say.

We stop at a payphone in a park near the Regatta Hotel. I grab the handset and pause, disturbed by what I'm feeling in the air.

They're out there in the dark. Stirrers, stumbling

through the night. At first they'll gather in the deserted places, the quiet places, and when there are enough of them together they won't bother hiding.

If Morrigan doesn't get on top of this soon, there will be a lot of suicides over the next few weeks, a lot of unexplained behavior. Bodies will disappear from morgues, people will see their deceased loved ones walking in the street, or wake with them in their bed. And there will be no joy in the occasion, because they are not loved ones, just something that possesses their memories: an imperfect and deadly mimic.

Stirrers are voids. They will turn a house cold, and they will swallow laughter. They are the worst aspects of time only sped up and grown cruelly cunning. Bad luck follows them.

They'll keep their distance from me, if they can. If they have a chance they'll try and kill me, from as great a distance as possible, with a gun or in a hit and run. They can sense me, but I can sense them as well. And I'm more practiced at it, and I've only just had to face off seven of the bastards in the Wesley. You could say my palate was refined.

Which was why I could tell that the man pushing the swing in the park was a Stirrer, even from a few hundred meters off.

I slide my knife across my palm, wincing a little. And then I come up on him casually, trying not to look like he's where I'm heading. It works for a while.

He finally feels my approach and turns, but now I've got up quite a head of steam. The Stirrer runs from the swing set toward me, but he doesn't quite inhabit the body properly. After all, people spend the first couple of decades of their life coming to terms with their bodies. It's one of the most obvious ways of telling them apart.

Their flesh will be bruised, the nails and hands will often be dirty. The longer they stay in the body the less clumsy they become, but there are limits. They will never attain the kind of grace that even a relatively clumsy person has—this isn't their universe.

The Stirrer slips, then gets to his feet. I grab his back, and he wrenches away, so I tackle him, a perfect round-the-legs tackle. My hand brushes cold flesh.

The Stirrer rushes through me, and it is like swallowing glass. I push myself away from the motionless body, my chest heaving.

"Rough stall?" Lissa looks at me with concern.

I nod, some stalls aren't too horrible and some are like a punch to the stomach. This was the latter. Jesus. Normally I would have called for a pick-up, someone to take the body and dispose of it, but that's not an option, now.

The Stirrer opens its eyes, sits up: sees me. Its panicked expression is almost comical. It lets out a groan and struggles to its feet, legs shaking. The blood on my hand must have dried too much to have a permanent effect.

I reopen the wound, fresh blood flows.

The Stirrer stands there, unsteadily. Its eyes dart left and right of me, looking for some sort of escape route.

"Fuck off back to the Underworld," I growl, and slap my hand against its face. The body drops. This stall doesn't hurt as much. The Stirrer hadn't inhabited the body long enough to get a good hold on it, but there's more pain to it than there ought to be.

"That's not good," Lissa says. And it isn't. That was way too fast.

The Stirrer's eyes flicker. And I do it again, this time sitting on its chest while I get out my knife.

I slice open one of my fingers, making a fresh wound, and touch the Stirrer's cheek. There's a definite finality to that stall, like a door slamming shut. The body stills for good. Nothing will get through now, as long as I stay alive.

I get to my feet. We have to keep moving.

"The world's gone to hell," I say as I dash across the park, Lissa by my side.

"Not yet," she says.

And I know she's right. Things can get a whole lot worse, and they probably will.

"I have to see, Mr. D," I say. "There's no way I can leave Brisbane with this going on. It's obviously getting out of Morrigan's control."

"And I'm telling you that's not going to help any-more—at least, not now, maybe later. You just need to stay alive for a little longer, get out of Brisbane. Come back later."

"But if that's what Morrigan wants—"

"I think he wants you in Brisbane. But regardless, I want you alive. Neither of us know enough about Schisms to hang around, except I can guarantee this much: all the other regions will have closed down communication. They don't want word of this spreading. Something like this could see a whole heap of madness. No, you need to keep moving, and Brisbane's not big enough for that to work."

I head back to the payphone on the edge of the park and dial a number I know off by heart.

"I thought it would be you," Tim says. His voice is

strained, the kind of strained that the last few days will engender. I look at my watch: it's three-thirty in the morning.

"Not getting many calls?"

"Too many, but I just thought it would be you. I'm glad to hear your voice."

I'm glad to hear his as well. "We need to meet," I say.

"The Place?"

"Yeah, that'll do. I have to get out of Brisbane." It's not far away, I can easily walk it.

"I'm going to have to organize a few things," Tim says. "You going to be safe until mid morning?"

"Yeah. I think I can manage that." I'm not sure if I can, but Tim knows what he's doing.

"You OK?"

"No. You?"

"Not at all."

Honesty is such a wonderful thing.

20

Delightful," Tim says, glaring at a gob of spit on the ground by his foot. It's fluorescent green and ants have encircled it like a besieging army, a boiling hungry black mass. "That your handiwork?"

I shake my head, thinking about some of my recent handiwork. "If I start spitting that sort of stuff you'll know I'm not long for this world."

I doubt I'm long for this world as it is, but neither of us goes there. I'm feeling very rough this morning. The souls have kept coming, and the drain I slept in last night was hardly salubrious. I reckon I've slept maybe three hours in the last twenty-four. I know I don't smell that good.

The first thing Tim did was throw some clothes at me. I've got my backpack with me, but it doesn't hurt to have some more. They feel better than what I was wearing, not exactly a perfect fit. The jeans are OK, a little loose around the waist, but my wrists jut a good ten centimeters out of the sleeves. I'm rolling them up as Tim gets to work on his third cigarette.

We used to smoke cigarettes here, when we'd first got our licenses. Or sometimes a little weed, but not for a long time. Tim offers me a cigarette, but I decline. "Yeah, stupid idea." But he lights one up and has a puff.

"The Place" is a small park in Paddington. Very suburban, but old-Brisbane suburban. Big weatherboard Queenslanders surround us, all of them in far better condition than the one I'd belted my way out of in Albion, but essentially the same design. Their verandahs are empty. No one is that interested in being outside.

Tim has driven here, in yet another car that I don't recognize. I apprise him of the situation in detail that I didn't want to disclose over the phone. Tim's opinion I trust, though he doesn't need to know anything about the binding ceremony. Lissa corrects me often enough that, even though Tim can't hear her side of the conversation, he laughs. "You're sounding like your parents."

I glare at him. "Cute. Real bloody cute."

"Schism, you think," Tim says. "I've heard of them."

"Really?"

"You'd be surprised how much the government's got on you. Think about it, Steve. Technically you don't exist. And what are the rules binding government in dealing with things that don't exist?"

"If this goes wrong everybody dies, Tim."

"Which is why we think there should be tighter state controls."

"Do you really think that?"

Tim grinds his cigarette out beneath his boot. "Look at what's happening. Do you think we could fuck this up as badly?" Tim sighs. "But fuck that. Other than Sally and the kids, you're all the family I've got left. You know that me and Aunt Teagan don't get on."

"Who does?"

"Lots of people, just not her family."

"Have you talked to Sally?"

"As much as I can. I don't trust the phone lines either. She says she's sorry. We all are."

"Yeah."

"If locking you up in a room would keep you safe, I would, but you'd find a way to get into trouble." Tim knows me better than I know myself sometimes. "I can understand this is as scary as all hell. But I agree with Lissa, you have to get out of town. I've spoken to Alex, did that after I got off the phone with you. He'll be here soon."

"You know Don's son?"

"You really need to be more sociable, Steve. Maybe it's guilt or something, but we Black Sheep stick together."

"That's a bit ironic."

Tim ignores me. "I've talked to Alex, and he's got a car for you. You take that, and you get the hell out of here until it all cools down, or whatever it needs to do."

I don't think it will cool down. Not in the way Tim means or hopes. "What about you?"

"Some of us have to work for a living," Tim says, and now he's the one trying to sound all casual. He snorts. "Look, don't you worry about me. I can take care of myself. It's what I do for a living. Anyway, you think my minister could take a crap without me?"

That's policy advisors for you. "Maybe I will have a cigarette." But it's a mistake, I'm coughing after the first puff.

"Smoking never took with you," Tim says wryly, picking out his fourth cigarette in half an hour. "Lucky bastard."

Alex pulls into the park flashing his headlights. Lissa shakes her head. "You call that a car?"

"Hey, don't diss my wheels." I'm not sounding that convincing.

Even Tim laughs. "I can't remember the last time I saw one of that...um...vintage on the road."

Alex opens the door and gets out of the multi-coloured, mid-seventies Corolla sedan. It's a patchwork of orange, black and electric green. He looks from me to Tim, who is actually laughing so hard he can't breathe. I'm not far behind my cousin. It's the first time I've laughed like that in—well, in a long time.

"What's so funny?" Alex demands.

21

There's a full tank of petrol. That'll get you on your way. Wherever that is." Alex chucks me a phone, and a handful of sim cards. "You'll get one call with each of those, I reckon. Probably more, but better safe than sorry. They've probably got the network tapped. Morrigan doesn't do anything by halves. Chuck them away when you're done."

"I will. I'm sorry about your father."

Alex stops me with a look. "I know you are. Let's just keep you alive, eh."

He tosses me the keys. I unlock the front passenger door and put the phone on the seat.

God knows where Alex got the car from, probably the same place as the various other bits of contraband sitting under the blanket behind the front seat. I've got a feeling that if I open the glove box I'll find half a kilo of something or other. I open it. There's a yellowing service manual, which looks like it should be in a museum, a wad of cash that must come into thousands of dollars, a charger for my mp3 player, and a pair of aviator sunglasses. What the hell, I slip the sunnies on.

"Well, I'll be your wing girl, Maverick," Lissa says, flicking me a salute.

"Shut up, you."

I look at all that money. With that and the money I took from my place I have an alarming amount of cash. "If any cop stops me, I reckon I'm in trouble."

Alex shakes his head. "If any *officer of the law* stops you, you get them to call this number." He hands me something he's written on a Post-it note.

"They call this number, and I'll be fine?"

Alex grimaces. "It's by no means a Get Out of Jail Free card. If you drive carefully no one's going to stop you."

"Don't worry, Officer, I don't intend to get any traffic infringements."

Tim chuckles, but Alex doesn't. He looks at his watch. "I'd wait an hour or so before heading out of the city. Go with the traffic. You'll be harder to follow."

"Harder to tell if I'm being followed, too."

Alex shakes his head. "Nah, these guys are pretty obvious. You'll know if someone's following you."

"And what do I do if they are?"

"You drive, as fast as you can."

Lissa snorts. "Which won't be very fast in that car."

I thank Alex for everything including the number, which I slip into my wallet. Alex's eyes follow the movement.

"I just hope you don't have to use it," he says.

My face is raw. The only razor I could get my hands on was as blunt as a toy pocketknife, but I need to look clean-shaven. My stubble marks me more obviously than anything else, though I can't say I like the bare face beneath. At least the hair's looking good. I'm wired on adrenaline and cups of strong black coffee, and driving an old bomb out of Brisbane, following the Western Freeway. It's the fastest route out of the city if you want to head toward the low mountains that make up the granite belt. Up in the mountains, as low as they are, the air will be cool, even this late in spring—and the mobile reception should be terrible.

The car is older than I am, though Alex assured me it would run like a dream...Yeah, a patchwork dream. Lissa's already calling it Steven's Amazing Technicolor Dream Car. And I must admit that the car *is* running smoothly. Corollas from this era are about as unstoppable as the Terminator, and every bit as ugly.

"Any tunes?" Lissa asks.

I try the radio. Only AM. We get a couple of stations playing classical, and a talkback radio show, all leavened with a fair bit of static. Lissa sticks her head through the front windscreen, which is quite disconcerting.

"That explains it," she says. "The aerial's been broken off."

The stereo itself is fairly new. I link up my mp3 and we have music. Radiohead, intercut with Midlake, is a perfect soundtrack for my mood.

The sun's setting. Brilliant in its suspension of red dust, it's the starkest, most beautiful sunset I've ever seen, and I'm driving into it like some character out of a movie, crashing into the apocalypse. Number Four and the Hill are sliding away from me. And while that should be some sort of relief, all it does is leave a bad taste in my mouth. I'm deserting my city, and this is no movie.

• • •

We stop at Stanthorpe, about 200 kilometers southwest of Brisbane. I get a single room on the ground floor of a boxy old hotel, best for a quick exit. The carpet is about the same era as my car, a combination of curlicues and some sort of vomit-colored flowers—why were the seventies all about vomit colors? It's the ugliest thing I've ever seen, almost hypnotically ugly. But it's a survivor; you can barely make out the cigarette burns, which is something you can't say for the bedside table or the tablecloth which, while perfectly clean, is dotted with melty holes. There's a no smoking sign on the wall by the door.

The first thing I do is mark the doors and windows with a brace symbol.

The second thing is open a beer from the fridge.

I'm sitting there, in my underpants and a T-shirt, counting the cigarette burns on the tablecloth when I look up and into Lissa's eyes. "What do you do when I'm sleeping?" I ask her.

"Look at you," she says, and I laugh.

"Seriously?"

"Seriously. I look at you and I think. You'd be surprised how patient you can be when all you are is thought."

Thought is so fragile. A strong wind could blow it away like a dandelion. That fills me with a dreadful sorrow.

"How long's this binding going to hold?"

"I don't know. Do you want to break it?"

"No!"

"Are you sure about that? You've only had grief since I came along."

"Less than some of my girlfriends," I say.

"Girlfriend, eh?"

"It's more of a marriage. After all, we're bound together."

"Well, at least you haven't started nagging me yet," Lissa says, giving me a dirty look. "And the only sex we've had resulted in your orgasm. You didn't even expect me to fake one. So I suppose it's a marriage all right."

"Ha! I'll have you know we de Selbys are extremely generous lovers. Besides, you're a ghost."

"I still have my urges," Lissa says, a little defensively.

"Well, I wish you had more corporeality," I say.

"So do I."

We stop ourselves there. Our eyes meet, and we both turn sharply away.

I finish my beer, then walk to the bathroom and clean my teeth with a finger and some salt. I wonder if I'm being a dickhead. Probably. More than probably. I know it with deep certainty, and I'm suddenly ashamed. This girl brings out the best and the worst in me.

I've experienced more with Lissa, and with more intensity than with anyone else I've known, including Robyn— then I catch myself. It's the first time I've thought of her in what feels like days. Well, that's something at least. And here we are in this old hotel room which smells of smoke and cheap instant coffee, the traffic rumbling outside, the road's endless breath. It's the lovers' cliché, this.

I step out of the bathroom and look at Lissa. Those amazing green eyes hold me again. This time she doesn't turn away.

"You can have a quick wank if you want," Lissa says, and smirks.

I grimace. "I'm going to sleep."

After switching off the light there's half an hour of restless tossing and turning on a mattress that's firm and soft in all the wrong places.

Lissa chuckles. "Go on. You'll feel better for it," she whispers in my ear.

"Shut up."

22

I never sleep well in strange places, and that's all I've had these past few nights. At least the hotel is better than a highway underpass or a stormwater drain. My sleep is light and dream-fractured. There's a lot of running. I keep seeing the faces of my family and they're yelling at me, but I can't hear what they're saying. All I get is the urgency. And then there are a couple of nightmares on high rotation. I'm dreaming of:

Bicycles. They're tumbling from the sky.

Wheels spinning, gears shifting, and when they strike the ground they make skullish craters, the orbits of which cage vivid green eyes. Every death's head skull stares at me with Lissa's eyes.

It's not that far away, a voice whispers.

A bicycle strikes me hard. Gears grind down my arm. I drop to a crouch, cover my head with my hands. Warm blood trails from my wrist.

Duck and cover doesn't work anymore. It never really did.

I recognize the voice, it's—

I remember the first time I saw Mr. D. I was about ten and Dad had taken me to work. Even then I had a clear idea of what my parents did. Death was never such a big deal in my family. Cruelty, unfairness, rugby league— these were often spoken of—but not death, other than in the same way one spoke about the weather.

So I guess I was in something of a privileged position. Most kids my age were just starting to realize that such a thing as their own demise was possible, where I already considered it a natural part of existence.

Dad had told me it was time, but I hadn't really understood until he took me into Number Four. There was Morrigan, who scruffed up my hair. Number Four tingled around me with all the odd pressures of multiple worlds pulling and pushing at my skin like ghostly fingers. It was a peculiar sensation, and unsettling.

Then I saw Mr. D and he terrified me.

"Is this your boy, Michael?"

Dad nodded. "This is Steven."

"My, he's grown."

I realized that he must have seen me before. Well, I knew that I hadn't seen him—how could I forget? His face, it shifted, a hundred different expressions in a second, and yet it was the same face. He crouched down to my height, and smiled warmly.

"You were just a baby when I saw you last. Have you had a good life so far? Do you want to be a Pomp like your father?"

I nodded my head, confused. "Yes, sir," I said.

"Oh, none of that. Mr. D will do fine. The age of

formalities is deader than I am." He looked up at Dad. "He's certainly your boy," he said. "Very brave."

I didn't feel brave at all.

He looked back at me, and I saw something in his eyes, and it horrified me. There, reflected back at me, was a man on his haunches, face covered in blood, howling. And a knife: a stone knife.

I let out a gasp.

Death held my hand, his fingers as cold and hard as porcelain in the middle of winter, and he squeezed. "What's wrong?"

"N-nothing."

"Not yet, anyway," Mr. D said, and he smiled such a dreadful and terrible smile that I have never forgotten it.

And I dream of it still, even when I don't realize that's what I'm dreaming of. Shit, that grin creeps up on me when I'm least expecting it. There was a bit of the madness of Brueghel's "Triumph of Death" in it, though I didn't know that at the time, and something else. Something cruel and mocking and unlike anything I'd ever seen.

I have spoken to Mr. D since, and nothing like that has happened again. Of course, it doesn't matter anymore, but it did then, and it haunted me for over a decade. It's true, isn't it? You drag your childhood with you wherever you go. You drag it, and it sometimes chases you.

I wake, and then realize that I'm not awake. The sheets cover me, and then they don't. I'm naked, standing in the doorway, and they're out there, a shuffling presence, a crowd of wrongness rapidly extending through the country.

You need to hurry, Steven. I can feel every single one of them. They shouldn't be here. But of course they are, there's no one to stop them.

You wait out here, and it will be too late.
You have to call me.

I turn to see who is talking, and I know, and am not surprised.

Mr. D is a broken doll on the floor. He's a drip in the ceiling. A patch on the floor. He's smiling.

And then Lissa's there and she's gripping an axe. The smile on her face is no less threatening than Mr. D's, and it's saying the same thing. Death. Death. Death. In one neat movement the axe is swinging toward my head. I hear it crunch into my face and—

I wake to dawn, feeling less than rested. My face aches and I know I've come from some place terrible.

"Not a good sleep?" Lissa's looking down at me.

The image of an axe flashes in my mind. It takes a lot not to flinch.

"What do you think?" I rub my eyes and yawn one of those endless yawns that threatens to drag you back into sleep. It's early, no later than 5:30, but I don't want to return to my sleeping. I don't want to slip back into those dreams.

"You talk a lot in your sleep, you know," Lissa says.

"I have a lot on my mind."

"And you drool all over your pillow."

I wave feebly in her direction, then drag myself out of bed and stumble to the bathroom. There's a hell of a lot of blood in there, more blood than any portent has given me before.

I don't know where the blood comes from, even now. I've never found a satisfactory answer, which is fine, when most of the time it's only a splatter here or there. But this bathroom has more in common with an abattoir. I almost throw up.

"Come and have a look at this," I say.

She's by my side in an instant. "Oh, that's not good."

"What the hell is going on?"

"I don't think Morrigan has everything under as much control as he would like."

That's an understatement. I grab the showerhead and start hosing the blood away. I feel like some mafia hitman cleaning up after a brutal kill, only there's no body, thank Christ. It's gone fairly quickly but the stench remains and, with it, the feeling of things coming. A dark wave on the verge of breaking.

I shower, soap myself down, rinse and do it all again. Maybe fleeing the city wasn't such a good idea after all. But if that portent is correct there is a stir happening somewhere near, a big one.

"I have to do something about it," I say.

"He may be able to track you, if you do."

"My job is to facilitate death," my voice sounds high and unfamiliar in my ears, "not to allow murder, and if I don't stop this stir, I'm a party to it."

"How many stirs do you think are happening now, right around the country?"

I glare at her. "I know, but I'm near this one."

23

I get dressed and take a drive.

It's easy to sense, more than ever. The Stirrer's presence is a magnet, and I follow the line of least resistance toward it. It's as though the car has a mind of its own. I barely have to turn the wheel.

Lissa's silent the whole way, and I don't know if she's angry with me or worried, maybe a bit of both.

We end up at the local hospital, almost in the center of Stanthorpe.

The staff there let me through when I raise one hand to reveal the scars criss-crossing it. They look harried and frightened. I guess that there have been a lot of things going bump, and then murderous, in the night lately.

One of the senior doctors meets me near the reception desk.

"I'm here to deal with your problem," I say.

"Thank Christ. We've never had to wait this long."

I can tell. Everyone here is strung out and weak. The Stirrer is drawing their essence away. There's a vase of dead flowers by the reception desk. The doctor looks at that.

"Not again," he says, tipping the dead things into a bin. "Keeps happening."

And there's no stopping this, until I do something about it. Soon, the sicker, older patients will pass on, and more Stirrers will appear, and more life will be drawn out of the world. It's reaching tipping point and I'm gripped with a sudden urgency to get this thing done.

"Where is it?" I ask. I hardly need to, I can feel it.

"The Safe Room," he says.

Out here in the regional areas it can take a day or so before someone is available to pomp a Stirrer. They don't make a big fuss about it, but most regional hospitals have ways of dealing with their Stirrers.

We walk through the hospital, descending a level by way of a narrow stairwell. With every step, the sense of wrongness increases. The air closes in, grows heavy with foulness.

Another senior doctor's waiting by a door. He mops at his sweaty brow with a handkerchief.

"We've had to lock the lower room," he says, relieved as all hell to see me. "This one is a bit more active than usual."

I nod, hoping that I look more confident than I feel.

"This is too dangerous," Lissa says again, though her eyes say otherwise. I'm doing the right thing, the only thing.

The door is marked in all four corners with the brace symbol. My Pomp eyes can see them glowing. They're lucky, Sam made these markings.

"Sam's alive," I say to Lissa.

The doctor looks at me questioningly. He can't see Lissa, of course. "Sam's one of my workmates. She's in trouble."

This guy doesn't know the least of it. "Yeah, we all are."

My fingers brush one of the brace symbols. I swear and yank my hand away from it. "Hot," I say, blisters forming on my fingertips.

The Stirrer has pushed its will against this door for quite some time. The sort of will that can generate friction is unnerving. Actually it's downright terrifying. A muscle in my left thigh starts to quiver, fast enough to hurt. *Suck it up*, I think. *You're here to do a job.*

I turn to the doctor. "The moment I'm through, lock the door and refresh those symbols. The brace is weakening." I toss him a little tin of brace paint. "Don't open this door until I ask you."

He nods. I look over at Lissa. "Don't go in there," she says.

"I have to." She looks away, but just as quickly turns back to me. "Don't let it hurt you."

The doctor glances at me.

"Sorry," I say. "Nervous tic."

"Just watch who you're calling a nervous tic," Lissa says.

I open the door, and it closes behind me. Maybe I should just turn around, head back out and think this through. I can't see the Stirrer, but I can feel it. I realize that with all that talk of trouble and doom, I'd forgotten to ask who was in here, or how big they might be.

Then it grabs my legs with its hands. Huge hands. They squeeze down hard.

Big mistake. My touch stuns it, but not enough. I slice open my palm and stall it, but it's painful, rough as all hell. This Stirrer's grown fat on the energy it's drawn from the hospital. I can feel its pure, wild hatred as it scrabbles through me like shards of glass, or knives slicing, cutting inside me. Almost the moment it's gone there's another Stirrer within the body. I stall that too, an easier stall since the soul's not been as long in the body, hasn't put down roots. I reach for my knife. I need more blood to do this properly. The next Stirrer to inhabit the body crash tackles me, knocking the breath from my lungs. The knife flies from my hands and skitters along the floor.

I scramble toward it, knocking over a tray of instruments. Sharp things tumble on me, stuff sharper than my knife. I feel around, both hands scratching over the tiles. Who the hell puts blades in a "safe room"?

The Stirrer is up. It's clumsy but quick, stomping toward me. One of its boots crashes down on my hand and words slur in its unfamiliar mouth: "Not this time." Then I see the flash of a blade, a cruel, hideous looking mortuary instrument.

I howl as the Stirrer's boot grinds down on my knuckles. It's a purer pain than that of a stall. I clench my teeth. All I can smell is blood, and death. Things have never been so clear. It lifts its boot up to put in another grinding stomp and I drive my shoulder into its leg, hard. Something snaps—I pray that it isn't my collarbone—and there's another swift stall. Then I'm cutting my hand on the nearest knife I can find... hell, there's a dozen cutting edges scattered across the floor. I slam my bloody palm against the Stirrer's face, just as its eyes open.

"Not this time," I say, my voice barely a whisper.

Pure hate regards me, then all life, and un-life, slips from its features and it's just a dead body.

I limp out of the room.

"Steven, Steven," Lissa says. "What did they do to you?"

I look at her. I realize just how frightened I was that she wouldn't be here when I came through the door, but here she is. Relief flows through me. I find myself shaking.

"I'm OK," I say. "I'm OK."

The doctor frowns at me.

"Sorry," I say, "just mumbling to myself again."

He drags a chair toward me. "Sit," he demands.

I look at the door out of here, then the chair. Gravity decides for me. Before I know it I have a blanket over my shoulders and a cup of tea in my good hand.

"You're not going anywhere until I look at that hand."

"And when will that be? I have to keep moving."

"When you finish that tea."

As determined as I am to get out of here, it takes me a while to drink the tea. It's sweet and too milky, everything I hate about tea, and it's the most delicious cup I've ever had.

"Nothing broken," the doctor says. "You were lucky. Now let's look at that palm."

He winces. Even Lissa winces. "Any deeper and you'd have needed stitches."

"Yeah, I was in a bit of a rush. I'm not usually so amateurish."

He looks at the scars that criss-cross my palm, and shakes his head. It's all part of the job these days, it seems, deeper and deeper cuts, more blood.

I get slowly to my feet. I'm still a bit shaky. "I have

to go," I say, and nod back at the open doorway to the morgue. "Burn the body. As quickly as you can, and any other body that comes down here. These are strange times."

"It's going to get worse?" he asks.

"I think so."

"Jesus, it's real end-of-days stuff."

"Regionally, yes," I say, and when he looks at me questioningly, I shrug. I don't have time to explain Pomp jargon. "I have to go. Someone will be coming for me, it may be too late already."

"Thank you," the doctor says.

I wish I could do more. But I'm only one person, and I've got my own problems. I get into the Corolla and head out of town.

"They know where to look now," Lissa says.

"I don't know how long we can stay out bush."

"A few more days," Lissa says. "We'll come back when he least expects it."

And then what? A few more days for things to get worse, for more horrible dreams? "I think he's going to expect it whenever I go back to Brisbane."

"Maybe. Maybe not."

I drive up north, inland across the dry plains. The land is flat and vast, but it doesn't feel anywhere near big enough to hide me.

We find a caravan park in a small country town, as far from anywhere as I've ever been. I pay cash for a couple of nights. The owner doesn't look at me, just my money.

It's hot and dry during the day, and cold at night, with a sky clear enough to see the wash of stars that make up the

Milky Way. You can lose yourself in that sky. Morrigan certainly couldn't get me there.

If I sense a Stirrer—and I do, even if it's hundreds of kilometers away—I go to it. And every night I use a different sim card and try and call one of the other regions. No one answers. The Regional Managers know what's going on, Lissa's absolutely certain of it, and they're not going to help.

They don't want this spreading across the sea. They don't want this in their backyard.

24

It's the third day in the same town and we're on our way to the local supermarket—Lissa and I have agreed on some music, Simon and Garfunkel, which is better than the Abba she suggested, and I just knew she wasn't in the mood for Aerosmith—when I notice the black car following us. I don't like the way it feels.

We pass the supermarket and start heading out of town. Lissa glances at me.

"We could be in trouble," I say.

Lissa looks behind us. "That's one way of putting it."

"Country towns, eh? You go out shopping and this happens."

The car's going fast, even for the straight stretch of road we're on, and it stinks of Stirrers. I put on a bit more speed but the Corolla doesn't have too much to give. We take a corner, way too fast, and the wheels slip a bit. The car shudders, but we stay on the road. The stereo hisses with the Stirrers' presence, the music rising and falling in intensity.

The black car's closing the gap between us, and then

I realize I've seen it before. It's the Chevrolet Lissa and I had watched race down Milton Road after Sam. Its grille is dark with dead bugs. It's been driving all night.

I put the pedal to the metal, squeezing every bit of speed out of the car, my knuckles white around the steering wheel. But in every moment that passes I get a clearer, closer view of our pursuers. Don and Derek! At least Lissa's not there. The Chevy's V8 engine is soon drowning out my sputtering four cylinders.

Don neatly swings the car into the next lane and it roars up beside me. The stereo's breathing nothing but static now.

Derek smiles at me. There's a rifle in his hands and a predatory look sketched across his face that somehow combines the Stirrer's hatred of life and Derek's almost palpable dislike of me. His shirt flutters in the wind and I can see the gaping hole where his chest should be.

He fires through the window. I've got the windows open—the only aircon you can get in a '74 Corolla—so there's no explosion of glass. The bullet misses me by just inches. I'm so glad Stirrer Derek isn't using a shotgun or most of my face would be missing now in a red spray of shot.

The road narrows up ahead. I smack my foot down on the brakes and the tires smoke. The Chevy shoots past. I'm already spinning around, my foot hard on the accelerator, choking on the smell of burning oil and smoke. Lissa's yelling, I'm yelling—shrieking, really. Various forces that I'd understand more about if I'd listened in my high school physics classes tug at us as we turn, and it's a near thing between rolling the car, colliding with a tree and getting back on the road. We make it, somehow, judder up to speed and head back the way we'd come. Simon and Garfunkel crackle back into life.

"Thank Christ," I say, though my relief's short-lived. In the rear-view mirror the Chevy turns neatly, far more neatly than I could ever have pulled off, and tears back after us. What else was I expecting?

"Steven!" Lissa's pointing frantically in front of us. That's when we nearly collide with a police car, head on.

It's only through luck that we both veer to our left.

I keep going, and the cop performs a textbook hand-brake turn.

Then the Chevy clips the back of the cop car and hurtles through the air, flipping over. It slides down the road on its roof.

I bring the Corolla to a shuddering, squealing, rattling halt. I can't leave the cop with these Stirrers, even if the Chevy is totaled. He's a target, and if they take him they've just got another agent for their cause, and a cop car. Time to put an end to their aggressive expansion.

I take a deep breath and turn the Corolla around. This would be all so very *Mad Max* if I was driving a V8, and if it wasn't me. Lissa doesn't say anything until I stop the car off the road by the smoking wreck. She knows what I have to do. I swing open the door. Lissa follows, staying back, the Stirrers' combined presence pulling at her.

Only one of them is getting out of the car. Don. I slide my knife across my palm.

But that's bad enough. I'm gagging at the sight of him. Most of his chest is crushed against his back and his heart flutters beneath the wreckage of his meat and bones. He's the perfect picture of a Romero zombie, except the bastard is lowering a rifle to point at my chest. I'm thinking about the standoff at Albion, only this time Don *is* going to shoot me.

Why couldn't the gun have been totaled in the crash?

"Hey!" the cop shouts.

Don spins and aims the rifle at the cop. I sprint toward him, grab the Stirrer by the arm and feel him slide through me. But almost at once there's another one in the body. It stalls through, too, and then another one. Every stall is rough and breath-snatching. The Stirrers are getting stronger, and the rate at which they are re-entering bodies is rapidly increasing. I feel each one's rage at its too-swift passing, and there's so many of them.

Lissa's frantic behind me. There's nothing she can do. We both know that. But it doesn't make it any easier.

Stirrer Don is a bloody spinning door, and I'm standing on the precipice of a vast and horrible invasion. The body jerks and I grit my teeth against the motion. Each Stirrer gets a single movement in. They're orchestrating it, each entering spirit moving in sync with the previous one. Jesus knows how they're doing it, but I'm getting an elbow in the head. The movement is little more than a series of stop motion convulsions, but the elbow is no less persuasive. And every stall is tearing through me, so I'm hardly at my best.

This is going to kill me. I let go, and the gun rises up again. But I've not stopped. My knife is out again. I slice open my hand, deeper this time.

The Stirrer snarls at me, the rifle against my chest. He fires. The bullet must just clip something, blood's washing over my face. I swing my head hard against his and with that bloody contact the body drops to the ground.

The cop has his gun aimed at me.

I lift my hands in the air, then remember the weapon, and let the knife fall.

"Don't shoot!" I'm almost screaming. I don't want to die like this. The car is now an inferno behind me, and my back is hot. I'm dripping with grimy sweat and blood's sliding down my wrist and face.

"Get down," the cop roars. He hits the ground, covering his face with his hands.

I'm on my chest with a bone-juddering dive. The Chevy explodes. And there's more heat striking me, and bits of car spilling from the sky in a heavy metal rain. I stay there a moment, coughing with all that smoke and dust, then slowly get to my feet.

The cop is already up, peering over at the corpse.

"He's dead," I say. "He was before I touched him."

"I know. That body's been dead for a couple of days at least," the cop says. His eyes widen at something behind me. He shakes his head. "I've seen some flaming weird shit lately. But this, you've got to be kidding me..."

The second Stirrer has pulled itself from the car. Derek's body is burning, but it doesn't stop it from shambling toward us: another rifle raised. Shit, give dead people firearms and soon enough it's all they know. Shoot this, blast that.

The cop doesn't hesitate. He fires twice, both scarily accurate headshots. "Supposed to work on zombies, isn't it?"

"Only in the movies," I say. "Slows them a little though."

The Stirrer hasn't done more than stumble though there's barely anything left of its head. It shoots, and misses. If it still had eyes it wouldn't have. And its presence is offending me, driving me mad. This isn't Derek, but this is as close as I'm going to get. I know what I need to do.

I rush at the flaming body. My knees almost hit me in the chest I'm running so hard. My shoulder slams into Derek's stomach, tipping him onto his arse, and he lands with a grunt. I drive my bloody palm against his flesh, and then roll away, extinguishing flames as I go.

Not well enough, obviously, because the cop drenches me with a fire extinguisher.

"My hair! How's my hair?" I demand, and the cop laughs, and then we're both laughing the crazed laughter of the utterly terrified.

"You're insane." He stretches. Joints crack, and he looks from the corpses to me, and back again. "Sorry about this, mate, but you're going to have to come with me."

"I've got a number for you to call," I say, and I can't quite hide the desperation in my voice.

He raises an eyebrow. His shoulders tighten belligerently almost instantly.

I give Alex's special number to him. The cop walks away and when he comes back, holding two shovels and some gauze, he's pale.

"You've got some very powerful friends," he says. "He said to tell you that it's getting bad in the city. And not to use that number again. Oh, and you're to help me, so dig."

After I bandage my hand (the wound in my scalp has stopped bleeding) we dig two holes for the bodies. My back's screaming by the time I'm done. I'm a Pomp, not a gravedigger. My hand's not much better.

"You all right?" the cop asks, wiping sweat from his brow. We've worked in silence, though I can see there's a good dozen or so questions he's desperate to ask me, and that he can tell I have no intention of answering them.

"Not really," I say. "About as good as you'd expect."

He laughs at that. "Yeah. You seem to have a complicated life."

"You don't know the half of it."

The cop goes back to his sedan. The back end is dinged up badly but it still looks driveable. The radio's already screeching with something or other. He says a few things into the handset and looks set to drive away, but doesn't. He comes back to me and shakes my good hand.

"Good luck." He looks at me, grimly. "Yeah, and I'd prefer it if you didn't come back through my town again. Not if you're bringing this kind of trouble."

"No problem," I say. "Trouble's probably going to come anyway."

"Thought as much. Anything I can do?"

"Run, if you get the chance."

He nods. He doesn't look like the sort who would run.

Lissa's waiting in the car. "That was close."

"You're telling me." I start the engine. God, how I want to kiss her, but that's not going to happen.

We drive for hours, heading to the coast, me pushing the car as hard as I dare. I'm running but I'm not sure where.

I stop at a deserted truckstop. While I'm washing my hands, and splashing water on my face, cleaning off as much of the sweat and blood as possible, I think about what needs to be done. I have to bring this back to Morrigan somehow. I can't keep running, and Morrigan is sure to find me eventually. If that prick were here right now, I'd—

I look up, and Morrigan's walking out of a cubicle. I blink and he's still there. I scramble for my gun.

"You really should think before you start wishing for things, my boy." He's wearing a short-sleeved shirt. The tattoos of sparrows on his arms are no longer bloody. The last time I saw him—wounded and frail—couldn't be a greater contrast to this Morrigan before me. I have never seen him looking so strong. He almost glows. Wholesale murder does wonders for the complexion, it seems.

On the other hand I'm pale, washed out, and what fingernails I have that aren't broken are dirty and black with blood. I wave the pistol in his face. "Get out of here!"

"Why are you so frightened? If I really wanted to kill you right now, you'd be dead. All in good time."

I steady the pistol, aim it at his face. It's one thing to know that he's behind all this, another entirely to hear it from his lips. I hesitate.

He blinks. "Are you going to shoot me with that?"

I pull the trigger. Nothing happens. Morrigan laughs dryly. "You always were such a stupid little fuck. You will see my messenger soon, just so you know how serious I am."

He's gone before I release the safety. I feel Number Four—I feel the Underworld—open then close.

Lissa's through the wall, her gaze swinging this way and that. "You're shaking."

I am, fear's running through me. I want to cry. I want to hit something. "Morrigan was here. How the hell did he do that?"

Lissa grimaces. "Morrigan is Ankou. He can shift."

"Shift where?"

"Anywhere he wants to."

"I thought that was an RM thing."

"It takes some effort, but Ankous can do it, too. Besides, his powers are increasing. That bastard really kept you in the dark. And I didn't feel anything, not until he was gone. He must have been waiting. You should have called for me."

"And what could you have done except put yourself in danger?"

Lissa shrugs. "I could have been here."

I try Tim's phone. No answer, it just switches through to his voicemail. I don't leave a message, there's no point. He's in trouble, he has to be. Lissa suggests that he might just have his phone switched off, but even she looks worried.

We head down the coast, driving until I'm too exhausted to drive anymore which is far too soon, but I know that I'm going to wake up with the car wrapped around a tree if I don't stop. I pull into the first motel in Noosaville with a vacant sign, not caring that I look a sight, though the bored teen at the counter hardly glances at me as I pay for a room.

I'm exhausted, but manage to have a shower.

Steam fills the room. Tim's in trouble, he has to be. I've been out here for days and I still know so little, except that Morrigan doesn't seem to have a lot of difficulty finding me. If I stay out here, there's no one to help Tim. How could I ever face Sally again?

The truth is, Morrigan can kill me whenever he wants.

It's three o'clock in the morning and I'm standing in the doorway, shaking, after another dream of bicycles. Even here I can feel it—the Stirrers building in the west and the south. I've had as much rest as I'm going to get.

"We have to go back, now. I can't spend another moment out here."

Lissa nods. "This was never going to be easy, Steven. But what do you really know?"

"That this has to stop. I'm learning nothing out here, except that Morrigan can get me."

So much for escape, it really was a bad fit. I'm a Pomp, death is calling me, and the rough madness of the Stirrers. Maybe that's what Morrigan expected, maybe he knew I couldn't keep away for long. "We have to finish this."

"It's going to be tough, going back."

"Yeah. But what else can I do?"

"I'm worried about what it's going to do to you," Lissa says. "I don't want to see you hurting."

"Hurting more than I am now?"

Lissa nods at last. "I guess you're ready. It's time to find Mr. D."

I grab my backpack—it's already packed—and open the door.

Lissa stands there. The Stirrer.

"We need to talk," she says.

25

My knife is in my belt. I can get it out in a moment. I look Lissa—I mean, the Stirrer—up and down. It doesn't seem to be armed.

"Well?" it asks.

I can either fight and run, or step back from the door.

I let the Stirrer in. She/it is unarmed and walks quickly by me and sits on the bed. The room shifts with her presence—the life in it starts bleeding away. I can feel all those poor microscopic creatures that fill any space on the earth dying. A silent shriek fills the room.

Lissa fumes at her body, and the Stirrer either ignores her or can't see her.

My eyes dart between the two of them. My Lissa, and this facsimile. Its presence startles me. This is a first, a Stirrer not trying to kill me. Just having her here is unsettling enough. They're Lissa's eyes, but they're not. The mocking wit has been replaced by a hatred that is at odds with her words.

"Morrigan wants you back in Brisbane. The killing's over with. He says it's time you returned."

This immediately rings false. I have no position of power to negotiate from.

She must read this in my expression. "He needs you back, Steve." The informal address is wrong and its callous eyes narrow. "He says it has to stop, for the sake of the region."

"I don't believe her," Lissa says.

Neither do I. Her presence itself is a continuous nexus of death. As long as this Stirrer and its ilk exist, the dying cannot stop—it can only accelerate.

"I don't believe you," I say to Stirrer Lissa. I can see that this is going to get confusing very quickly. I'm so used to waiting for Lissa's opinion. And that's just what he's given me, a deal dressed in the most persuasive face possible for me. The bastard has wrong-footed me.

"He wants to negotiate?" I don't know why, but my words send a shudder down my spine. I move toward the door.

"Yes." Then Stirrer Lissa realizes what I'm doing. She gets up from the bed, but it's too late. "You little prick!"

I dash over the threshold and slam the door shut then mark it with the brace symbol. At once it's hot to touch. It will take a while for her to break through.

She's swearing on the other side of the door. But not as much as my Lissa.

Then I'm in the car, rattling down the road. Heading away from the motel as fast as I can.

"I couldn't stall her," I say.

"Why not?"

"Because it's you."

"It's not me," Lissa says. "It isn't. Everything that it

remembers, everything that it knows—that I knew—contains nothing of the me that you know."

"I know, you're right. But it's you."

"Oh, Steven. I could kill you."

Well, I couldn't kill her. Not even a malevolent copy of her. Not ever.

We're on the road to Brisbane. Stirrer Lissa was right, it's time to negotiate, but not with Morrigan. No matter the pain, it's time to talk to Mr. D.

We drive south down the Bruce Highway, heading through the lightening landscape toward Brisbane. The flat plains on either side of us are broken only by the warty ruptures of ancient volcanoes, now silent. It's a tired country, and an old one, and I know what it feels like.

My brain is somewhat similar, my thoughts worn down, broken only by the sudden adrenal jolt that I'm actually doing this, crashing toward the last place any sane person would want to. There's a fair bit of traffic going the other way, people already starting to flee the city. I shake my head at the folly of that, even if it's a lesson I've only just learned. You can't escape death. It has a habit of following you.

We're in Brisbane early in the morning before peak-hour traffic—before even its first suggestion, just trucks and taxis on the road—and I get the feeling that it's not going to get too busy. The souls of the newly dead are hitting me: an altogether different and unwelcome traffic. They're stale and prickly and every one of them turns my stomach. Each has felt the touch of a Stirrer. I wonder if Sam is still out there, and how she might be feeling, having had to deal with all this urban pomping virtually alone.

I head to the inner-city suburb of Toowong. It wasn't so

long ago that I fled from here, though it feels like an absolute age. I park the car in a side street, under a drooping poinciana tree, slip on my backpack then walk to the CityCat terminal on the river and wait for a ferry. This is the most convenient place, Lissa tells me. I don't want to telegraph my movements too much, though I already suspect that Morrigan has more than a good idea about where I am.

As we sit on the dock waiting, I sketch an upside down triangle on the bench, pick at a scab until it bleeds and mark the triangle with my blood. Anything to make a Stirrer uncomfortable.

"Bugs Bunny or Daffy Duck?" I ask Lissa, because there's never a moment that's too dark to talk cartoons.

"Mickey Mouse. I can't stand Warner Brothers cartoons."

"Shit, are you serious? You can't be serious." So those badges aren't ironic. *You can never tell.*

"I love Mickey Mouse," she says, tapping the badge on her sleeve. "Finest fictional creation of the twentieth century."

"Finest creation of the—Oh my, you seem to have forgotten Batman, not to mention Superman. What's Mickey Mouse got besides a whiny voice and big ears?"

"Universality," Lissa says. "No Mickey Mouse, no Disney, no manga, no anime. Besides, he rocks."

"He's a bloody wimp. I can't believe anyone actually likes Mickey Mouse, well, anyone above the age of four. Now, I'm a Bugs Bunny man. He's like some sort of trickster god."

"He's just Brer Rabbit."

"That's like saying *Firefly*'s Mal was *just* Han Solo. He wasn't."

Lissa rolls her eyes. "There's no point in having this conversation with you. You're too much of a nerd."

I'm just nervous as hell, that's what I am. There's a CityCat coasting in, the pontoon rocks with its approach. The blue and white catamaran's engines hum; its forward lights blink. "At least I don't like Mickey Mouse. Next you're going to tell me you don't like the Simpsons."

"Well…Nah, just kidding."

The CityCat docks, and we get on. I nearly buy two tickets—even now it's hard to escape the habit, the belief that she's actually there. It's early and the CityCat's almost empty, but there are still some passengers, all of them looking a little startled by the hour, which is odd. People up at this time tend to be annoyingly bright and chirpy. I wonder if they're feeling what I feel. Being this close to a Regional Apocalypse it would make sense. Unprotected, even the chirpiest of the chirpy would start to present with symptoms of fatigue and despair. I sit out front, and the cat pulls away from the pier. It slides toward the city, the skyline brightening in the distance.

It would almost be a normal day except there are bodies floating in the river. As I watch, someone topples from the edge of the CityCat and what's left of their soul burns through me. No one even notices.

Lissa points to a metal tower on the side of the river across from Toowong. It looks like a lighthouse but is actually an old reconditioned gas-stripping tower. It was used to clean coal gas for the city, stripping it of impurities, but now it's just a landmark on the West End side of the river. "That's where we need to go to get at Mr. D," she says. "I can feel it."

And looking at it, I know she's right. The tower has a

sort of gentle gravity—it draws the eye, like Lissa draws the eye. This is why we had to come back to Brisbane. There's a certain density of souls in the city that the rest of Queensland doesn't have. The population here is big enough to make such a place possible. I can't believe I've never noticed it before. Now I find it hard to look at anything else. It's the tower or Lissa. Both entrance and terrify me.

"Why are you sticking around?" I ask. She tilts her head at me. "I mean, *how* are you sticking around? You should be gone already, even with the binding. Everybody else is gone."

"The Underworld is pulling at me all the time," Lissa says, "but I don't want to go. I'm a Pomp, and I know what I'm doing. I know the tricks, there's all manner of stalls. The binding is just one of them."

I'm wondering how I don't know this. I wish I'd never bought into Morrigan's philosophy. There was so much I just didn't bother learning. I'd been too busy doing nothing, earning money, not really caring where it had come from, and moping after Robyn.

"But that's only part of it," she says. "There are two things holding me here. Hate—I really want to get the bastard who did this to me—and something else."

"What's the other thing?" I ask.

"You."

The city has never looked more beautiful than it does now. I smile, and Lissa's smiling too. She's never looked more gorgeous. Ah, I tumble so fast, but this is different. I want to hold her hand, but I can't. I want to wrap my arms around her, and I can't. She's all I want but to touch her would destroy her, and take away the little that we have. This perfect moment is nothing but a lie.

Lissa coughs. "You've got that whole geek–cool thing going on, like Cory Doctorow or—"

"Who's Cory Doctorow?"

"Science-fiction writer, and cute."

I don't know what to say about that. So I just say nothing, pull my jacket tight about me, shove my hands deep in its pockets and wait until we get to our stop.

We turn our backs to South Bank and head toward the tower in West End. There's hardly a soul about, though someone's swimming at the little fake beach there by the river. The tower's a half-hour tramp along the bank and it's still a good walk away when it starts to rain. And it's not just rain. I can't believe that I didn't see this coming.

Brisbane is beautiful in the rain, and it doesn't rain nearly enough. The city's been drying up for decades, so I feel kind of mean-spirited cursing it, but this rain is something else. It's the fiercest downpour I can remember. The sky's so dark, and my vision so limited, that it could be the middle of the night. But even then I'd see more clearly, because there would be streetlights.

The wind builds quickly as we walk, growing from breeze to gale to something else, the river churns past us, black as the sky. Storm-tossed things crash past us: outdoor furniture, rubbish and signage. Every step toward the tower is a struggle.

"This isn't normal," Lissa says.

I look at her. "It used to be. This is about as close to a Brisbane storm as I've seen in years. But it feels wrong."

We just grin and bear it, and I find myself almost knocked on my arse on several occasions, but it isn't enough to stop us.

• • •

"So they've built a fence around it," I say. "A high, rattling, shaking in the wind, fence."

There are Moreton Bay figs thrashing in the wind behind the fence, which looks like it could take off into the air at any moment.

"You can climb over it." Lissa is already on the other side, a broad smirk on her face. "It's hardly a fence at all. Hardly any barbed wire."

"Yeah," I say uncertainly. I hadn't actually noticed the barbed wire. The rain is streaming off the figs that rise up behind the fence, their root buttresses like knuckles bunched above the ground. I remember reading about this now. They're the reason this tall, portable (possibly too portable) fence has been erected—the trees are unsafe. The tower just happens to sit directly behind them. Metal spotlights shudder stupidly in the wind, making shaky shadow puppets of everything.

It seems some sort of fungus has gotten into the roots of the trees. It's visible even as I near the top of the fence, a dark stain penetrating the wood. I wonder what that might be like if it ever affected the One Tree. The fence can't support my weight, it wobbles, creaks, and then slams onto the muddy, but hard, ground. I'm face down in it, and winded.

"Well, that's one way to do it."

"Yeah, really elegant. I'm a bloody Pomp, not James Bond."

I get to my feet, slowly. Nothing seems to be broken. I check the straps on my backpack and wipe mud from my jeans. *Great, just great.* I take a couple of deep breaths, then consider the tower. "So how do we do this?"

Lightning strikes the tower before us. I'm momentarily blinded, my ears ring. There has to be a better way—with less thunder and great balls of fire. Lissa's unaffected by it all, and I'm reminded again that she's not of this world anymore. The storm, the lightning, all of it is an inconvenience.

Then a Stirrer drops from the nearest tree and comes barreling toward us.

"Steven!" Lissa shouts, and she's suddenly in front of me but, of course, it crashes through her. If I hadn't bound her to me she'd be gone.

I don't have enough warning to do more than tense as its shoulder slams into my stomach. I crumple over its back then hit the muddy ground again, with a groan.

"You should never have come here." I recognize the voice, Tremaine. The Stirrer looms over me. "But I'm glad you did."

Hatred breeds hatred. Stirrer Tremaine has it in for me far worse than the living one ever did. "Morrigan will be here soon, but I can kick the shit out of you before that."

"Have a go, Flatty," I say, hardly from a position of strength.

Tremaine swings a boot at me and I grab it, catching it mere centimeters from my face. The kick jolts through my body. He yanks his foot, but I'm holding on tight and I've got a good grip. I push him hard. He's on his back. I stagger to my feet, I have to finish this quickly. I need to get into the tower before Morrigan arrives. I kick him, then bend down. I slap my hand against his face and realize that he's wearing some sort of mask. I feel his smile beneath it.

"Not so easy is it?"

My hand yanks the mask free. He punches me in the stomach and I throw up all over his face.

Seems that blood isn't the only way to stall a Stirrer. He gasps then shudders, and is still.

"Christ," Lissa says from behind me. "You're an innovator."

I'm too shaky and sore to be embarrassed. The rain is crashing down with even greater force and my stomach is an ache that extends all the way to my mouth. And I know what I've been fighting for—just another gateway to pain. To make it even worse, a soul pomps through me. People never stop dying. The taste of blood is added to the delightful mix of vomit and terror.

"We have to get this over and done with," I manage.

"Follow me, mud boy," Lissa says quietly, her voice carrying easily above the storm.

We circle the tower once. It's metal, a rusty red. Up close it looks even more like a lighthouse than anything as industrial as a gas stripper.

"Follow you where? There's no way in, besides it'll be full of baffles and gas-stripping stuff. Maybe we need to do this outside?" I've decided I really don't want to go in there. I'm feeling sick with fear. "Yeah, out here would be better."

Lissa shakes her head. "Put your hand against the wall."

I brush a hand across the cold metal, hesitantly. "See, nothing." I'm lying though, there's a definite buzz to the metal, and the moment I touch it I can hear bells tolling in my skull.

Lissa gives me her darkest grin. "I'm sorry, Steve. But this isn't that easy. You know it isn't. Keep your hand on the wall. And you're going to need the craft knife."

I pull the knife from my pocket.

"There's a reason why this is so hard to do."

I understand that. We can't be encouraging people to cross over into the Underworld, even to the edge of the Underworld. It's easy enough to enter Number Four. Sure it requires a little blood, but only a pinprick, because that is an entranceway sanctioned by Mr. D. This is something else. This is a back doorway and its lock is much more complicated, much more demanding.

Lissa points to a spot on the back of my hand. "There," she says.

I know what to do. I drive that craft knife right through to my palm. I tear my throat with the scream.

The tower jolts and I leap back, my hand burning. The wound has healed, but darkly, and where the wound was is now a smoking scar. And where my hand was there is now a door. It opens inward with the force of the wind, clanging against the inside of the tower.

"Go the magic and shit," I growl.

"You always this cynical?"

I nod, peering through the doorway. It's dark in there. "Sometimes, but mostly only when I'm half frozen to death and covered in mud, and I've just driven a knife through my hand. After you."

Lissa walks through and I follow, closing the door behind me. It's an effort against the wind, but when it shuts it stays shut.

26

So what do we do now?" I shrug the pack from my shoulders.

We're in the gloom of the tower, in a space that shouldn't be. We're somewhere between worlds—a bubble of time and space, its surface marbled with possibilities, and far too many of them are grim. Whether I succeed or fail has never mattered more than now. The walls of the tower are marked at regular intervals with glowing brace symbols. No Stirrer could enter this place.

The air is rank with a back-of-the-throat burning odor of cat piss and vomit. Magic door and what not, it still bloody stinks. There's crushed up fast-food wrappers and soft-drink cans cluttering the floor, and a used condom opposite the door—hardly a clinical place for what I imagine is about to be done. But then maybe that's the point of it. Maybe it has to be rough and raw, and there's certainly something in the air, a little like the quiet expectancy of the doorway to Number Four.

The rain is loud against the metal walls, and the trees

outside sound like they are thrashing in the storm as though the riverfront's become some giant's moshpit. Inside the tower, everything rattles and creaks and groans. What's more, there is a bell tolling in the distance: really bloody portentous. I feel like I'm on some sort of carnival ride, one that is exceedingly fast and poorly maintained.

"It's going to hurt," Lissa says. "More than the knife through your hand."

"I know it's going to hurt."

"No, you don't. You just think you do."

"Look, are you trying to talk me out of this? If that's the case I would have been more open to persuasion before we made our way through the storm, before I fell in the mud and was nearly struck by lightning, and before being almost kicked to death by Tremaine. And just where else are we going to go anyway?"

"Have you got that marker and the *craft* knife?" Even now in the dark, with me scared and sweating, she can't help but smirk. Somehow, it helps.

I dig around in my pack and pull out the marker. The knife is clenched in my hand.

"So you're a Pomp, right," she says. I nod. "Well, you're going to have to be your own conduit. You're going to have to pass through yourself into the land of the dead. Well, to its edges, anyway. You don't want to go too far in—the further you go, the harder it is to come back."

"I'm going to the Underworld? I'm sure every Stirrer I've faced could have sent me there much less painfully."

"And much more permanently," Lissa says.

"Then how am I going to draw Mr. D out? If he's still around."

"He'll be around; he's trapped or hidden somewhere.

This ceremony will not only bring you firmly into the Underworld, it'll also break through whatever's holding him. It's essentially a summoning ceremony, but one where you show a *real* commitment."

"Mr. D won't be happy. You know what he's like."

"Yeah. But trust me, he *will* be impressed. Do you have a handkerchief or tissue?"

I feel in my pockets. Nothing.

"Then you'll have to use your shirt. You're going to need to soak it in blood."

"All right then." I take off my shirt.

Lissa whistles and I give her a look. It's not like she hasn't seen it all before. But it breaks the tension, and then she's all business.

"You need to cut here and here." She points to two points on my shoulders. "It's absolutely necessary that you sever the arteries there, and only *those* arteries. They're the portal wounds. I'm sorry, Steve. You've got to bleed for this to work. Profusely. Mark those points with your pen."

I shiver, my skin is all gooseflesh. She reaches out a hand to touch me, and stops just before contact. I look into her eyes and can see her recognition of my fear.

"You'll be all right. The binding ritual went perfectly. Just don't forget that shirt."

The binding had been a quick wank—a little messy, but hardly fatal. I've never felt as close to death as I am now. The precipice is before me and I'm the one who has to step off it. If I look too intently at the edge I know I'm not going to do it.

The adrenaline from the fight and the stabbing of my hand is fading. All I have to do this with is me, terrified and tired me. If I die, at least it'll be on my own terms. That has to mean something.

I mark the two spots Lissa has pointed to. The first one is going to be easy, if driving a knife into your own flesh is ever easy. I click the knife blade free of its plastic sheath. It glows dimly.

Everything is silent. I can't hear the storm. My entire universe has narrowed down to this. There's such a thrumming tension running through me that I could snap. Then all of a sudden my head is pounding, beating time with my heart. This is more horrible than I could have thought, and I haven't even started. *Calm down. Calm down. Calm down.*

I take a breath, and push the knife into my flesh. It's hard to apply the right amount of pressure. My hands don't want to do it, and a lot of me agrees with my hands. Most of me in fact.

But, shit, I *need* to.

I push and cut. At first there is no pain. That doesn't last.

"Oh, God." Blood spurts, ridiculously and vividly. I drop to my knees.

"Breathe," Lissa says, as though I am giving birth, somehow. I feel naked before her, stripped down to my essence. "Breathe. I'm here with you, Steven. I'm here."

I never realized just how far blood could jet from a wound, and its bursts are fast and forceful because my heart is racing. I'm shaking. Part of me is wondering just how much time I have before I lose consciousness, but that isn't going to get me anywhere. I clamp down on my thoughts with whatever will I have remaining, because there's only one action left to me.

I drive the knife into the shuddering meat of my other shoulder, my hands sticky and slippery with my own blood.

"The shirt," she says.

I've dropped it. Christ, I've gone and dropped it!

A bell is ringing. *Ha!* The voice of Eric Tremaine is rattling around in my head. *How the hell did you survive this far?*

I swing my head left and right, searching for the shirt. I'm clumsy, drunk with the loss of blood and the pain and the shock. My vision is spotting, narrowing down. There it is! Away from the mess of my wounds, untouched by blood. Definitely unsanguine. *How the fuck did that happen?*

It's you, Tremaine says, buried in my head somewhere, a new voice for my own self-loathing. *You.* Derek's there too, and they're both laughing, having a right old time, slapping each other on the back like the old chums they are. *See you in hell.*

I scramble desperately toward the shirt, through the blood that was once part of me and that is still pouring from me, though with less and less urgency now. *The well is dry, gentlemen. The well is dry.* I reach out one bloody paw and grab the shirt. "Lissa—"

Darkness smothers me like death.

PART TWO

THE ORPHEUS
MANEUVER

27

You come out of that sort of dark and you know you're done. You're dead, or you've brought the Underworld to you—and there's not a lot of difference between the two states.

Lissa's looking at me, her gaze heavy with something—pain maybe, or relief. We're in the tower. Only we're not. We've made it through to the fringes of the Underworld. I can feel it, not just in the silence, because there is no storm on this side, but in my flesh, just as I do when I'm at the office, only this is purer, darker and more terrible.

"I'm—" That's all I manage, my body is startling me. It's not how I remember it: except it is. The wounds are gone.

And there is no blood. Anywhere. Not a single drop of it within the curved space of the tower. I open my hand and there is the shirt so, yeah, there is some blood. The material is dark and dry with it. I fold it up and put it in my pocket. My backpack is next to me. I grab another shirt and slip it on.

I'm whole, and hale, except the cherub tattoo on my biceps is burning, as though it has only just been inked. I ignore it. Quite frankly I've experienced much worse in the last few days. The air, too, is fresh. No cat or drunk has ever marked this place.

"You did good," Lissa says. "For a moment... I thought you did too good."

And I want to kiss her. Her lips lack their usual blue-tinged pallor. In fact, her cheeks are flushed. There's not even a moment's hesitation. It's the only time I'll ever get the chance. I reach over and I touch her face, and it's warm against my fingers.

"Jesus," I say, and I can feel the pupils of my eyes expanding so fast they hurt.

"Here," she says, "in this place, we can touch. Here, we're the same." She holds my hand against her face. That contact of warm skin against warm skin is electric, and her beautiful eyes are wide. "But I don't know for how long. Steve, I can feel the One Tree calling me. I've denied it for so long."

I pull her to me, hardly hearing her.

"I—"

Then we're kissing. And I'm on fire. There is part of me railing against this madness. We're in the land of the dead. There is no time for this. But, really, my sense of time is gone. It has been since I drove the knife into that first artery. In a heartbeat such reservations burn away, and all I want is her.

Lissa pulls at my shirt, and I'm tugging at her blouse, and trying to get my jeans off at the same time.

I stumble out of them, awkward as all hell, but it doesn't matter. Nothing does except her. Her skin is soft against my chest. My lips find the hollow of her neck, my arms find an aching rest against her back, and there's a synergy, a perfect motion between us. I kiss her gently, then slide down, my lips grazing her skin, feeling her shudder through my lips.

I'm on my knees tugging at her clothes, then burying my face in her, rough and soft and wet. I'm tasting her, devouring her with a hunger that I never knew I had, that I never believed I could deserve.

"Steven," she breathes.

I am so hard. How can I have an erection here? How can I feel this way? The questions fall from me. They have to, because I want this so much.

I slide up against her. My body feels like it's fused with hers, that we've somehow melded together. I can feel her heart beating beneath her breast. It's crashing and pounding like mine, and here, in this gateway to the Underworld, it dazes me. Then I remember that we're not yet one, and then we are. And that should be enough to bring me to orgasm, the long lack of such sensations, the liquid heat of it. But I don't and I don't and when we do it's an epiphany of fire.

"Oh, my," she says.

"Oh, my," I say right back. My body is sore, but it's a good sore.

I kiss her so hard my lips hurt. I run a thumb along her cheek, then hold her head gently, staring into her eyes, trying to peer into the green-gated glory of her soul.

She smiles at me, and it's a different sort of smile. Not sardonic in the least. I feel for the first time that I've gotten past the armor, that I'm really seeing her.

Still there's part of me that's thinking, *Well, only one*

place to go from here, can't beat that, and another part is yelling, *Shut up, shut up, shut up!* and there's another part that's just beaming, grinning like crazy. My head's become an awfully crowded, complicated space.

Sex with a dead girl. That sets a new low for Pomps. Except we're both sort of dead now.

And, here's the thing: I don't care.

I open the door.

There's a cold wind blowing, strong and smelling of rain, a memory of the world I had just left. I shiver and pull my duffel coat about me.

The ritual was a success. We're somewhere, and I have the means to bring Mr. D to me and, perhaps, find a way to end Morrigan's Schism. And, hell, I'm in love. Totally in love. I almost spin. Buried in all this dreadfulness, I've found a perfect moment. I'm happy for the first time in longer than I care to admit.

I glance around.

We're in Death's neighborhood, but not George Street. We're in the park in the Underworld equivalent of West End—the tower is behind me. The river's flowing in front of me, but has a dark luster more like licorice than water. It's Brisbane but not Brisbane. There are gaps, places where the wind whistles through from... There's one near the tower, between it and the river, and I peer into its depths. Someone stares up at me and there is a jolt of recognition. I'm looking at my face. It winks at me, and then is gone, and I'm staring into a dark space as deep as the one I fell into to get here. Why the hell am I down there?

I look up, my eyes taking a while to adjust to the light. Across the river are the Underworld versions of the suburbs of Toowong and Auchenflower. In the living world the Corolla is in Toowong, in Auchenflower my house is nothing more than a pile of smoldering wood. Traffic is congested along Coronation Drive, and behind it all Mount Coot-tha rises, and it's there that the dead gather. Here the mountain is topped by a tree, a Moreton Bay fig, that reaches into the sky, its lower branches extending over the inner suburbs, its roots sliding all over the mountain, and descending into the city in great blades of wood.

The One Tree is a blazing cynosure above the city: the death tree where everybody in Australia goes when they die. The Hill squats beneath it, its stony surface blazing with a red fire. I've never seen it burn like that. Usually it's a dim blue light like something you'd expect in a public toilet to dissuade junkies from shooting up. I wonder if Lissa has any idea what it means.

"Lissa, you might want to see this." I walk back to the tower and poke my head in the door. "Lissa?"

She's gone. There's just the empty tower.

I feel her absence like a punch to the stomach. Now I understand what Lissa meant when she said we didn't have much time. She'd held on to me longer than she should have as it was, binding or not. Coming this close to the Underworld was going to draw her away from me faster than anything else. I should have realized that, but then I've been distracted of late. It's not much of an excuse. And it is no salve to my pain.

I take a deep breath, pull the blood-soaked shirt from my back pocket and drop it on the ground. Nothing happens. There is no sense of change or a magical burst of power. There is no sudden rising darkness that takes the form of Mr. D. It's just me looking at my blood on my shirt.

"What the hell are you doing, idiot?" Morrigan is standing on the edge of the road. He looks pale, almost ill. "I can't believe that—"

"Well, you wanted me dead."

"Do you not know how difficult that ceremony is?" And it's almost the Morrigan of old, the mentor, the one I've known since I've had memory.

"I know it intimately," I say.

"Bullshit," he snarls. "That ceremony has worked just once in three generations, and the man who did it then was raving mad. It's not supposed to work. You're mad, crazy." He's sounding crazy himself. Spit flecks his lips.

I shrug. "Maybe, but it worked."

"You're the luckiest man I have ever met." Then he wrinkles his nose. "I can smell the sex on you. Where's your sense of propriety? You did all this to get into Lissa's pants? I'm quite disappointed." And he sounds disappointed, genuinely dismayed.

"Lissa—"

"She's gone." He nods to the tree behind and above us. "You know how these things go. You're quite welcome to join her. Yes, there's an open invitation for you, care to take it up?" He looks hopeful, and I'm thinking maybe that's the way to go. With all this running around, I was heading in that direction anyway. But there's also a part of me that wants to wipe that smug grin off his face.

"Nah. Not just yet."

Morrigan rushes toward me, his hands clenched. Something cracks in the air, a thin sound, like a tire iron scraping over concrete. Morrigan backs away.

A shadow forms, coalesces, out of the air.

Morrigan pales. "You."

"Yes, me. Richard, you should go." The voice is dry and quiet, little more than a whisper. "This is still my kingdom, and you do not have a clue what you have set in motion ... Not really."

The man standing between us doesn't look like he should be particularly imposing. His suit is conservative, even a little threadbare, and his hair is parted neatly to one side. But he's imposing all right. And his anger fills the air with a dull and steady buzz. It makes my stomach roil, and he isn't even looking at me.

There is a soft exhalation, and Morrigan is gone. It's just me and the RM. Mr. D looks at me with such a wild expression that, for a moment, I wish I was with Morrigan. Then he grins warmly, though that's not all I see. There are too many faces for that.

"I've wanted to do that for days, but Morrigan is canny. It took your summoning to free me from the place he'd thrown me into. A broom closet, would you believe? Of all the bloody places, and not even a magazine to read. Steven, you've gone to rather a lot of trouble to see me. Shall we walk?"

It is a peculiar sensation talking to Mr. D. The man is slight and rather handsome, but also vast and power-hungry and grinning. He moves slowly, carefully, and sometimes he doesn't move at all, and yet he's shambling, racing, rushing around you, and checking and peering, like a doctor on speed doing an examination or a spider binding its prey in its web.

"How bad is it, Steven?" Mr. D asks.

"Well, I'm here aren't I?"

"You have a point. I would have expected Tremaine, your father, or even Sam."

"I can't tell you about Sam. But Dad's gone. Tremaine, too."

"So everyone senior?"

"They're dead," I say, and Death nods.

"I felt them, but I couldn't be sure. Everyone dies eventually. Call me biased, but that's what life's about. Even I can die, and without my Pomps, my position here is… tenuous. Morrigan knows that. He knows that my power is at an end—the prick."

I clench my jaw. "It isn't fair."

Mr. D laughs. "Nothing's fair, Steven. Not in the games we play."

I catch a movement out of the corner of my eye. An engine roars. And then an SUV strikes Mr. D from behind.

It nearly takes me too, but I'm just that little bit closer to the gutter, and Mr. D's hand pushes out precisely at the moment of impact, throwing me to one side. Death slides under the wheels. Bones crack like thunder. The SUV pulls away and shoots down the street.

I run to Mr. D's side, I try and help him. I didn't know Death could bleed, but he's bleeding all right. His clothes are sticky with it. There's blood leaking from his ears, and his lips and teeth are rubicund. I start dragging him off the road.

"Get away, Steven," he says, and pushes my hands from him. He's still strong—I'm flung from the road, the breath knocked out of me.

Mr. D stands, his legs shaking, his face messed up. One of his eyes has closed over. "Perhaps you should run," he says to me.

But I'm stuck to the spot. The SUV has come back and it hurtles into him. This time it turns in a tight circle and hits him again, then again. Morrigan's behind the wheel, smug as all hell, and by the time he's done, Mr. D is a lump of blood and rags on the ground. Finally I regain the will to move.

"Don't even think about it." Dad steps from the passenger-side door and points a rifle at my head.

"Dad, I—"

"How thick are you, Steven? I'm not your father," he says in my father's usual irritated tone. How can I think of him as anything but my dad? But the moment my eyes meet his, there can be no doubt. There's a wild, tripping madness there, and a vast alien hatred. His skin glows with a lurid, sickly light. Stirrers shouldn't inhabit the Underworld this way. Its true form is slowly burning through his flesh.

A week ago this was my father, though that animated spark has gone and has been replaced by the enemy. Still, if you're going to die, die pissing something off. "Dad—"

He swings the rifle at my head.

"None of that," Morrigan says, sliding out of the SUV.

The rifle butt stops just centimeters from my skull.

Morrigan rolls Mr. D's body over with his foot, and smiles. "So it's done. Death be not proud and all that," he says, rubbing his hands gleefully. This is Morrigan as I have never seen him. So damn happy. He terrifies me, more than Mr. D ever did. "Death is dead."

"Why?" I demand, and Morrigan wags a finger in my face.

"Need to know basis only, I'm afraid. And you know too much as it is. But don't be too sorry for him. The bastard deserves every last instant of pain." Morrigan glances over at Dad. "End it."

Dad fires.

At the same time cold fingers run over my flesh. Everywhere. They're brushing everything. I'm smothered in a rushing, tapping, piercing density of ice.

A voice whispers in my ears. "The rules are changing, Steven."

Then I'm in that dark space again, and the last thing I hear is Morrigan's weary voice.

"Oh, fuck," he says.

28

Crack!

That's how I wake, with a jolt and a deep gasping breath, as though I've been drowning.

Crack! The door nearby shudders.

Crack!

Dust, centuries old, spills from the top of the bookcases that line one wall.

Crack!

Mr. D sneezes. "Don't worry, I made this office with my own two hands. The doors are reinforced with my own blood, and the blood of my enemies. There's a bit of strength in them yet. Do you take milk?"

I nod my head as Mr. D pours my tea into a fine china cup. I've been here once before, so long ago that I'd almost forgotten about it. It's the inner sanctum, the throne room. Mr. D's big chair is up at the other end of a long wooden desk, and it's covered with carvings of figures running, fighting, dying, all of them gripping daggers, and is utterly incongruous with the metal, plastic and leather business chairs that face the desk. Morrigan covets that deathly throne. It shivers and sighs and seems to stare back at me. I feel the intensity of its regard. How can an inanimate object have such a tangled scowling presence? I can't imagine anyone ever wanting to sit in such a thing.

The desk is submerged in paper—scrunched up balls of it, rough teetering piles of it, and all of it covered in Mr. D's dense scrawl. Post-it notes fringe one side of the desk.

Mr. D catches me glancing at the papery chaos. "I never bothered with a computer for the real work." He lifts a hand and Post-its flutter like jaundiced butterflies from the table toward his wrist. "Who needs one, eh? Though I do like my Twitter." He reads the notes that he'd called to him, and frowns. "There are too many names I know on these things."

I'm quick to forget about that, though. Something else has grabbed my attention. Mr. D really does have the original "Triumph of Death" on his wall. There are all those skeletons getting jiggy with the damned. Mr. D has always seemed a little too smug about this picture for my liking, but here it is, in all its splendor.

I walk up to it and shudder. Looking closely, I don't see the Orcus in those skeletons, or Pomps, I see Stirrers. And I'm thinking about that impending Regional Apocalypse.

"Quite a piece of work, isn't it?" Mr. D says. "I, um... procured that for myself a long time ago. One of the benefits of this job. Well, it was."

"What the fuck is going on?" I ask, turning away from the picture. It's bigger than I expected, and I can feel all those mad eyes staring at the back of my neck.

Mr. D sends the Post-it notes fluttering back to the desk. "Death and death and death, I'm afraid."

There's an almighty crack and the door behind him shudders. We both jump.

"Well, that was a big one." Mr. D passes me my cup and saucer. His mind is already wandering to a new topic. It's not just his face that jumps around.

"There are other spaces, other places, and they proceed endlessly, universes and universes. One day, death may not be needed. But we're a long way from that." Death sips his tea casually, even as the door and bookcases shake. "I keep up with my reading. I like physics, I like the possibility that one day death will be irrelevant. After all, death is merely a transitional state. The body is devoured, and made alive again in all the creatures that devour it. And the souls of those gone are absorbed into the One Tree, sinking through it to eventually track across the skies of the Deepest Dark.

"Death's job, Steven, is to shape the Underworld, to bring to it a neatness, a less savage afterlife. And that's all I've ever done, managed my little alternate universe. Other RMs do it differently, but we're all here to provide a peaceful transition, to make sure the dying continues as it should, and to stop the Stirrers. That's the position Morrigan hungers for."

I'm still a couple of steps behind. I think I always will be. "He killed you. How are we even here?"

"Think about it." Mr. D taps his skull.

"I'm a Pomp—"

Death nods, and takes a loud slurp of his tea. Lissa would hate him. He also takes sugar. Mom would have hated him too. "Exactly. You pomped me here and I took you with me. Things are different for RMs—the manner of our deaths—particularly in such situations as this.

We're given some leeway. You being a Pomp meant I could use you as a portal to get us here. When that door they're so desperately trying to break down does, things will become a little more...final. The rules are changing, Steven. I'm not the first RM of Australia, nor will I be the last unless, of course, we have come to that time when death is made redundant." The door jolts, metal shrieks. Mr. D considers the door. "I'm quite certain that we haven't reached that point yet, not even close. For one, you're still breathing." He finishes his tea and gestures toward mine, frowning. "You haven't touched yours."

Crack!

Mr. D turns toward the sound. "Don't worry, we've time enough, believe me."

The dark carried me here half an hour ago and Death made tea with all the speed of a man who has no idea of the concept of the word "hurry" or "apocalypse."

I wish I could say that I share his lack of urgency, but I want out of here. And I want answers. "So what is Morrigan planning? To become the new RM?"

"Morrigan has always been extremely diligent in the application of his duties. It was only a matter of time before he wanted my job." Mr. D shakes his head ruefully. "Something much easier to recognize with hindsight, of course."

"So what can I do?" I look down at my cup.

"The first thing would be to get young Lissa Jones down from the tree."

"But the rules..." I have no idea how I can even reach the One Tree, let alone rescue Lissa.

But if there's a way...Mr. D better not be messing with me. I want Lissa back. I need her.

"Everything comes to a close, even the efficacy of paradigms, Steven. And besides, you must realize the rules are remarkably flexible. After all, you're here having tea with me, aren't you? Well, you would be if you actually had a sip."

I can't drink the tea. I'm too keyed up. "This hasn't happened before, how can Morrigan—"

Mr. D laughs and regards me with his affably vicious eyes. "Of course it's happened before. When these… Schisms occur there are no survivors, not if the new RM is doing his job. And let me tell you, I did my job most thoroughly."

"Oh."

Mr. D isn't quite the friendly fellow he was a moment before, and I wonder who or what I am really locked in this office with. If you scratch the surface of any business you start to find dirt, I guess. But it's disappointing. "So you…"

Mr. D nods his head. "Don't feel sorry for me, de Selby. But I am pissed off. I didn't see this coming. I knew it was inevitable, of course, but that hardly means I was expecting it, and certainly not from Morrigan. He was just too good. A stickler for the rules. A fellow always creating new efficiencies. I was lulled, Steven. I thought he had my back, not a knife pointed at it. I'd forgotten how it goes, you see." He grins at me. "I was a very nasty man, Steven."

Mr. D moves close and pats my back. "I still am, though I'd like to say I was an idealist, and I can assure you that I never dealt with the Stirrers. Morrigan is opening doors that should never be opened.

"Pomps are the front line in a war that has been going on since the Big Bang, between life and the absence of life. Ultimately it's a war that we probably have no chance of winning. Our enemy is powerful. You don't give Stirrers an edge, you *never* give them an edge. And certainly not now.

"Morrigan is very likely to discover that he won't be RM for very long. Once enough Stirrers are through there won't be anything living to bring over. Morrigan's made death too efficient for his own good."

I'm still a couple of steps behind, but I have to bring something to the conversation. "If you hadn't sent those crows I wouldn't have survived, and I would have lost Lissa sooner than I did."

Mr. D turns his changeable face toward me. "Crows? I didn't send any crows. I've had no control over my avian Pomps since Morrigan pushed me in the broom closet."

"Well, if you didn't, who did?"

"Crows like to see things out to their own conclusion. Perhaps they wanted to even things up a little. After all, my Schism may have been brutal—and it was, believe me, it was—but Morrigan has taken it to a whole new level. You shouldn't deal with Stirrers. I don't know if I can stress that enough. Absolutely no good can come of it."

"So what do I do?"

"Well, first things first, be careful: you can die here. Morrigan is going to want to stop you, and his influence in the Underworld is strong. You need to find Lissa. Love's far more powerful than you can believe, and you are going to need allies."

He's suggesting an Orpheus Maneuver. I thought they were impossible. They've certainly never worked before, as far as I know. Otherwise they'd have been named after something other than their most spectacular failure.

You can't just go to Hell and back whenever you choose. It exacts a price. It demands pain and suffering. Bringing someone else back is even harder. Orpheus failed and he was the best of us. I can't see how a Brisbane boy is ever going to better that.

My face burns. "What about my parents, would they make powerful allies?"

His eyes flare, and he jabs a bony finger at me. "Are you trying to bargain with an RM? Believe me, it doesn't work."

"Paradigm shift," I remind him, and I feel pretty cool, eye to eye, with Death. Is he really Death anymore?

Mr. D chuckles. "Now that's the spirit, but it would take a greater paradigm shift than anything we're capable of to bring them back. Bigger than that of the Hungry Death of old." My jaw drops at that. I'd always thought the Hungry Death was a myth, a scary story. "I'm sorry Steven, but they're too far gone."

"Thought it was worth a try."

"Everything is. The Boatman Charon, now he's the one you want to make a bargain with. Indeed, you'll have to. Or Neti, Aunt Neti, but no, she's probably best avoided for now."

The door cracks, louder than ever before. We both swing our heads toward it. Fragments of the frame tumble to the floor. There's not much left in it.

"One more thing. You're going to need this." Mr. D hands me a key. The metal is warm and oily, in fact it feels disturbingly livid. "It's my key to Number Four. The iron was shaped around the finger bone of the first death—the Hungry Death—so they say. I can't be sure of that, but it's old and powerful. Keep it on your person and Stirrers won't feel you. Morrigan won't change the locks. He can't, not until every Pomp is gone. Make sure he's never able to, Steven."

The door cracks explosively and splinters strike us both. Dust fills the room—serious dust, the dust of the dead, and it's heady stuff.

Mr. D's grinning and then he coughs. "Take a deep breath, Steven. I'm sending you to the place beneath the Underworld, the Deepest Dark. It's a short cut to the One Tree. You'll feel it drawing you. There will be a bicycle there. I like bicycles. Just keep riding until that breath gives out."

The mention of the bike startles me. I hope this one isn't going to fall on me. Mr. D sighs. "There's much about the nature of a Schism that Morrigan doesn't understand. That's about the only advantage you have. Once you find Lissa, you're not going to be able to run anymore." His shifting gaze settles on me, his face swims in the dust. "Things are going to get very nasty before the end, de Selby. And you're going to have to approach them head on. I'm sorry, but you've not seen anything yet."

I don't know what to say to that. I *try* to say something, but my lungs fill with dust, and all I manage to do is cough.

Mr. D pats my hand, and smiles. "Finally, lad, for what's ahead it's best not to think about it too much. We all die in the end."

And then I'm gone again.

29

The Deepest Dark is loud with the creaking of the limbs of the One Tree, but the sounds are carried to me through an air more viscous than air has any right to be. The vibrations of the One Tree judder through me. I am in the underbelly of the Underworld.

I'm crouching on ground knotted and ridged with questing root tips. Dripping from them like a luminous fluid are the souls of the dead, their time in Hell done. They slide into the air, first just as balls of light, but soon they take a roughly human shape—a life's habit, a life's form, is hard to undo.

Here, down is up and up is down. Above my head is the great abyss that all souls rise/fall into. What happens after, I'm not sure. Souls coruscate across the dark like stars, heading to places our words cannot encompass, because no stories come back from there. Nothing comes back from there.

For a while, despite my urgency, I am held by that

sight. Captivated. The time will come when I'll know it intimately—maybe soon—but not now.

The air crackles with the whispers of those long dead, coming down through the roots of the tree.

"It was only a cold. A passing that became passing."

"Miss her."

"Miss her."

"Sorry, never finished before I finished."

"And...And...And..."

"Sometimes it rains, and all I am is the rain. Can you feel me?"

"Here...Here..."

It is a tumbling cacophony of bad poetry. Maybe that's what people are, ultimately. These chattering final thoughts, crowded and messy.

I lower my gaze and try and shut out the sound.

Here in the dark, I reach out, and my questing fingers find the bicycle that Death has somehow left me. "Yes."

Yes, yes, the bicycle echoes. *Ride. Ride.*

I clamber onto the seat. I haven't ridden a bike since I was twelve, but you never forget. OK, maybe you do. The bike shakes beneath me and I wrestle with the handlebars.

Care. Care, it whispers.

Once I start pedaling, I'm in the groove. Easy. Sort of.

I ride in the darkness, the bicycle wobbling between my legs. The dark is a deep cold liquid pressure around me. My ribs complain, everything feels like it's going to implode. My breath grows stale in my lungs. Suffocation looms.

I make the mistake of looking up into the dark again and see the souls there, drifting slowly, spinning and orbiting one another. Some are twitching but most are still, and they extend into the weightless abyss above.

I get the sense that, if I look too long, my flesh, or whatever this is that inhabits this space, will hollow and lighten, and I will lift and rise into that dark. It's already starting to happen, and it's not altogether unpleasant. I've stopped riding. The bike tips, and I fall on my side. It doesn't hurt. I get to my feet, and I realize that my grip is tenuous. I've also noticed that the urge to breathe has disappeared. I'm starting to get awfully casual about the whole thing.

A crack has opened up before me, and I peer down. Light spills from it and I'm gazing into my own stupid mug. It's a bemused face, a little sleepy, an I-just-had-sex face. Then I remember why I'm doing this: Lissa. I don't know what future we have together, but I want to create the possibility of one.

I wink at myself, clamber back on my bike and keep riding. There's a long way to go.

I follow my instincts, taking one narrow road, then another, rising up one hillock then down the next. I pick up speed as my confidence returns, and I start to accept my surroundings rather than gawking at them. This isn't so hard.

Slowly the darkness becomes something else. A green glow reveals the streets of some under-under city. And it's the first time I start to have any serious doubts. There's a familiar wrongness about the place. It shouldn't be here. The root tips that extend over this part of the Deepest Dark are dying—curling up and blackening. The air is foul and choking. But it's where I need to ride.

There's a hall in the middle of the city and a door is

open. Something vaguely humanoid slips through it. Its eyes are huge, its face narrow, and its long mouth opens to reveal teeth. There are rather a lot of them, and they look sharp.

Then I realize where I am.

I've never seen one in its natural form, but I know what it is immediately. The hate-filled eyes glare at me. If looks could kill... I'm staring at a Stirrer. And this is the city Devour. I'm in the heartland of Stirrers. I'm a dead man.

The Stirrer sniffs at the air, and takes a step toward me. How the hell do you stall a Stirrer in the Deepest Dark?

It takes another step toward me.

The bicycle shudders between my legs. *Flight*, it whispers. *Haste*.

Good idea.

The Stirrer howls. It's a shrill and horrible sound that tightens my skin, and I pedal faster.

Not much time, the bicycle says.

I know what it means. The world closes in as I pedal through the streets, clumsily jumping gutters when I need to. The whole place is lit like the radium dial on an old watch. The sky above here is absent of souls, it's a patch of utter darkness. A wind crashes down from the dark, and it's frigid. I'm really not meant to be here. This place is telling me that in no uncertain terms.

A quick glance over my shoulder reveals a dozen Stirrers loping after me. They're making ground. The under-under world increases its pressure against my flesh. I start pedaling as hard as I can. And then the bike stops, just jolts to a halt. Unfortunately I don't, and I'm flying over the handlebars. I flip in the air, then land on my back. I open my eyes, all my breath gone now.

The Stirrers race toward me, their great mouths widening. I look at all those teeth. They grab my bike first. It lets out a shrill scream. The air closes about me like a vice. The fastest Stirrer grabs my leg and I—

I can breathe again.

The Deepest Dark is gone, and I'm…well…I'm in the Underworld again. The familiar smells of rosewater, rot and doughnuts fill my nostrils, the odor overpowering everything else, but for the dim hint of Stirrers. Here I am as deep in the Underworld as I have ever been and it is shockingly familiar.

I'm standing and shivering at the top of Mount Coottha—well, the Underworld equivalent. It's actually quite crowded here. But whether these people are dead or, like me, just visiting, I'm not sure. I think about what it takes to reach this place if you're not dead, and I doubt they're like me. But then there are tourists to every realm. Even Everest can be crowded at this time of year. People are gathered at Mount Coot-tha's lookout, built in the gap between two mighty root buttresses, gazing idly down on the city.

A baroque, brass curlicue-covered CityCat—looking like something a cartoonist might draw after a couple of tabs of acid, all flourishes and shadows, everything either sharp-edged or ridged with flowers—piloted no doubt by one of Charon's many employees, is cruising the black coils of the river below. Shadows clamber over it. The Brisbane River is one of the many tributaries of the Styx, and if you blink you can see, momentarily, the multitude of other rivers intersecting it so that the river below looks less like a cogent single stream and more like the vascular and shifting fingers of a delta or the veins of a lung.

The suburbs below, stretching out to the city and south to the Gold Coast (well, their Underworld equivalents) are, for the same reason as the river, a difficult thing to look upon. Buildings are fused together, different histories fold over each other. If you blink, sometimes the city isn't there at all, just a great forest. Only the sky is a relative constant, and the constellations that mark it are those that I know, though the dark is a little more crowded. Shapes stream through the spaces between the stars—spiraling ropes of birds and bats, or things that look like birds and bats, their cries distant and shrill, and meaningless.

The land of the dead is actually a little more happening than I guessed. We don't see this side of the world from our offices. Absurdly, I wonder, can people have mortgages here? What are the interest rates like? Have those fragments of the living clung onto that much?

But then I stop thinking about that because my left biceps starts to burn with a horrible liquid fire, more than the stinging ache that had bothered me by the tower. I grab it, and the flesh twists beneath my fingers. My tatt is taking a three-dimensional form: a nose and face pushes out from my skin. I try to push it back, and tiny teeth nip my palm. I snatch my hand away with a yelp. The tattoo draws a deep breath. The sensation of air entering my arm isn't pleasant.

Tiny eyes roll up in its cherubic head to meet my gaze.

"Shit." My voice is a whisper.

"You're telling me," the cherub says. It stretches its wings, which is a truly disconcerting feeling, as though someone is moving rods beneath my flesh. "What the—? I'm stuck on your arm. Oh, and where's my body?"

"You're just a symbol," I say, thinking, *I've grown a bloody inkling.*

The cherub squints at me. "One pissed off symbol. This is Hell."

"I'm sorry, I never thought about giving you a body."

"No, I mean, what are we doing in Hell? You're not dead, yes?"

I shrug. "I guess. It's complicated."

"No, it's not. Don't you sound so damn uncertain. That sort of uncertainty is going to keep you here."

"But here's the thing. I *am* uncertain. I've got no bloody idea what the fuck it is I'm doing here. Or even how to start getting Lissa back."

"You need a guide. Call me Virgil."

"You worked for Dante, I suppose."

"Ha. Maybe we should get a coffee first." The cherub says, and I don't argue. "The name's Wal."

"I thought your name was Virgil," I say.

"Don't get cute on me, buddy."

"What kind of name is Wal?"

"Better than Stevie wouldn't you say?"

We reach the cafe and I sit in pretty much the same seat that I sat in not so long ago when I was rendezvousing with Morrigan in the living version of this place. A lot's happened since then. The creaking of the tree dominates, louder than I have ever heard it. It's calling me, I realize. This is truly what it must feel like to be dead. There's a mesmeric quality to the sound and it generates a hunger in my chest.

I've pomped all my adult life, but I've never felt this

before. This is what I'm going to have to fight against, if I ever want Lissa back.

I run through the coffee choices.

"Sweet Jesus. All I want is coffee. What the hell is a flat white?" Wal peers at the crow growing out of the barista's neck. "What do you recommend?"

The crow cocks its head.

"Just get him something easy," I say.

The barista sniffs. "You saying we're not up to the task? Saying we can't make good coffee?"

"No, I—"

"We'll make you good coffee," the crow says. "You'll like it. Now what do you want?"

"Long black, no milk."

"Ah, typical," the barista sneers. "Fucking tourist."

The tree creaks like it's ready to tumble. Should it fall, the whole weight of it would surely break the thin shell of the earth and drive the city into that chill abyss beneath. I realize I've heard that creaking ever since I sliced open my arteries with the craft knife. It's a background noise that has lifted startlingly in volume, shocking me when I least expect it.

I sip my coffee out of a paper cup. It's cold and tastes burnt and a little ashy, but no matter, I'm still getting over the fact that my money is good here.

I look at my change. The money is subtly, slyly different. The plastic of the notes is a bleached white. The faces printed on it are the same, but the flesh hangs loose, the eye sockets are empty, and the expressions contained within change every time I glance at them. They shift from mute terror to mad laughter in an eye blink. Except for the coins and the five-dollar note—there the

Queen's face is serene and motionless. She's still alive, I guess.

The cherub grins at that. "I can't believe that after a century of federation, you're not a bloody republic yet."

Wal grips a chai latte in its wings, taking loud sips every few minutes that disquietingly warms my left biceps. I don't understand why *my* coffee is so cold.

I'm not terribly comfortable with the whole thing, but he seems to be enjoying his latte. "Haven't had a cup like that since, well, I can't remember. I do remember old Vic was still queen, and it wasn't as milky."

"Nor was it chai, I'd wager. Which hardly makes it coffee."

Wal grunts. "Maybe we need to keep going."

"How familiar are you with the Underworld?"

"I've been here a few times, day trips mostly. Been a long time between visits. So you're a Pomp. It explains a lot. The Underworld's different for you guys. It doesn't like you lot messing around. It gets you out of the way as quickly as possible. You can't change the order of things around here, mate. Your girlfriend will be up in the tree, and if she's been fighting her death like you say, then it may be faster for her."

"What'll be faster?"

"Assimilation. The tree's going to want to absorb her."

I'm looking at him, not comprehending at all.

"By your blank look, it seems to me that you are a pretty typical Pomp." I'm immediately defensive. But Wal doesn't allow me time to respond. "I don't know how you've lasted so long. What do you think a tree does?"

I shrug. "Grow."

"Nah. Well, yes, but *how* does it grow? It absorbs stuff,

and it leaches stuff, too. This tree's just a wooden sieve. It separates the soul, and puts it where it belongs.

"It's the memory of the world, and a reflection, distorted of course, by the memory of it, because memory distorts everything. And it's the resorption of all that psychic energy, all those souls. The tree does that. Without this place, you'd have souls running amok everywhere, and Stirrers. Shit, there'd be so much confusion they could just walk in and take everything. Which is, from what I've heard, exactly what's been going on."

"So Lissa's being absorbed?"

Wal grimaces, his eyes lifting toward me. "Slow on the bloody uptake, aren't you? Yes and, like I said, it's going to be quick. As far as the tree is concerned, Lissa's been dead too long already."

And then I notice the armed Stirrers walking through the crowd in the lower section of the lookout. Stirrers here? How brazen.

I have to get going before they spot me. I know they can't sense me because I'm holding Mr. D's key, but they'll find me soon enough if I stick around here. They approach the barista. Great. He points vaguely in my direction, with an arm and a wing, and the Stirrers head my way.

I move as quickly as I can, hopefully without drawing attention to myself, to the base of the tree trunk. Once there, I can see stairs carved into the wood. The stairs stop at each branch after winding a lazy, but steep, circle around the tree. I start taking the stairs three at a time. It's a long way to the first branch, and even longer to the top.

"Slow and steady, eh," Wal says. "You'll wear yourself out at this rate."

"I don't have time," I gasp at him.

By the third circuit I'm hunched over, my hands gripping the rough bark of the One Tree, and I'm throwing up my coffee.

"You right?" Wal peers up at me.

"Fine, just some bad coffee."

"Just try not to get any of it on me."

Several times I pass dead folk heading where I'm heading, though none of them seem in any hurry. They look at me disinterestedly. There are a few I recognize, like John from the Wesley morgue, who nods at me. The sight of him disturbs me. But we don't talk, there's no time for that. All of us are too focused on our respective destinations. And I'm too out of breath.

There is only one person who passes me.

Mr. D comes silently from behind. He doesn't look at me as he goes, his shoulders hunched, his face set. The RM just walks higher and higher into the tree, and though he hardly seems to be walking at all, he's soon out of sight.

So he's finally gone. I'm seriously without allies.

"There's a place for all the Deaths—for the whole Orcus—high, right at the top of the tree. It's called the Negotiation," Wal says.

"What's up there?"

"Something you don't need to consider right now. One thing at a time."

And that one thing for me is these steps, one after another, over and over. It could be worse. I could be carrying a rock above my head.

As I climb, Hell unfolds beneath me, attended all the while by the creaking branches of the tree and the cold fingers of wind blown in from the sea. It's a beautiful sight, awe-inspiring in its vastness, the colors muted but varied. It's city, forest and sea. It's a sky streaked with blood-orange clouds. It's every sunset I've ever seen, every first glimmering star. I'm determined not to get used to it.

This place is death to me. Beautiful or not, that's all this kingdom is about.

30

I reach the first branch, and know at once that it's not the right one. It's a sensation buried in the meat of me, a certainty that is almost comforting, because it suggests that I might know where I'm going.

A little further up there is the scent of familiar souls, of family—cinnamon, pepper, wood smoke, a faint hint of aftershave and lavender. Maybe it'll be the next branch, or the one after that.

I stop to catch my breath and peer along the wooden limb. It's a gently swaying woodscape, and all along it there are people. Most are lying down, some stand, but the tree is absorbing all of them. Wood sheathes their flesh. It's a macabre yet somewhat serene vision. There is no pain here, just a slow letting go.

Then I see the Stirrer. A big one. It'd take two of me to fit in it. It's walking between the dead, peering at this body or that. Above its head heat shimmers, but that's not what catches my eye.

In one hand the Stirrer's holding a machete. It looks

at me and grunts loudly. Shit. Mr. D's key means it can't feel me, but it certainly recognizes me. I lingered here too long.

It runs toward me, along the branch, and I don't wait around. I start up with a stuttering, desperate sort of run. I get back to the next set of stairs.

By the first circuit up from the branch it's obvious that it's going to catch up with me, and soon. My legs are burning, I don't have much pace left. I pass one then another of the dead, making my way around them as quickly as I can on the vertiginous stairway. The Stirrer isn't far behind me. I hear him push them off and their screams echo up to me.

"The bastard," Wal says. "They're going to have to do that climb again."

It's hard to find much sympathy for the dead, the worst has already happened to them. I know how resilient souls are. Me, on the other hand...I'm doing my best to avoid that outcome. I get flashes of the machete and the easy way the Stirrer holds the weapon in its hands. The thought of it slicing into the back of my legs is about the only thing that's giving me any strength.

I manage to reach the next branch, and I don't have any climb left in me. I stagger-run out onto its flat, windy, shuddering expanse. I'm panting and dripping with sweat, my legs rubbery. The edge is too close. I stare around me. In the distance a helicopter circles, looking for something that I suspect is me. I don't know what I'm going to do, but I need to do it here.

I only have a few moments to catch my breath.

"Stirrers are different here," Wal says.

"How so?"

"The Stirrers here must still inhabit bodies, but in this place between the living world and their city in the Deepest Dark, the bodies are tenuous things. The Stirrers don't fit well. There's a kind of friction of wrongness that exists between the bodies they inhabit and the Underworld."

"That's good, right?"

"Not really, they're stronger. The Underworld is much closer to their element and their true form will struggle to escape the flesh."

Wonderful. Exactly what I wanted to hear.

But there's no time to worry. The Stirrer's here and it comes at me, waving its machete in the air. Its host body is smoking, overheating. Flesh bubbles almost hypnotically, and ectoplasm the color and consistency of mascara streams down its cheeks. I'm fighting a zombie Robert Smith.

"You don't belong here," the Stirrer says in a singsongy sort of voice.

"Neither do you. Morrigan should never have brought you here."

The Stirrer shakes his head. "Come the Negotiation he will be the new RM. This will be his kingdom to rule."

So it hasn't happened yet.

The Stirrer swings the machete at my head, and I duck. My legs, weak from all that stair-climbing, shake beneath me, but they still have enough spring in them for me to swing up and drive the palm of my hand into its chest. It grunts and something shifts beneath its skin: the true Stirrer within. The form within the form strikes out at me. Its little claws or teeth rend its host's flesh. I tear my hand away. The Stirrer's skin is hot and there's a stinging red welt across my palm.

It's not what I was expecting. The Stirrer hasn't gone anywhere.

"Oh, yeah. Stalling won't work for you here," Wal says.

Now he tells me.

But the Stirrer is regarding me cautiously, and where my hand touched its flesh is a palm-sized black hole. It backs away. I've hurt it somehow, and I need to press the one advantage I have. I charge the Stirrer.

It hurls the machete at me, an easy, brutal gesture, and the pommel strikes me hard in the sternum, knocking me off my feet. The Stirrer looms over me and Wal's wings are a desperate blur to my left, as though he's trying to lift me through wing power alone.

"Get up, get up, get up," he urges, and I try, but it's too late.

The Stirrer grabs me and lifts me above its head. Smoke streams from its points of contact with my flesh. I can smell myself cooking, but I'm not the only one suffering—bits of its undead fingers are falling away like wet sponge cake and slopping onto the branch.

It stumbles and curses in an alien tongue, then something collides with it. The Stirrer stops, shakes its leg. Its fingers loosen their grip now, just when I don't want them to. We're a long way up, and the edge of the tree is so near. I can see the city and the dark beyond. I'd very much like to stay up here rather than go hurtling down.

There's an oddly familiar growl coming from the Stirrer's ankles. I look down and there is Molly. Her jaws are wrapped around the Stirrer's ankles. She looks at me and her expression is like, *Well, come on, help me out here!*

I slam my fist into the Stirrer's temple, hard enough

that my knuckles crack. It shudders, releases its grip on me, and I fall. I swing out at the branch, grabbing as I go, but my grip is slippery at best. I slide over the edge until I'm holding on by my fingertips, my feet dangling over all that empty space. I get the feeling that if I fall I won't be climbing back up as anything living. Wal's wings are a hummingbird blur again; as though that's going to do any good.

Molly grabs at my wrist, as gently as she can, and pulls. Together we get up onto the branch and I lie there panting. I reach up and hug her. "Molly," I say. "Molly, I'm so sorry."

The Stirrer stays back. Bits of it have fallen away, and whatever's left has slipped so that it looks like a poorly made human collage.

Molly's smiling that beautiful grin of hers. She stays by my side for a moment, then crashes toward the Stirrer, barreling into its legs. The Stirrer topples forward, sliding past me and over the edge of the branch. Its slide slows and Molly leaps onto its back. She starts to burn, but she's everywhere, snarling and biting. The Stirrer's eyes are wide with terror or rage, Molly snapping at its neck. It reaches out for the branch, and gets a grip. Then, with the sound of wet paper tearing, wrist and hand separate. And they're gone.

I stumble toward the edge.

I watch Molly and the Stirrer fall away like some sort of flaming comet, rushing to the dark earth beneath us. The earth opens up, or low dark clouds scud in, because they are suddenly out of sight. Besides, I can hardly see at all. My eyes are wet with tears.

"Molly," I say. "Molly Millions."

I stare down at the dark where they fell. I'm beginning to understand this place better and what it means to come here. In essence it's just a way of losing what you love a second time. "Maybe I should have let Lissa go," I say.

Wal's head turns up toward me. "Ah, bullshit," he says. "Think of all the people who have suffered to get you here. Everyone suffers to get here. And you're ready to give up."

"Maybe."

Wal sighs. "That's just the Underworld talking. It's going to get worse, but if you want Morrigan to rule here, if you're happy to have him get away with all the killing, then who am I to argue? After all, the best I can get is living on your arm. It's *not* inhibiting at all."

Wal's right. I give myself a few more moments at the edge and then I climb again, following the stairs up into more crowded branches. Here, the stairs and the branches intertwine. We climb a tight bundle of fleshy tendrils, and we follow wooden handholds, hammered into the trunk of the tree, sticky with sap. Upward, always upward, and soon we're on another broad branch.

And, there, I see my parents.

The tree has begun to wrap around Mom and Dad's legs with woody vines rising from the trunk. Mom looks up, her eyes are dull. Death is already settling down her humanity, letting her sink into the tree and the universal thought or whatever it is that exists beyond the flesh and the memory of flesh. Soon she and Dad will be nothing but whispers and light dripping from the roots of the tree.

It's always faster with Pomps, maybe because we have an idea of what to expect, and we're cool with it. Slipping into some sort of universal truth is so much better than spending your eternity in heaven or whatever. Still, when Mom sees me her eyes widen and the dullness fades away.

"Steven. Oh, no. I was hoping that—"

"It's OK, Mom. I'm not dead."

Mum gives Dad a significant look. She might as well be giving him the crazy signal. Dad frowns.

"Seriously, both of you. I'm not."

"Then what in the seven bloody hells are you doing here? The living aren't meant for this place, Pomp or not."

"I'm looking for Lissa."

"Oh, the Jones girl! An Orpheus Maneuver, eh?" Dad gives me an extremely wicked look. "You know where she is, love?"

Mom has always had a greater sensitivity to the dead. We both look at her. Mom lifts her head and breathes deeply. "Oh, but there are a lot of Stirrers on the tree! They're like termites. They're going to be hard to get rid of, and it makes it difficult to... Yes! I can feel her. She's on the next level. She came in fast, which means she'll leave fast. If you weren't here I'd think you were with her." She glances over at Dad. "He was certainly all over her."

I redden at that. "Yeah, well..."

Dad winks at me, and Mom sighs. "But Steven, if you *are* here, it's not bad. It's marvelous, in fact. I've not felt... It's... Well..." Finally she shakes her head.

I know what she means. It is terrible and marvelous at once. The things I've seen getting here, things not even hinted at from our vantage point at Number Four. It's the sort of stuff you're not supposed to know until you're dead.

I don't know what I am here in the Underworld, except I'm not that. Definitely not dead, not yet. I kiss Mom's forehead. Her skin is cold against my lips. I'm finally getting the chance to say goodbye, but it isn't any easier.

"I love you, Mom."

"I love you, Steven." She blinks. "Get out of here as quickly as you can."

Dad nods. "Go get her, Steve," he says. "She's a good one."

"I could try and send you back," I say, and there's a slight pleading tone in my voice.

"No, I've died once. That's enough for me, Steve. I'd like to say I miss you but that's for the living, and your mother and I, well, we're not living anymore." He smiles, looks over to Mom, and she nods her head—wow, they actually agree on something. "Get her, Steve," he says. "And then, stop Morrigan. I can feel what he's doing even here. He's an idiot. You can't deal with the enemy and not expect grim consequences."

I look at them one last time, then clamber up the interconnecting branch.

"Oh, and I'm glad you got rid of that beard!" Mom shouts after me.

31

I look down and notice that, not too far below, there are Stirrers with machine guns. One of them points up at me. I hear a distant crack, crack, cracking and the wood near my feet explodes. I get out of the way, quick smart.

Even more worrying is the helicopter racing over the city toward this branch.

I don't know how long I've got, but I can hear the chopper drawing nearer. It's a peculiar looking thing, with huge, flat tear-shaped blades that look as though they're made of brass. But the Stirrers in its cockpit are grim-and melty-faced and all of them are carrying guns—old AK-47s. Morrigan's ambitions are huge, but he's still obviously working on a budget. One of the chopper crew points in my direction.

"That can't be good," Wal says, less than helpfully.

All I can do is try and climb faster.

The wind is picking up: salt driven on the air. A storm rushes along the surface of the sea, pelting toward the city. I grin into the wind, feeling somehow recharged by it. Out there beyond the edge of the city the great dark sea is crashing against the shore. Even here things rage and swell and live a kind of life, and my cares fall away from me all at once.

I'm wearing that smile on my face when I see her, but it doesn't last.

The One Tree has bound itself around her with rough fingers of bark. Lissa's eyes are milky with death. There is no recognition there. I might already be too late.

One of her fingers wiggles.

I touch it, and feel the slightest warmth, just the barest hint of life.

I don't want to be here and, above all, I don't want her to be here. If I could tear down the Underworld I would. But I don't have that power, just my love and my will. I'm terrified of failing, I'm terrified of succeeding. The only thing I don't doubt are my feelings for her.

The branch fights me all the way. It grows thorns. It snaps at my fingers with little teeth. I bleed pulling the bark off her, and maybe that's what does it, because the tree gives her up at last. I lay her gently onto the branch.

I touch her face. There's a flat warmth to her flesh that is almost worse than the cold I was expecting. Her eyes are dull, barely green at all, and nowhere near the startling, quick to fire color that I remember.

I hold her in my arms. She is still. I can't feel any more warmth. I lower my lips to hers and a force, a presence, a fire passes through me in a brief, agonizing flash. The tree shakes. Something howls, the light dims and I get a vague sense that the whole Underworld has paused. Even the storm seems to be waiting.

Then Lissa coughs and shudders. Her eyes widen. "Steven?"

"Lissa." *My darling Lissa.*

Her face wrinkles. "Steven, this isn't some sort of cruel joke, is it?"

"It better not be." I'm grinning again, a smile so wide that it hurts. My hand rests on her cheek; her skin is warming. And her eyes, they're no longer as flat, as lifeless. Shit, of course that could just be wishful thinking—that's gotten me here as much as anything else, even if Wal doesn't believe it.

"So how do we do this?" I ask her, and she frowns.

"Do what?"

"I'm taking you back."

"There's no... You can't. Not an Orpheus Maneuver," Lissa says. "You'll get yourself killed."

"That's been on the cards for about a week now," I say.

"No, you have to leave me here. You can't."

"Another bloody optimist," Wal says. "How do you two get out of bed in the morning?"

Lissa's eyes regain some of their gleam. "Who's your little friend?" she asks.

"Little friend!" Wal snorts. "This woman lacks sensitivity. Throw her back, Steve. There's more fish in the sea."

"Hmm, I don't like him either," Lissa says. "He's much better as a tatt."

Introductions are quickly made above the increasingly vocal wind. The dark clouds bunching up near the horizon are sliding toward us fast.

"I'm getting you out of here," I say.

"But the thing is that Orpheus Maneuvers always fail."

"Paradigm shift," I say, then kiss her.

She kisses me back. Her flesh warms, then burns. I feel her excitement. Her hands are getting busy at the back of my head, pulling me in closer, and I'm holding her face. When we finally pull away she looks into my eyes.

"I love you, Steven. Find me," she says.

There is a sudden blinding brightness.

I'm on the One Tree alone. Lissa's gone. I'm not sure where, the Deepest Dark or back to the land of the living. I stand there looking out at the Underworld, and stare at all those bodies closest to me, wrapped in tree. Most of them are Pomps. The nearest one is Don.

"How about a kiss then," he says and grins lasciviously.

I roll my eyes.

"Good to see you, de Selby," he says, though he's already slipping into that post-caring dead state. "Morrigan. Did he send you here?"

"No, Mr. D, after he died. Morrigan tried though, and he's going to pay."

"You make sure he does. I'd just paid off the place in Bulimba and Sam had moved in. Not bad, eh? I spent my childhood in a bloody caravan in Caboolture, and there I was with a classy lady like Sam. She's still alive, isn't she?"

"Yeah, I haven't felt her here."

"Good."

"He'll pay, I promise." I feel that sense of urgency winding up in me again. I need to find Lissa again. And then we'll make Morrigan pay for what he's done.

"Good on you, kid," he says. "Now get going, there isn't much time."

There are cries in the distance. Stirrers. I walk to the edge of the tree. Peering over it, I can see dozens of them rushing up the stairs. Bodies tumble everywhere as the Stirrers push them out of the way.

"I'm not sure how I get out of here."

"There's really only one way," Derek says. He's standing behind me. The tree has yet to take him. "Make sure you get Morrigan." The bastard has his hand in the small of my back. He hardly has to push at all.

I tumble off the tree. There are cries, I hear gunshots, but they can't hurt me now. I'm moving too fast. I spin in slow circles as the ground rushes up. It's terrifying, my stomach is a dozen flips behind me, and I think it's so unfair that, even here, my body holds on tight to vertigo.

"Sorry," Wal says, "sometimes this doesn't work."

"Now you tell me."

The ground beneath me opens its great earthy maw and I'm enveloped in loamy darkness, and then I'm out, and once more in the whispering Deepest Dark.

Lissa's soul is a brilliance in the dark. It coruscates, and I recognize it immediately with a certainty that only years of pomping, and true love, can provide. Oh, how I love her. She's my Lissa, and I'd go through Hell a thousand, thousand times to find her. And if I lost her I would do it again.

I reach for her soul and it bites me, bites and scratches in a way that no light should. I yowl into the void, but I hold on. The soul is chaos in brilliant form. It is all that is love and hate, it is all that is passion and hopelessness, and madness. It is so definitely madness. But so is what I'm doing.

I am holding her essence.

I bring it to my chest and Lissa's soul passes through me. It's a fierce liquid pain, and one I've never known before, but there's also a rightness to it and an intimacy that goes far deeper than what we shared when we made love. It spreads through my flesh, seeps into my bones.

A Pomp is a gateway, a conduit, and that doorway can extend back to the living world. I don't fight it, just let it happen. Until it's over.

At last, I release my breath.

She's gone. Again. I look up into the sky, where all the souls are flickering like stars, shining and waiting, waiting perhaps for the love that is life to call them back again. And I realize that this is what we're fighting for, this aching brilliance. This is what the Stirrers want to destroy.

And suddenly I'm scared, because it seems so fragile. I felt the essence of Lissa, held it in my hands, though already the clear memory of it is fading. My flesh cannot hold it, shouldn't hold it. Life is longing, it isn't certainty. That is what is most wonderful, and awful, about it.

I take a deep breath in the cold. It's time I went home. Time I faced Morrigan.

32

Do you think that did it?" I take a few jumping steps, to try and get the blood flowing. Dust lifts in a fine silvery cloud into the air.

Wal sighs. "Hard to say. You're mixing up the natural order of things, and while I'd be the first to say that nature and supernature could do with a kick in the teeth sometimes, it can be difficult."

"You're saying that after everything I've done—after being macheted at, shot at, pushed off the branches of the One Tree and falling, falling, falling—that I still may not get home?"

"That's exactly what I'm saying, Dorothy," Wal says. "You're not even wearing any slippers, and if I remember correctly there is no place like your home, because it blew up. As I said, it can be difficult."

"Sure is," whispers a dry old voice. I turn toward the sound and there is Charon. At last.

He's the tallest—why is everybody so tall in the Underworld?—gauntest man I have ever seen. Bones are barely contained by his skin and jut like bruised wings from his hollow cheeks. His fingers and wrists seem to contain a fraction too little flesh to enclose the meat and skeleton beneath.

"Been waiting for you," I say. You can't pull an Orpheus Maneuver and not expect to talk to the Old Man. "Where's the boat?"

"That metaphor really isn't appropriate anymore. Besides, I've got staff. They drive the hydrofoils, the UnderCityCats, for me."

"So how do I get back?"

"My, you are a tubby bugger," he says, swinging his hand faster than my eye can follow. He pinches my stomach with fingers hard as stone.

"I'm not fat," I say.

"You're a regular bloody buddha." Charon shakes his head, and lifts up one of his wrists. "This, my matey, is size zero. You don't get any leaner. Well, perhaps there are a few fashion models who do, but they're on a fast track to this place. The world's gone to fat, particularly the bits of it that exist on the back of the other bits. When did you last go hungry, Mr. de Selby?"

I shrug. I'm starving now, in fact. I can't remember the last time I ate.

Charon isn't one for silence, I suppose he gets plenty of it. "Yes, well, you'd know if you ever really had—"

"So how do I get back?" This could go on for a while.

"Hmm, it was *you* who interrupted me." He frowns. "I had a peek at your dossier. It's highly unusual for you, but these are highly unusual times. The Negotiation is going to be very interesting, I think, more interesting than any of those dickheads upstairs expect." He pulls a packet of

Winnie Blues from his pocket and picks out a cigarette. "Want one?"

"I don't smoke. Not when I'm sober, anyway."

The Boatman grimaces. "C'mon, this is the Deepest Dark. Indulge yourself."

I shake my head, and he puts them away. "Let me tell you though, you will—and sober too, that's a total one hundred percent prophecy—or maybe you won't. Now, back to the question. You don't leave—"

"I have to. I have to get out of here, there's unfinished business."

"Funny, I meet a lot of people who say that here. It's as though life owes you a neat ending," Charon says flatly. "And once again you interrupt. You don't leave, not all of you. You have to leave something of yourself behind."

"I'd not heard of that condition."

"Probably forgotten. It's been a while since anyone's done this—kudos to you on that, too, boyo. Think about it, even The Orpheus left something of himself when he tried to escape the Underworld."

"Eurydice," says Wal somewhat irrelevantly.

"Yes, your little arm face is right. Though obviously back in the day, Hell was all about cruel and unusual punishment. The Orpheus left his heart behind and so do you."

The Boatman coughs, and thumps his chest with a bony hand. The sound echoes loudly in every direction, booming back at us. I imagine that whatever beats beneath those ribs, if it beats at all, is dusty and ancient and probably needs the occasional jolt.

"Well, not exactly your heart," he says, once he gets his breath back. "I'm obviously getting metaphorical, you know, figuratively speaking. The Orpheus looked back. It saved his life though, because I can tell you if he hadn't left Eurydice behind he wouldn't have gotten back himself. The fellow was far too cocky."

"Cold comfort though, isn't it?" I say.

"This is Hell, this is the flaming capital of cold comfort, mate." The Boatman looks down at his feet. He's wearing rubber thongs. They're huge, but his feet overhang them by a good three or so inches, and his long toes end in nails painted black. He crouches, picks at something beneath a toenail. "Besides, if you go back, what are you going back into? That blocked artery is still going to be there, or that embolism. It's a revolving door for most people. Even Deaths aren't afforded the privilege of immortality, just a very, very long existence. Until Schism time, that is. That's how Deaths work."

I'm not in the mood for a long lecture. "Can I nominate what stays behind?"

"No." Charon lifts from the crouch and looms over me, bending down to regard me with eyes dark and dangerous. "Crikey, that's just being cheeky."

I hold his bleak gaze. "So it can be anything?"

"Yes."

"Like, say, the left ventricle of my heart?"

"Always getting back to the heart. You're heart-centric. There are a lot of other organs that are essential now, aren't there? And, each of them, including the heart, would be covered under the word 'anything,' though it would hardly be in the spirit of the deal. Look, it's a risk. But we can't have the living, not even Pomps, coming here and expecting it to be easy."

"I never expected it to be easy." The truth is, I hadn't

really had a clue about what to expect or, until Mr. D gave me the option, that it would be possible.

"You're in the Underworld, Steven. You're not on *The Price is Right*, or jumping a fence." He scratches his head. "Well, it's exactly like both, only the price of losing is death—the fence is fatally electric, probably has skulls painted all over it, or it's made out of skulls."

Wal looks up at me, and rolls his eyes. "You've got to hope for the best, mate," he says. His little wings flutter in that disturbing way that scrapes the bones beneath my flesh.

"Yeah," I say, "because everything's been working out well so far."

"You sent Lissa back, didn't you? And you're still alive—well, sort of, if we ignore technicalities." I look down at him, unmoved. "The other option, of course, is that you stay here," Wal huffs.

"In that regard," Charon says, rubbing his long hands together, "we can be very accommodating. I'm much happier bringing people here than taking them back. It seems wrong. In fact, it doesn't just seem wrong, it *is* wrong. That whole natural order of things, you know."

He's right. There's no point in arguing. I nod my head. "OK. Send me back, take what you will."

He grins. "That's my job. Now, you know the deal."

"The giving up something?"

"No, the other one."

"Which is?"

"Don't look back... and run."

And I want to argue the logic of that. After all, we just spoke about The Orpheus and his looking back, but it's too late. Charon claps his hands, once. There is a deep booming sound that reverberates through my body so that I feel as though I'm some sort of living bell.

Charon's gone.

The air feels and smells different, at once fresher and fouler. The scent of newly turned dirt. A warm breeze blows against my skin. Then all that's gone and I'm walking down a metal corridor lit with the blue lights of the Underworld, my footfalls ringing loudly. I'm not walking toward the light, but through the light.

I can smell doughnuts again, then something like burning tires.

"What do you reckon, Wal?" My voice carries uncertainly through the air.

The cherub is remarkably silent. I consider staring at my arm, but I'm not exactly sure what constitutes looking back. These rules can be extremely loose and terribly precise.

Then something chuckles, and it's not Wal.

I remember Charon's other advice. I run all right. The Underworld never lets you get too casual with it. I put on as much speed as I can, but it doesn't seem to do any good.

I run through hot and cold spaces, wet and dry. The air alternately clings to me or pushes. This is the edge of life and death, both forces are tugging at me, even as I go. I'm hoping for some sort of tidal shift, that life will start to grow more potent, and soon.

There are noises. Liquid, horrible noises, and scurryings, and more laughter.

The blue lights flicker.

I know not to look back, but that laughing...Something is drawing nearer, every footfall louder than the last one, every step faster than my own, and I'm no longer running, but sprinting, crashing down the hallway. Strobing blue lights line the walls. It's as though I'm racing down a long, halogen-lit disco, only whatever is behind me is more terrible than anything a disco ever produced.

It slobbers and howls. For a moment I think of Cerberus, the Hound of Hell, but then it's cackling, and dragging bones or bells along the ground.

I want to look back. I want to know what it is that will have me, to see if I've actually put any distance between us. The want is burning a hole between my shoulders, my skin is tight. The hairs on the back of my neck rise. But I keep my head down, keep sprinting until the tendons in my legs tear, until the muscles in my flesh burn.

And then I trip over, and I'm sliding on the floor.

It's on top of me and over me, and it's sliding into me, crashing into my mouth, my ears, my pores.

I don't scream until I'm back in the tower, but by then it's too late. I'm standing woozily, naked and blood-stained in the cold.

I know now why you can't look back: you see what's chasing you, and you may as well give up, may as well not bother running, because it is terrible and remorseless. Life, the living world, was what pursued me down that hallway. And it caught me, wrapped me in the mad vitality of its arms and flesh and showed me that it was as cruel as death ever is.

And here I am, back in the land of the living.

33

I don't even get time to laugh, because a moment later souls start rushing and scraping through me. They're zeroing in on me. It doesn't hurt as much as it once did, maybe because I've been to Hell and back.

All of a sudden I know that, other than Morrigan, I'm the last Pomp alive in Australia. Sam—well, her spirit—is here, looking extremely pissed off.

"The bastard got me too, Steve," she says. "They'll be coming for you now. All of them."

"I'm sorry," I say.

"Don't be sorry, just get moving. He was fast. I was driving through the outer suburbs around Logan, heading toward the PA hospital. He shifted right into the fucking car."

I nod my head. "Apparently he can do that now."

"He said to tell you he has what you want. That's all. Then he shot me. And here I am."

"Yeah, I'm so sorry, Sam." I'm not sure what I'm sorry about. Everything, I suppose. But the words catch in my throat. Sam doesn't deserve to be pomped by me, she should be the one still alive.

"So am I," Sam says, "but it had to happen. Mom died from a stroke, a series of them. I swore that I'd never die in bed but I never expected Morrigan to fulfil my wish. He was my friend. I've known him for nearly thirty years."

"He was everyone's friend," I say. "Don's waiting for you."

"He bloody better be." Sam frowns. "There's something different about you." She looks around the tiny interior of the iron tower. "Where's Lissa?"

Her words are little more than a breath, then Sam's gone, too. I call Lissa's name. Nothing.

There is no one in the tower except for me now. The place stinks of old blood, and there is indeed blood everywhere—my blood. Oddly enough I feel remarkably sanguine. Whatever I had lost was replaced, though that doesn't mean I am without wounds.

Where I had cut to reach the portal arteries there are two thick nuggets of scar. They have healed, but they ache, and when my fingers find the rough cicatrices of my knife work, I have to grit my teeth with the pain. The tattoo of Wal is gone as well, and where it was there is nothing but pale skin.

I'm shivering, and naked. My backpack has come with me but it and its contents are coated with mud—a final residue of the Underworld, perhaps. I scrape off what I can and quickly get dressed. My clothes are a little stiff, and my every movement hurts. I manage it. The cold has seeped into the fabric, and now it is pressed up against me. I feel like I've dragged myself out of icy water onto an icy shore.

"Lissa." I can't feel her, and if she was anywhere nearby I would be able to.

There's nothing.

I've lost her. I almost had her. We almost got a chance at a life together. I failed her and I failed my future. I sit in the tower, my knees pulled up to my chest, and sob.

Finally, I get up, wipe my hands on my jeans and step out of the tower. There's only so much grief I can allow myself. I am alive and I am still hunted. The storm's passed, gone on to drench someone else, or has dissolved into the ether. And it must have passed a while ago. The air is dry again.

By the tower is a bike, and on the bike, a note.

If you're reading this then you are most probably alive.
Welcome back, Steven. Now ride.
   They'll be coming for you.
   D

My watch says it's ten o'clock in the morning, Sunday. I've been gone since Friday. It's one of those beautiful days when the sky is so eye-searingly bright that it's almost beyond blue, and there's a warm breeze coming in off the river. I want to take pleasure from it, but I can't.

Besides, there's little pleasure to be had. I can taste Stirrers, they're filling my city. It's as though the air has thickened with some sort of grease. A bleak psychic cloud smudges the city as heavily as any stormfront. Tomorrow, if not tonight, things are going to tip into Regional Apocalypse. But that's not my biggest concern.

I quickly run through my possessions.

I've got Death's key to Number Four and my knife. I've

still got an mp3 with about two hours worth of charge, as well as my phone, around $2000 in hundred-dollar notes and a couple of twenties. Oh, and a bike.

The world isn't exactly my oyster, but I've looked Death in the face and that counts for something. Well, I'm going to make it count for something. This is going to hurt Morrigan.

I ride out from under the cover of the trees and over the fallen-down fence, putting the iron tower behind me, then cycle into West End. It's an inner-city suburb, but leafy and crowded with shops and cafes. Made up of detritus and dreams, there's a vitality to West End, a sense of community. It's old Brisbane with tatty finery and make-up. Maybe that's why some of the shops are still open. People cling to whatever normalcy they can when the world falls down around them.

Two Stirrers walk down Boundary Street. Both smile at me while I slide my knife down my palm. "It's not going to make any difference," one says.

I stall them. It certainly clears the air here, though.

I walk into the nearest cafe and order a long black from staff who may have served more disheveled customers, but not many. The coffee is scalding and it strips away a little of the cold within me. It's far better stuff than they have in the Underworld.

Lissa's gone. There's nothing I can do about that, except get angry.

Coffee done, I buy a new shirt and a pair of black jeans, then a hat and sunglasses, to avoid attention and the increasing glare of the sun. I slip my old clothes into a bin.

Then I insert a new sim card into my phone and call

Tim. There's no answer. I try his home number, it rings out. So does his work number. Morrigan has Tim without a doubt. I try Alex.

He answers the phone in a couple of rings. "Steve," he says.

"He's got Tim."

"The prick," Alex says. "The whole bloody city's going to hell here."

"Yeah," I say, "Regional Apocalypse."

Alex snorts. "Never liked that Morrigan. Always seemed too smug if you ask me."

"Listen, I'm sorry to pull you into this."

"Don't give me that shit. You're not pulling me into this. When my father died, Morrigan dragged me into it, willing or not," Alex says. "You've got nothing to be sorry for. As far as I see it, you're the only one who can stop this."

"Maybe, but I'm sorry anyway." Still, that realization makes it easier to ask him for the things I need.

Alex sounds a little surprised by the time I'm through with my list, but his voice is resolute. "I can get all of that. I'll see you at four. The Place?"

"Yeah."

I throw out the sim card and then ride as fast as I can to the Corolla in Toowong, hoping it's still where I left it. To my surprise it is, obviously not an attractive enough vehicle for anyone to steal. I open the driver's side door and sit down behind the wheel. The car feels so empty without her.

Working as a Pomp, you have a pretty good idea of the forecast, even if you don't know the specifics. But I'd never really understood until I'd failed Lissa so badly. There's always pain coming. There's always loss on its way. That's a given. Doing this job, you know it more than most. It makes you appreciate the little things all that much more. Sometimes that's worse, because the more you hold onto something the harder it is to let it go. Life and death are all about letting go.

That's the one lesson the universe will keep teaching you: that until you stop breathing, until you let go, life is loss, and loss is pain. Sometimes though, if you're lucky, you can find some grace. I'd seen it enough at funerals, a kind of beaten dignity. Maybe that's all you can hope for. Maybe that's all I can hope for.

I'd promised my parents that I'd do my best to go on, and that drove me, hard. Jesus, I'm lucky I had a chance to say goodbye, most Pomps don't even get that. Shit, I'd only managed because of Lissa. And now she was gone.

Alex is waiting for me. He smiles, though I know he really wants to tell me that I look like shit. It's one of the ways he's different from his father. Don would have told me straight up.

"You got that aspirin?" I have a headache, but that's not what it's for.

He nods and passes the packet to me. I take a handful of the pills and swallow them.

"You sure that's a good thing to do?"

"It's not a good thing at all. But aspirin's the quickest way I know of to thin my blood," I say. "Have you got the suit?"

He nods. "Oh, and I got something else." He chucks a heavy black vest at me. I catch it with a grunt.

"What's this?"

"Something you didn't think of. It's Kevlar, the best I could manage."

"Good work."

"It won't protect your head, but it's better than nothing."

It's *far* better than nothing. The suit and the vest are even the right size. I don't ask how he managed it. I just change. The suit's an affectation really, ridiculous. But if I am going to my own funeral, if I am doing the work of a Pomp, then I want to be in a suit. I look at myself in the car door window. If it's at all possible I look thinner than I've ever been, but the suit fits well, partly because of the bulletproof vest. I almost look good. Even my hair.

Alex has managed to get me everything else I wanted. "Thanks. You did good."

"The CBD's virtually deserted." He grimaces. "I had to do a little bit of looting. For the greater good, I kept telling myself, for the greater good."

I shove everything in the sports bag (another item on the list) and dump that on the front seat. Alex is standing there, formidable as always, waiting. But probably not for what's coming.

Suddenly I'm telling him about Lissa. It's pouring out of me, and by the end of it Alex, Black Sheep or not, is looking at me sternly.

Then he grins, and chuckles. "You fell in love with a dead girl. Even I know that's unprofessional." Alex shakes his head. "But then again, Tim said you were always getting into trouble."

I laugh even though there are tears in my eyes.

Alex grabs my arm, and scowls. "Steve, if you have any chance of getting through this, and believe me when

I say I want you to, you're going to have to put everything aside, or Morrigan's won. You're not dead yet, and that's got to count for something, don't you think?"

"I've let stuff slide all my life," I say.

"Yeah, but that's different. Stuff was never going to get you killed. Morrigan murdered my dad, Steve. He murdered your parents, too. Now we both know the score when it comes to death, but it still hurts. I'm still not even sure how I feel about it. But there's one thing I do know— Morrigan's trying to kill you, and he'll succeed if you lose focus." He pats my arm. "Maybe Lissa's out there. Shit, man, you've been to the land of the dead. You went there and you came back. Just stop and think about that for a minute before you face the end of days, eh?"

"It isn't," I say.

"What?"

"It isn't the end. I'm not going to die." We both know that this is unlikely, but we both know that I have to try.

Alex grins. "Yeah, bloody right, you're not."

"Maybe you should think about leaving town for a while."

"And extend the misery a little longer? No thanks, mate. If this doesn't work, I'm going to the Regatta to drink till I want to die. You think Tim's alive?"

I shrug. "I haven't pomped him, but that doesn't mean anything. Morrigan could have, or his spirit's been left wandering. I'm sure there's plenty of souls in that position."

Alex takes a deep breath. "Let me come with you," he says.

Christ, I wish he could. Alex is a thousand times more capable than me. For one, he managed to get everything that I needed. I reckon he could storm Number Four in his sleep.

I shake my head. "There's too many Stirrers." I point over toward the center of the city. Their presence is a choking foulness in my throat. "Even you must be able to sense them now. You wouldn't last a minute being so close to so many. I could brace you, but if I go under, you're gone. I don't want to have that on my conscience."

I don't know if he looks angry or relieved. But I'm sure I've made the right decision. Alex is a Black Sheep, and a cop. He knows what I'm up against—and so do I. I'm trying not to think about it too much, because I need to believe that I might have a chance. I desperately need to believe that.

"Well," I say. "It was nice knowing you." I hand him a tin of brace paint. "This will keep you safe for a little longer."

Alex nods then slides the tin into a pocket and we shake hands, which seems at once ridiculously formal and apt.

"Good luck," Alex says.

"You too."

We stand there awkwardly, then the moment passes and we head to our respective cars.

Number Four is waiting for me. Morrigan is waiting, and I'm going to give him what he wants.

It's time to end this.

34

Number Four is on George Street, so I park in the Wintergarden car park. The big car park is empty but for a couple of deserted cars—all nicer than the Corolla, but it hasn't let me down yet. I'm less noticeable as a pedestrian, and I can reach George Street and Number Four directly from here. It's only a few blocks away and there's a nice circularity to it—though I only think of that once I've parked. The last time I was here I could have convinced myself that my life was normal. I yearn for that time. But it's lost to me now.

I pass through the food court where I first met Lissa and fell in love or lust or whatever it was at the beginning, just before she told me to run—in the other direction. Even then I knew to avoid Number Four, even if it was for all the wrong reasons.

Everywhere I look I see Lissa, the places she filled. I struggle to stop the rising anger that it brings, a bleak force that threatens to overpower me as much as any Stirrer.

It's now late in the afternoon and normally the CBD

would be crowded with Sunday shoppers, but it's a virtual ghost town as I walk up Elizabeth Street, past empty boutique stores and bus stops. None of the pubs and clubs are open, their doors are dead mouths gaping, their windows blank eyes staring. There are so many Stirrers in the city that my senses burn with them. What I'm feeling is far worse than the Wesley Hospital. It's a deep and sickening disquiet. Get too many Stirrers together and people sense the wrongness of the situation, in the same way they could sense Lissa on the bus seat next to me. The buses and trains would have been crowded this afternoon but people have stayed away, shops have shut early and no one would have been able to explain why.

It feels as though most of the Stirrers in the city have gathered here. Better near me than out in the suburbs.

As I approach Number Four, the key starts tingling in my grip, then it begins to burn. For all its heat I refuse to let it go. I'm not Death, and the key knows it, but that's the thing, there is currently no Regional Manager. I'm hoping that I haven't set off alarms, I just don't know.

But when I turn into George Street, that's the least of my worries.

Stirrers have gathered around Number Four. There are at least a hundred of them, and that density of death is going to kill. A void of that magnitude is going to drive people away if it doesn't just swallow them up before they get a chance to run. Of course they don't just consume people. The trees along the street are wilting, birds are falling out of the sky. As I watch a possum tumbles from a tree.

A hundred Stirrers at least and they're not scared of me. I cut both of my hands, deep and hard. It hurts, but I am so used to that sort of pain now. And I'm angry. I don't know if I've ever been angrier. The things Morrigan has stolen from me. The important pieces of my life. All I am now is pain and anger.

At their front is Jim McKean. It's appropriate that this should end with him. At least he doesn't have a shotgun now.

"Out of my way," I snarl.

"Try and stop us," Jim says. He's in a suit, not as nice as mine, but pretty stylish. I grab him with my weeping hands, and the Stirrer passes through me.

"It's my job." I let the body fall. The Stirrers pull back, wary of my blood.

Then someone points a gun in my face. I duck as it fires. I'm rolling. The Stirrer aims again, and then its chest implodes. It staggers back, dropping the gun, then steadies, looking for the weapon. There's a distant crack and a moment later the Stirrer's head is gone, too, and the body falls. I stall it before it has a chance to get up.

I throw my gaze around the street. Alex, it has to be Alex. He's ensconced himself in a building somewhere nearby. I've a sniper at my back. The Stirrers hesitate. There's another crack; another head explodes. I stall that one, too. They know they have no choice now. The circle closes.

And they're on me. It's worse than any rugby scrum, grabbing and gouging. But I'm stronger than any of them. I'm a Pomp, and I'm damn good at my job, and I've got nothing to live for, nothing to fear. Because I've seen the other side—shit, I've ridden a bicycle down its boulevards! They couldn't get me then and they're not going to get me now.

I tear the Stirrers away from their hosts, one after another, and I pay for it in my blood and my hurt. By the end I'm hoarse with screaming, but there is an end. Unbelievably, impossibly, there is. I lie there amongst the dead, my breathing ragged, until I have the strength to pull myself out of the mass of bodies. Blood streams from wounds all over my body, but that doesn't bother me. All it says is that I'm alive. Besides, I've experienced worse in the past few days. And I know that this is only the beginning.

And then a new wave of Stirrers pours around the corner and I'm striking out with fists coated in my own blood, and every time I connect another body stalls.

I recognize these faces. Most of these people were Pomps. It's terrible work, but I know that they would have done the same, that I'm honoring their memory, however desperately and clumsily. There are tears in my eyes, and an ache in my chest.

By the time I'm done there is a pile of corpses on George Street, but that's not my problem. I know that this mess will be cleaned up, if I succeed. And if I don't, then the region is doomed anyway.

This close to Number Four the building tugs at me, drawing me in. The big Mortmax Industries sign is winking, as though unable to hold a charge. The ground hums beneath my feet, and it's not due to passing traffic. There is none. The city is empty.

We recognize each other, Number Four and I, and it recognizes the key. I've never felt this connection to Number Four before. Remarkably, the thing I sense coming from it most is sympathy.

I peer through the window. It's no longer dark. There

are more people I know in there with clipboards, on mobile phones, a few are working in front of laptops. But when I say people, I mean they were people once. They're not anymore.

I've known this for some time but to see Morrigan actually working with the Stirrers still makes me shiver. Of course it makes sense. Stirrers, after all, are pure Pomps, even if they're otherworldly Pomps. It sure beats training new staff. We've been economically rationalized. Imperially screwed, as Don would have put it, a step up from royally fucked.

And here's the thing: his replacements haven't kept up their end of the bargain. We Pomps are not only easing the passage of the soul into the afterlife, we're also fighting an invasion, and Morrigan's not only sold us out, but he's sold out the whole continent.

Morrigan's pure eighties' Brisbane, never too frightened to tear down the old for the new. And I can see him getting ready to push this idea internationally as a more efficient facilitation of the pomping process. Morrigan's always been an early adopter, and the other regions' Ank ous keep an eye on what he does, and, generally, take it up quickly.

I wonder how many other Schisms he's set up. These could be tripping through the world, Schism after Schism, Regional Apocalypse after Regional Apocalypse. It may explain why not a single RM has answered my calls. No region's that parochial, and the various RMs are, in most cases, happy to step in when a takeover is liable to occur.

This time it's as though the rest of the world is holding its breath, waiting to see how this plays out. Well, they don't have to wait too long, damn them all to Hell. The landscape of death and life has changed for good. I know that, but I'm after some payback.

The door before me no longer emotes any of that odd sense of knowingness. It's just a door. There's no hunger there, or maybe my own hungers are matching it, somehow canceling it out. Maybe I just don't care anymore.

I pull out my pistol, release the safety—yeah, I'm learning—and then insert Mr. D's key in the lock.

The door opens. I step through it.

35

The first Stirrer I see is Mom. She's standing there by the front desk. I grab her with one bloody hand and the Stirrer evacuates her flesh. Her eyes widen and her body drops with a soft sigh. I've no time to lay it down gently. Though it hurts me deeply, I let it fall.

There are so many Stirrers in here. They're a dull scratching behind my eyes, an infection of all my senses. My only hope is that Mr. D's peculiar key is doing what he promised and dulling my presence to them.

I sprint down the hallway past a half dozen Stirrers. There's one at the desk, my Aunt Gloria, Tim's mother. That almost stops me in my tracks, but only for a moment. I hope Tim's somewhere ahead of me, and that he's unharmed. If he isn't, I've failed her.

Aunt Gloria's body doesn't notice me until I've leaped over the tabletop and grabbed her arm with my bloody fingers. It's another hurtful but final stall. Aunt Gloria's body slides from her chair.

The elevator door opens. It's empty. Stirrers are coming down the hallway after me.

I jab the button for the eighth floor. If Morrigan is anywhere it will be there. The door shuts and up I go.

The elevator door pings open. My cousin Jack sees me and his eyes widen. He comes at me with a ring binder. I dispatch Jack quickly.

"Could you please stop neutralizing my staff?" Morrigan asks. He's standing at his desk, his fingers resting on a glass paperweight of the world. He picks it up and puts it down. My gun is trained on him.

"Don't listen to the bastard," says a familiar voice from a corner of the office.

Tim's alive! I look over at him. He looks a little disheveled but is otherwise all right, even if he is tied down to a chair. I see where Morrigan has marked him with a brace. He's proofed against the Stirrers. That's a relief.

"You OK?"

He nods his head. "Better than expected."

"My staff haven't harmed him," says Morrigan.

"Your staff? These are Stirrers. They don't work for you." I glare at him.

"You're wrong there, Steven. We have an agreement, and it is to our mutual benefit. I don't think you understand how powerful I've become."

"Powerful or not, you can't trust them, surely?"

"It's not about trust," Morrigan says. "They do exactly what I tell them to do. They are under the strictest controls. My controls. You see, there's always a problem when you try to fuse an organic process with a bureaucratic one, Steven. Everything is open to corruption, but nothing more so when there is an ill fit, when two separate processes collide."

"Tell me about it," I say. "People start getting murdered in their beds. Friends turn on friends and family. It's definitely a flawed system. You should just kill everyone, then everything's smooth and simple."

Morrigan ignores me. "But I've managed it. Efficiencies will be improved. The Stirrers are much better than human Pomps. You keep them under enough control and everything works well."

"So what you're saying is that death works best without the living to screw it up?"

Morrigan nods his head. "All those noisy rituals, all those dumb beliefs drawing us away from the truth, and shaping the Underworld until it's a mess. You've been there, Steve. You can't tell me it works."

The truth is I can't, because if it had, I'd still be back there, drawn into the One Tree. "So, it has some problems," I say.

"Problems, Jesus!" Morrigan hisses. "I'm steering us toward uniformity here. My region will be like no other, and then the others will slip into line. There will be new efficiencies."

"You're trying to control Stirrers here. They don't care about your efficiencies."

"Poppycock," Morrigan says. "Total bullshit. You want to know what I did? I dragged Mortmax Industries up by the bootstraps. Turned it from a small family business into a well-oiled machine. I may have been born into pomping, Steven, but I chose this path. I didn't just drift around, expecting everything to fall in my lap.

"Have you ever worked a proper day's work in your life, Steven? Have you ever sat there, planning, setting out the future?"

We both know the answer to that, and there's a small part of me that's blaming him. It's not like he ever encouraged me to apply myself. "But I also never planned on killing everyone, never decided that the way forward was fucking contingent on slaughtering my friends."

Morrigan jabs a finger in my face. "We work for the Orcus! The way forward was always going to involve death. You're not a child, stop acting like one."

I step back. "Yeah, then what about the Stirrers on George Sreet? The Orcus would never allow that. Remember what this job is about?"

"You don't know what you're talking about," Morrigan says, but he doesn't seem as certain as he did. And he's shuddering, the bastard is as worn out by all the pomping as I am. And that shouldn't be happening if the Stirrers were actually helping him and not just waiting to devour Australia.

"I wish I didn't. I've pomped a hundred people today. All you've done is remove the people who held back the Stirrers. But it isn't too late. We can stop this. God knows it'll probably kill us, but we'd be halting a Regional Apocalypse."

Another Stirrer comes near enough for me to touch and I do. It takes the breath from me. Every time I do this, my heart tears in my chest. "You know it's true, Morrigan. We can do this. The Stirrers are older than life itself, and they want this universe for themselves. And you've let them in. You've opened the door wide and I don't even know if we can close it now."

"Steven, the moment I killed Mr. D, I put into motion something that can't be stopped. And I don't want it to."

"But maybe—"

There's a dark flash of pain, and I'm down. I hear my gun clatter to the ground. I'm not long after it.

My eyes open slowly. I don't know how long I've been out. Not that long, I think. The big glass paperweight of the world that struck my skull is next to me on the floor, and there's blood all over the thing. *Oh, the prick.*

"Good, you're awake," Morrigan says. "Now kill him, darling."

I look up. Blood is pouring into my eyes from the deep cut in my head, but there's Lissa's body. The evidence of all my failures. Not her, why did he choose her? She's holding a rifle.

She swings the gun up and fires.

The bullet strikes Morrigan in the chest. He stumbles backward a step, and then another. He stares at the wound in disbelief, then falls to the ground silently, his arm outstretched toward me.

"You're alive," I say, somewhat obviously.

She runs toward me and wraps her arms around me in what is the most wonderful embrace I have ever known. She's all hard breath against my neck. I kiss her.

She's alive. She's alive! I didn't fail her. I'm woozy, bleeding, possibly dying, and I can't stop smiling.

"Don't you ever do that again," Lissa says. "Don't you ever pull me out and leave me alone."

"I won't, I won't," I say. She pulls back and I drown in those eyes. "I thought you were gone. Jesus, I thought I'd lost you."

"Where else did you think I would be? My body was here. I'm so sorry, I've been doing my best to keep away from Morrigan, and the Stirrers, but trying to look like I'm not. It's exhausting, let me tell you."

"It's OK. We've made it." The words come slowly. I'm just so happy to see her.

Lissa shakes her head. "I don't think so. Look where we are."

But at least we're together again, I think, smiling. "How do I look?"

"Like shit, not a good impression at all. I thought you were dead." Lissa grabs my face gently, it hurts. "When you slipped away from me, or I slipped from you, there were all those Stirrers and their guns. I couldn't see how you'd survive that, but I thought if you did survive, you'd come here, and if not, the Stirrers could take me again."

"Have you managed to stall any of them?"

"Steve, I'm not a Pomp anymore. I died, remember? You brought me back. I don't have those powers, and there's no RM to give them to me. I'm not even sure I want them back. If I hadn't stolen some of Morrigan's brace paint I'd be dead."

"Good for you," I say. I'm really bleeding a lot. My vision's fading.

"You patronizing shit. Now, hold on, you're going to be OK."

I touch her oh-so-serious face. "It's a Regional Apocalypse. There are Stirrers everywhere. If you're powerless, you need to get out of here. As far away as possible."

"You're going to be OK," Lissa repeats.

"I really don't think so," Morrigan says. He's on his feet and looking as bad as I must, maybe even worse. We're mortal, even here in Number Four. Being Pomps we have no excuse for forgetting that. I don't want to die, but I know that's what's about to happen.

Morrigan lifts his rifle and aims it at me.

With whatever strength I have left, I push Lissa away from me, except she's already off me and rolling, her gun swinging up toward Morrigan.

And Morrigan's rifle fires, almost at the same time as Lissa's.

36

Well, I did my best. There's that howling wind again, rising through the dark, promising a storm. I'm dead. The One Tree is a siren call in my skull. I know where I am before I even open my eyes. Still, I don't expect to see Death looking down into my face. I bite back a yelp. The pain is gone, I'm whole, and shocked to the point of shuddering, then even that's gone. I'm just lying there beneath that prickly, various gaze.

"What are you doing here? You're dead."

"Dead, but still existing." Mr. D smiles. "Hi, Steven, I kind of hoped you'd kill each other, it brings you to the Negotiation on an even footing. So there are only two of you left, eh? All my wonderful employees, all of them gone."

"And Lissa, there's three."

Death shakes his head. "She's not a Pomp anymore, unless she chooses to take that role up again, and only if the new Death offers it to her. It's just you and Morrigan."

Lissa's got to be happy with that, but then I think of her there, cradling my body in her arms. Oh, Lissa. Yeah, it was never going to end well. But then nothing does. Everything is jagged at the end, truncated and cruel, love most of all, like a branch of the One Tree snapped off.

"Why am I here?"

"Because you're dead and Morrigan's dead, and you're the last two Pomps. And here you'll get to decide who gets to live again. The Negotiation always comes down to this. Morrigan vanquished me and he chose you as his opponent."

I notice Wal, hovering behind Mr. D. The cherub winks at me. He's in possession of a body now, chubby and bewinged, and I'm seeing far too much of his package. He flits this way and that, with a speed and grace that surprises me.

"It always comes to this," Mr. D says. "Start a Schism and it ends here on the uppermost branches of the One Tree, the point where all the Underworlds connect and the laws of living and dying are more flexible."

Then I see Morrigan off to Mr. D's right. His sparrows lift into the air and hover behind him like some winged cowl. Blinking, Morrigan pats his chest, then grins. The injuries we'd sustained are gone.

Around us in a ring are all the other RMs in their ceremonial garb. No corporate gear, just the long dark cloaks of the Orcus. The thirteen regions, the thirteen Deaths. I'm waiting for them to start chanting, "Fight. Fight. Fight."

Suddenly the Stirrer helicopter is lifting into view. Half a dozen machine guns fire. The Orcus laugh.

"Cheat!" Mr. D roars. He flicks one hand casually at it,

as though it is nothing more than some sort of annoying insect.

The chopper tips, then plummets away. A few minutes later there is a distant popping sound.

A savage smile is stretched across Morrigan's face. I can tell he didn't expect the helicopter assault to work, but Morrigan is the sort of person who will try anything once. He rubs his hands together. His sparrows spin off in two braids of shadow. They loop around him, with the precision of a troupe of stunt jet pilots, then return to their position behind his head. I look over at Wal, he gives me a jiggly shrug. I really wish the little guy was wearing pants.

"So this is it," Morrigan says. "The Negotiation."

"Yes," Mr. D says. "And don't think I've forgiven you for running me over. It's a most terribly ignominious way to die. A bullet in the back would have been preferable, or even a knife across the throat—at least that ends with an ear-to-ear smile—but you've never been one for the up close and personal, have you Morrigan? Everything is automated, everything is done at a distance. I don't understand that."

"Which is why your time is past." Morrigan moves in. "It's my time now. Things will run smoothly."

Mr. D swells. He broadens across the chest, and his limbs lengthen until he towers over Morrigan, and his face is all faces. It is ruptured meat and broken bone, and the furious swelling of flies and worms, and the quiet that comes after. Then it is Mr. D's face again, marked with a silent rage, and he's his usual stick-thin size. "Not just yet," he says. "I stay to see this out. Those rules remain. This, as you said, is a negotiation, The Negotiation. But not between you and me, that has already played out. Between you and him."

He's pointing at me.

"At last." Morrigan's grin keeps getting bigger and bigger.

"This isn't fair," I whisper. Why is Morrigan looking so cheerful?

Mr. D spins to face me, and I see there's a measure of anger in all that rage just for me. "When is life or death fair?"

"Can we just finish this? I've had enough of your talk, years and years of your bloody talk," Morrigan says. "I have a lot of work to attend to."

"Of course you do," Mr. D snaps. "The creatures with which you have made your curly, crooked deals will ensure that. You were the one who started rolling the knuckle bones, Morrigan. But it is up to me to bring it to an end. I cede, I was outplayed, one by one you have gained my powers . . . but I wonder if you haven't outplayed yourself."

Morrigan sighs. "This is exactly why I began this in the first place. I'm tired of this slow, slow bureaucracy. You were never fast enough, nor efficient enough. I know I can do better. Just let me start. Just let me get it done."

Mr. D is having none of that. "The cleverest thing, of course, was that you left the weakest Pomp till last."

The penny drops. *Ker plunk.*

I realize how I've been manipulated. I glance over at Wal, and he shakes his head. Seems the idea's just struck him as well.

Everything was done to drive me to this place. I would have died a week and a half ago if Morrigan hadn't wanted it to end up here. He shaped everything, probably even Lissa's ability to stay in the land of the living. I don't know how I know that but, here, on top of the tree, I'm certain of it. Lissa came and went too conveniently. Now I understand why Morrigan looked so shocked to see me in the Underworld, and why he had grown so angry at me attempting the ceremony. It hadn't, as I'd thought, been a remnant of avuncular concern. If I had died then, he'd have been forced to fight one of the other more capable Pomps. And he'd counted on me. Of course, he'd adjusted quickly. He'd known I would pomp Mr. D on the side of that road, and had even hurried it along by getting my Stirrer father to fire at me.

I understand now why Mr. D hadn't known about the crows. By that stage Morrigan even had control over them. And why Lissa survived "unnoticed" around all those Stirrers. I was never meant to die, just to believe I was going to, until he had me where he wanted.

I think about all those other Pomps better able to challenge Morrigan physically or experientially. Morrigan was behind every step I've taken and, looking at it, I can sense his smiling presence in everything. He's known me all my life, knows how I think.

The dickhead even used me as bait.

"You did this because you thought I'd be the easiest one to beat," I say.

Morrigan looks over at me like I'm a pet he's extremely fond of. "Steven, you were my best choice. Why do you think you've managed to keep your position as a Pomp all these years?" He shakes his head. "Even then, you nearly ended up killing yourself a half-dozen times. Why did you go home? That bomb wasn't meant for you, just to keep you away so you wouldn't have a chance to regroup.

I needed you running, not thinking, because even *your* brain starts to consider things eventually."

Morrigan planted that bomb there himself. Now I know why Molly hadn't seemed worried when I got home. She knew Morrigan, he'd actually taken her for a few walks a couple of weeks ago. My hands clench to fists.

Mr. D motions for me to stop. "Not yet, boy," he whispers. Then, more loudly, he says, "Of course, Steven is quite different now. Your attempts at engineered mayhem were perhaps a little too realistic. I rather think you underestimated him. Now, you have to face the consequences."

Then it sinks in. What this is all about. The heat of my rage chills.

"I don't want to be RM," I say, and it sounds a little whiny. "That's never what I wanted. I was just trying to survive, that's all."

There's a gasp from all the attendant Deaths. It's as though they can't understand why anyone wouldn't hunger for this job. Mr. D did and Morrigan does, but they have known me in one way or another since I was child. My ambitions have never been as focused or as cruel.

Honestly, I hadn't even thought about it. Maybe I'd had some hazy idea that after beating Morrigan (not that I'd ever really believed that I could) all the other Deaths would gather together and vote on a new Regional Manager. But I'd really only been thinking about the corporate veneer, not the rough and callous beast that lies beneath it.

OK, I'm screwed.

Mr. D brings his bleak eyes to bear on me. "You want to give all this to him? You want Morrigan to get away with everything he's done, and become the new RM?"

I don't say anything. My gaze slips from Mr. D to

Morrigan. There's a bad taste in my mouth that has nothing to do with Stirrers. Bloody Morrigan. He knew I wouldn't want this.

Morrigan smiles. "Then it's easy. The Negotiation's done. I desire this, I have the will, and I most definitely have applied the way. Send me back," he says to Mr. D.

Our old boss shakes his head; he even waggles his finger. "That's not how it works," he says. "No, we're talking about death here. And death is brutal."

"No," I say. "I'll do what it takes, but I don't want to be Regional Manager."

Mr. D sighs. "Look, Steven, it's time you grew up. You've drifted along, cashed your checks and done your job, but little more. If this job hadn't existed, you'd be a video-store clerk, getting angrier and more bored. Sometimes the world hands you something and you have to take it."

"You don't have to," Morrigan says. "We can negotiate."

Mr. D nods his head. "Of course you can. The problem is that this Negotiation is done with knives. And it has begun."

The other Regional Managers draw in close, their black cloaks flapping in the wind like a murder of crows. There is a deep and awful sense of anticipation. Blood lust glints in their eyes, brighter than hair in a shampoo commercial. This is the moment they've been waiting for, the reason calls have remained unanswered, why Australia hangs, teetering on the brink.

I look down at my feet where a stone dagger, the length of my forearm, lies. The damn thing wasn't there a moment ago. It shivers with a hungry anticipation that is palpable and more than the sum of the gathered RMs'. The only one not hungry for this is me.

Morrigan fits in here. He knows this game, he will excel at it.

"You either pick it up, or there's no resurrection for you, Steven," Mr. D says, impatiently. "Hurry."

Morrigan has already snatched his dagger up from the ground and is running at me. All right then. I get the feeling that this isn't one of those cases where, if I die willingly, I get the job and Morrigan is hurled into the depths of Hell.

Do I want this?

Do I really have any choice?

I crouch down quickly and snatch the blade up. It's heavy but well balanced, as though it wants to cut, its point dipping and rising, seeking out Morrigan's blood. The hilt's cold, with a spreading iciness that runs up my arm and envelops my flesh. Morrigan is already on me, swinging his dagger down. Out of the corner of my eye I can see Wal, up against Morrigan's flock of sparrows. He's snatching at them, but they're fast. His skin is already flecked with tiny wounds.

A storm explodes about us as I meet Morrigan's strike. It's a violent raging gale, cold and laden with stinging raindrops. Morrigan has attacked me with such force that I stumble. Somehow I'm meeting his next strike, then I realize that the dagger is guiding me, because there's no way I should have been able to block that blow. There should be a stone dagger jutting from my windpipe. My knife is already slicing through the air, cutting off another jab.

Oddly enough, and this is the hardest thing, winning this is going to be a matter of trust. If I fight against the dagger I am going to slow my response time. I realize that I'm not exactly going with the flow when Morrigan's blade draws a red line across my chest. I pull away just in time. The cuts mark my skin millimeters above my nipples.

It burns like hell. I'm lucky that this competition isn't to the first blood. By the end of it there's going to be so much of it. Our hearts are pumping and the knives slice deep.

I back away.

A sudden gust hits the branch and it flexes. Now it's wet and slippery, and I stumble backward and fall, which is what saves me as Morrigan slashes out. My cheek flaps open, a raw line of pain across my face. Better that than my eye.

Morrigan's hungry for it and I'm just me—I'm hesitating, fighting the blade. It's only going to be a matter of time. My death is imminent and Morrigan knows it. The bastard is grinning like the Cheshire Cat.

I think of Lissa, everything that she has had to endure, and just what Morrigan might do to her if he wins. I want her. I want to be with her. My lips curl, and my cheek tears a little more. Salty rain rushes into the wound, splashing against my teeth. I get back on my feet.

Fucking Morrigan.

He swings up and under at my chest and I grab at his wrist and catch it before the blade strikes my skin. I don't even know where that move came from, but I hold his wrist and twist, muscles juddering in my arms.

He winces, and I loosen my grip, though I'm still holding on too tight for him to pull away. I duck away from his flailing free hand, but not before it strikes me in the side of the head.

His eyes narrow. "That's the story of your life, Steven. Do you really want this?"

"I want to live. I want my family back."

"Neither is going to happen. So just give it up."

He punches down on my wrist and snatches his hand from my grip, but as he pulls away, my knife hand is swinging around and it catches him in the middle of his palm.

I yank the blade toward me, tearing flesh. "How's it feel?" I growl. "Hurts doesn't it?"

He kicks up and catches me hard in the crotch. I stumble back again, the tree shaking beneath my feet. Mr. D looks on, his face expressionless. The other Deaths are motionless, captivated. Each face is a rictus of pleasure. There's blood in the water and the sharks are circling—their eyes might be blank and cold, but their jaws are working, widening into that most devouring sort of smile.

I slide on my arse away from Morrigan. The stone blade is slick with rain and blood but I hold it tightly. All I can taste and smell is the iron scent of my beating heart. Morrigan casually kicks me in the chest, and ribs break. I'm nothing but pain, and searching eyes.

"You really drew this out, de Selby," Morrigan says. "Just like your bloody father, he never knew how to get to the point. It's only fair that I draw it out now, at the end. And to think you took up the blade. You even considered that you might be able to make it as one of the Orcus."

He kicks me again. And my chest is on fire, a liquid fire that has me gasping. "Look at them, boy! Look at them! They'd eat you alive in under a minute."

Then his boot finds my mouth, once, twice. I spit out teeth.

My mouth can barely contain all the blood in it. I can't catch my breath. All I'm breathing is ruddy and choking.

My vision spots as Morrigan transfers the blade from one hand to the other. My brain is empty but for the pain. I can't even move.

He drives the knife toward me. I weave—well, fall—to the right. Oh, the pure broken-ribbed agony of it. Surely there's not much life left in me, there can't be. But there's something, a wild and raging vitality, and it burns inside me. I can barely see, my eyelids are swelling with blood, everything is torn and battered from the toes up, and it doesn't matter. This is what death comes to. This is what it is all about.

Morrigan scowls. "Just die. It's over, don't you get that? It's over."

Wal's in trouble too. He's a blur in the near distance, hemmed in by all those sparrows. He's snatching them out of the sky, and hurling them down. But there's more than he can handle. Inky wounds streak his flesh. Sparrows are snapping at his wings. One breaks, and he falls. The sparrows are all over him, smothering him, pecking, devouring.

I scramble backward, trailing blood, and spit out another tooth.

Well, fuck it. It's over.

I smile. Nothing else. Just that broken grin. Morrigan charges at me, driving down toward my chest with his stony knife.

My breath roars in my head. My mind goes blank. I duck away from his blade.

Morrigan stumbles, and in that moment—in the absence of my own will—my own stone knife guides me, subsumes me, so that all I am is something cutting and deathly. There's a force, ancient and hungry, bound by its own cruel covenants, and it propels my hand. The blade glides forward, almost languidly, and it slams into Morrigan's left eye with a wet detonation.

He screams and I push the knife in further. I get to my feet—I don't know how, but I do—and he stands with me. Morrigan and I are one thing, swaying, unsteady, joined with a dreadful intimacy by the bloody length of the knife.

"Not enough," he mumbles, but there is no force in him, just the soft exclamation of a dying man. "Not enough."

I don't know if he is talking about him or me. His words mean nothing. He's carried on my blade, blood bubbling from his eye. I wrench his knife from his loosening grip and slash it across his throat. I'm screaming. All I am is death, violent, terrible death. There is no room for me, just this.

It scares me. I see the edge and somehow step back. I let go of the knives. And it's me again, and I'm horrified.

Morrigan's body spills blood as it topples to the broad limb of the tree. It shudders once, then is still. And he lies there, an old man, bent and broken and bloody, and I killed him. The Negotiation is ended. Jesus, how did it end up this way?

"Good work," Mr. D says.

"No, it wasn't." That's all I can manage. My breath is whistling through the hole in my cheek. Every heaving breath is agony, and it feels like I'm leaking fluids from every pore and orifice. As the rain lightens and the storm heads out, deeper into the Underworld or out of it altogether, I'm ready for death myself.

Mr. D pats my back, and the touch is gentle, but even that hurts enough to send a painful shudder through me.

"Yes, it was. You know, you're the first person to ever win a Negotiation who hadn't engineered it in the first place. I don't know what that means, but—"

"Some fucking negotiation!" I spit blood. It splatters across the rough bark of the tree.

"It's not finished yet. You've won the right to exist, to be RM, to sit upon the throne of Death, to have the high six-figure salary."

Mr. D's fingers drive into my back. Agony runs through me. It's jagged and dirty and I scream. Then the deeper pain melts from me. Ribs shift beneath my chest. The torn cheek knits closed. I'm almost a whole man again, except I'm more than that. Something passes from Mr. D to me, a coiling and vast prescience. Mr. D is diminished and I, well, I don't know what I am anymore.

"So it's over?"

Mr. D shakes his head. "Steven, it's only beginning."

Go the cliché, but he's right. Oh, is he ever right. There's no sense of closure, merely a cruel momentum. When am I ever going to get a chance to stop, to mourn?

37

The other Regional Managers crowd around. They're quick, as management always is to recover from shock outcomes, each one slick and ready to engage in damage control. It's all I can do to stop scowling at them. Not a single one of them stepped in to help while my family and workmates were being slaughtered. But is there any point railing against death?

I'm going to find out, but not today. Healed or not, I'm exhausted.

I look up and Wal winks at me, then winks out of existence. I glance at my arm, and he's back there, a motionless 2D inky presence, smiling benignly. This job has some perks after all.

The sparrows are all gone.

No one else seems to have noticed either event. New Zealand's Regional Manager, Kiri, nods at me, then grins a huge grin. The sort that shows far too many perfect teeth, all of them sharp. At least he doesn't go for Mr. D's theatrics, his face keeps the one terrifying visage. "Good one, eh mate." He slaps my back warmly. "Never liked Morrigan. He was a prick as far as I'm concerned."

Still, you didn't help, now, did you? There might be no point in remaining bitter, but I damn well intend staying pissed off about this for some time.

The UK Death smiles, as bloodthirsty as a lion. "I was hoping for Morrigan, I'm afraid." *Well, thank you. Let's let bygones be bygones, eh.* "But I'm sure you'll make a wonderful Regional Death." He doesn't sound sincere, but at least he's honest, and I realize what a minefield it is I've stepped into. A ruthless minefield built on countless little dirty deaths. They're all murderers, they're all ambitious, and they all see me as a new player, a new way of getting one over the others.

Africa's Deaths look on. There are three of them, all in suits well out of my price range. The only one that is less than eons old is South Africa—Neill something or other. I can tell their ages, now, just by looking at them. Some of these Regional Managers, particularly in Europe, are "only" a few hundred years old. The next youngest to me is only a hundred. But in each and every one of them I can see, suddenly and vividly, the sharp memory of the violence that was their Schism, their rise to power, and it sickens me, because none of them would have it any other way. And I can see in each Schism each poor idiot like me who was put to the knife. Already this is mine, this knowledge, this seeing, and I hate it.

Perhaps that is what needs to be done, perhaps only people who hunger for this can handle the job. Well, we'll see. I have a problem with perceived wisdom.

"Excellent," says Suzanne Whitman, the North American RM. She smiles warmly at me, and that grin is hungry and cruel at the same time. "Morrigan was too ambitious. I trust you'll still be organizing Brisbane's Death Moot in December?"

I look over at Mr. D. Death Moot? Shit, I'd forgotten about what amounts to the APEC for the Underworld, all those RMs in one room together for two days. And we're holding it in Brisbane this year. Mr. D nods his head.

Suzanne's still waiting for some sort of response, even as the One Tree gives me an image of her stabbing her own opponent in the heart, in her Negotiation.

"I suppose so," I say. God, I'm actually RM. I'm not even sure what that entails, but I know that I'll find out.

She shakes my hand and grins another deathly, horrifying grin. "Mr. de Selby, you are perhaps the luckiest person I have ever met. It's good to have you on board."

"Yeah, thank you," I say. "Every single last one of you."

"You're welcome," she says warmly and without the slightest hint of irony.

And then they're gone, and it's just me and Mr. D and Morrigan's body.

"You don't want to be offending your fellow RMs, Steven. In their defense, though none of them need defending, I wouldn't have stepped in to help any of them. In the event of a Schism you don't. It's bad form, and there are rules to be followed. That said, I wouldn't trust a single one of them, and they certainly won't trust you." Mr. D looks at me sternly. "You don't get to be RM unless you're prepared to kill everyone you love for it. Well…until now. And that's the worrying thing. Steven, you represent a change, and don't for a minute believe that any of those RMs won't try and exploit it. You've more sensitivity than all of them combined, and that means more chinks in your armor."

He leads me away from the Negotiation and all those bloody battles, enacted over and over again. "But I'll be around for a while, to ease the transition. It's traditional, and I can't tell you how glad I am it's you and not Morrigan that I will be advising. If you need me, you know where I'll be."

Mr. D motions at a treetop nearby and a small platform there which looks much more cozy than it ought to. There's a pile of books on a small table by an old wooden rocking chair. Classics, mainly. I even spy Asimov's *Foundation* and a few of P. K. Dick's. "I'm going to catch up on my reading, and enjoy the aspect, not to mention watching what you might do with it all."

The view's both fantastic and terrible at once. The city stretches into the distance, and then up rise the mountains of the Underworld like the shoulders of some mad beast, vaster and more enduring than the One Tree. At the mountains' base crashes the sea, its waves a raging, dizzying vastness. They slam into the stony cliffs and rise up hundreds of meters, their spume blown on the winds over the city. It's a mixture of salt and ash and fire.

Mr. D catches my gaze. "You really should go fishing there one of these days, once everything is sorted out. I'll instruct you, it's very relaxing." I wonder how a sea that huge and wild could ever be relaxing. "And the fish… Tremendous. Certainly a marvelous way to celebrate your victory."

I'm not really ready to celebrate anything. I'm not even sure if there is anything worth celebrating. I'm the new RM of Mortmax Industries, Australia, I've lost all my workmates and replaced them with the twelve most bloodthirsty people on the planet, and my only advisor is as bad as the rest of them. Don't trust anyone, Mr. D had said. Yeah, well, I'm starting with him.

I look at Morrigan's body, and I'm crying.

I'm angry and sad. And that's not exactly what I'm weeping about. It's more for the other things that I've lost, and so swiftly. The man's died twice to me. Ambition had proven as bad as a Stirrer, possessing him cruelly and completely. But he had chosen that path. I think about how long he must have been planning it all, working side by side with the people who he intended to kill.

It explains why he had been so easy on me over the years. He needed a patsy, someone he could manipulate. My, but he did a good job. I don't know how I feel about that right now, but it isn't good. I still can't believe that it came to this.

Less than a fortnight ago, Morrigan was as close to me as my parents, I was just heading back from a funeral, and I had no idea what it was to be in love. Things change so quickly. This job should have taught me that. All we have are moments and transitions. You never know what's going to come next.

Morrigan's body dissolves, and all I'm staring at is one of the creaking upper branches of the One Tree, marked with the faintest memory of Morrigan, one shadow hand, its palm outstretched.

I glance over at Mr. D. "Where did he go? I mean, am I going to have to worry about him coming back?"

"Good heavens, no." Mr. D jabs a finger at the branch and Morrigan's shadow. "Morrigan's nowhere and everywhere. He took the most deadly lottery in the world and he lost. Morrigan's soul has been as close to obliterated as anything can be in the universe." Mr. D snaps his fingers. His grin is chilling and satisfied, extremely satisfied.

I don't know what to say, or whether I'm pleased that I didn't know that I was fighting for, not just my life, but my afterlife as well. Who am I kidding? Like Mr. D told me, what feels like months but was just a couple of days ago: It's best not to think about it.

If I had known what I was probably going to lose, I'd never have been able to empty my brain. Not even that close to death. Killing is an emptying, and an absence of fear, an absence of empathy. It's also a state I never want to experience again.

"This is all going to change," I say. "It can't stay this way."

"You're the new Death, that's your prerogative," Mr. D says, with a generous shrug. "You can do what you want."

"Paradigm shift," I say, and I like the sound of that.

"The Underworld's your oyster, de Selby."

"Thanks a lot."

"You're welcome."

Then it hits me, worse than anything that Morrigan ever managed to throw at me. "Lissa's not a Pomp anymore."

"That's right."

"And she's surrounded by Stirrers."

Mr. D frowns. "Yes, you better do something about that." Like I said, Mr. D has no real sense of the pressing nature of certain events.

"How?"

"Oh, I think you'll find a way, de Selby." Mr. D waves a hand airily, then he is gone. Though I know he hasn't gone far from this empty triumph of death, I want him gone forever. But the truth is, I'm more terrified of his absence than I'm prepared to admit. Better the Death you know. Except I'm Death now, and I don't know anything.

I glance around me, at the great branching Moreton Bay fig that devours the hill below in rolling roots as wide and as tall as monstrous pyroclastic flows, and around which teems the suburbs of the Undercity of Brisbane. Cold salty air crashes against me. This place is as much mine as anyone's. It can bend to my will, but all I want is to get back to Number Four.

Easy, right?

38

What do you know, *it is*. Even if, as Wal once said, I have no ruby red slippers and my home is a smoldering wreck.

It's easy and painful. Shifting tears at my limbs. My flesh feels raked over. I scream. So much for an element of surprise. Every gaze is on me.

Lissa is in trouble, Stirrers surround her. Not that she's too worried. My girl appears to be pretty handy with a rifle. But, there are so many of them. And Tim's still stuck in his chair, though he's worked one hand free. He smiles at me.

"Hey," Lissa says, and she sounds so very, very happy. "You made it."

"Yeah. Where did all these guys come from?"

"Pending Regional Apocalypse," she says, matter of fact, and shoots another Stirrer in the head.

"Not anymore." I lift my hands, a motion perhaps too cinematic, too contrived, but I'm new to this shit. "Get out," I snarl at them, and my voice is louder and stronger than I remember it.

The Stirrers turn toward me, and they howl. It's a cry of distilled rage, a sound too much like the one I made in my fight against Morrigan. They are many, but I am Death here. I am the master conduit of this region, and I understand what that means at the most visceral level. I really do, and that almost shocks me to a stop. But the momentum's still building, and it's that momentum that takes me.

One of the Stirrers, Uncle Blake, still in his golf gear, raises a gun and fires. The bullet passes through me. It hurts, but then the hurt is gone.

"It's too late for that," I say. "Far too late. You didn't get what you wanted. You got me."

Oh, and they have *my* Pomps. I call them now and they come crashing down George Street, where another wave of Stirrers has gathered. The crows are pure death, as powerful as anything I have ever encountered. *We are here. We are here,* they caw. They beat at the sky with a thousand midnight-dark wings. For a moment I'm viewing the world through thousands of eyes, hearing the whoosh-whoosh of wings finding rough purchase in the air. Amazingly, I'm dealing with the vertiginous vision easily.

The crows descend in a storm of claws and beaks, and every Stirrer they touch is stalled.

It's hard keeping them under control. These aren't human Pomps, they're easily distracted, and the way they stall these bodies is different, more violent. It is a steady tearing of flesh from bone. But there are so many that the Stirrers can't keep up, they can't fill bodies fast enough. And the crows are taking their toll.

I can taste the meat, feel it pulling away from dead

bones. It should turn my stomach but it doesn't. These crows are mine. I am so intimately connected to them that this act, this devouring, seems natural. I wonder if this is what Mr. D had referred to as the Hungry Death.

But it isn't enough. Number Four is full of Stirrers, and the region itself, from the Cape to the Bight, is far worse than that. There are hundreds of them throughout the country. I look over at Lissa.

"So, are you open to becoming a Pomp again?"

"I want a raise," she says without hesitation. "A big one."

"Sounds good to me." I grab her hand, and transfer my essence into her, my fingers tingling as energy runs down my arm. For a moment I feel like I'm not just touching her flesh, but her soul again. It's frighteningly intimate. And the transfer is two-way, I feel something of her in me, something that gives me strength.

"Hey," Tim says, free now. "I want to help, too."

I raise an eyebrow. "Are you sure?" I'm not sure I really want to share that experience with anyone else, just yet.

"Just do it. Now. Do whatever the hell it is you have to do before I change my mind."

I glance at Lissa. She nods. We're going to need all the help we can get.

I reach over and hold his arm. The ability slides into him. He seems to fight it for a moment—a lifetime of Black Sheepdom I suppose—then gives in to it.

There's usually much more ceremony than this, not to mention contracts to be signed—and a bit of gloating, after all he *was* a Black Sheep—but we don't have time. Now, I have two Pomps. It's hardly an army, a once-dead girl and a Black Sheep, but I feel my strength increase, and the Stirrers are pausing, staring at us with their flat, undead eyes.

I open myself up to the Stirrers in Number Four, and I pull them through me. It is like nothing I have ever felt before. It is terrible and gorgeous at once. It is life, and it is life's ending, and there's so much wonder, so much pain, so much joy. Because death-like life is the contradiction and the certainty. It is the terror and the inescapable truth. And I embrace it.

I blink.

The Stirrers in Number Four are gone. The bodies are gone. *Is that it?* I think. *Surely that can't be it.*

And then it tears through me, worse than any pomp I've ever performed, because there are hundreds of souls, not just from here, but from all across the country, carried to me by the force and the will of the crows, the souls of Stirrers and people. Lost souls, angry souls, souls desperate for absolution, souls gripped in terror or madness, and I take them all because I am Australia's Death. I direct that raging torrent to the Underworld. I realize why a Regional Manager needs all his Pomps, and why he is so fragile without them. This is hard and awful, and utterly necessary.

I've stopped a Regional Apocalypse, but at a cost. People all across the country have paid with their lives. The Stirrers worked as fast as they could to turn people. There are hundreds more dead than there should be. Now I'm paying, because this dying business stops with me.

How could anyone want this? How could anyone kill for this?

Tim and Lissa grow paler by the moment, their lips bloody and cracked, but I'm taking most of it. I have to. This could kill them, and it may yet.

The Stirrers come first and each one is rough, a howling soul hurled into the abyss. But they're soon gone, all of them banished from my region. After them are the usual deaths. The misadventures and illnesses, the pointless tragedies as slow as cancer or as abrupt as a gunshot. It's all that dying darkness which the world holds up at the end though, of course, it's not the end. Not by a long shot. There's so much more. Every stage is precious and discrete, I understand that now. But there is continuity, and the responsibility of that begins and ends with me. I infiltrate the worlds of the living and the dead in a way I can hardly believe is possible.

And it's a dreadful agony.

Then I'm in a different space. If still feels like Number Four only it's different, somehow. Darker, colder, the only light a sickly green.

Stirrers surround me in their true form, narrow-faced, saw-toothed. Their vast emptiness is palpable and insulting, and all of a sudden I know them a little. Better than Morrigan ever could, deal or no deal.

I enter the dialog of their existence, see their world and ours through their eyes. They are old, older than death itself. I'm slammed with an epiphany. To them, the *living* world is the aberration, the new thing. They are not so much invaders but the usurped. Their time passed so long ago, but they refuse to acknowledge it. I could almost respect them for it if they didn't hate so desperately.

They cannot think of anything but our destruction. For two billion years at least they have focused on it. And we are but the latest opponent in what has been such a long campaign for them.

This is just the beginning.

Now I know why they were so eager to deal with Morrigan, why they sought such a disruption to the order of things, and that it wasn't just to cause mayhem.

Something is coming. Something big and dark—rising out of the darkest depths—and it was ancient before life began. I know at once that the Stirrers worship it and fear it in equal measure. It is drawing near, and I know that it has been here before.

In that moment of utter clarity, I look up, and it is not the ceiling of Number Four I see, but a space, an inky desolation through which howls a wind as cold and bleak as any I ever encountered in Hell. My body clenches, reacting against this place. My newly possessed power slides around me, sheathing me from this realm's touch, but even that is not enough to take the cold from it, nor the terror from what I see.

An eye the size of a continent rolls toward me in its orbit.

Its vast bulk strains against the dark and I cower beneath its alien scrutiny. There is a part of my brain that starts to lock down, a part of me that wants to curl up into the smallest ball it can and never look into that dark again.

But I hold its gaze for a fraction of a moment. The god's endless hatred and cruel hungers crash against me, but I do not quail, even as every bit of me chills. This is the creature that the Stirrers serve, the beast that their death and destruction feeds. Why have I not been told about this? It's one more thing to add to the misinformation that is my life.

The Stirrers call to it, and it shrieks back, a long sharp cry that sets reality rippling. Although I can see it clearly, the god is still so far away that my mind cannot fathom it.

I am Death, but I am nothing compared to this. And it is coming.

But it isn't here. Not yet, not today.

I snap back into the land of the living.

I'm not sure how long I've been gone but when I wake, Lissa's looking down at me and squeezing my hand.

"Where were you?" Lissa asks.

Tim's not far behind her, looking sick with worry and exhaustion. "You right, Steve?"

Maybe I should be asking him that.

I blink. I feel like I'm newly born or newly dead. Everything is tender. But that's not all of it. The world itself is clicking along at a slightly different pace...or am I? "I went everywhere," I say. "And I saw what's crashing toward us and it's terrible." I realize that I'm on my knees. There's a lot going on in my head, so many thoughts spinning tight orbits around each other, so many terrors. And there's so much to do.

For Christ's sake I'm holding a Death Moot in December. What the hell do you do, or even wear, at a Death Moot? But that is for later. Right now I can stop running. "It's done. For now. We've won, I guess." I touch Lissa's face. I could never get sick of that contact. "You're alive. We did it. We made it."

Tim clears his throat. I glance over at him.

"Mom, Dad. Did you see them?"

I shake my head. "They were gone."

Tim nods his head. "You tried though?"

"I didn't have much time."

"Yeah."

"Morrigan's gone," I say. "He paid for what he did. I made him pay."

Tim seems satisfied with that, and it's all I can give him. Lissa helps me get to my feet. I'm not that steady on them. She lets me hold her, and it feels good. Everything about her feels good.

"You're even cuter alive, you know," I say.

Lissa arches one eyebrow, her lips twitch. "Do you ever take anything seriously?"

"My hair. I take my hair way seriously."

"I hate to say it, but I think you're thinning on top."

Tim snorts. "She's right, you know. I didn't want to say anything but..."

"Really?" Shit, I know that baldness is hereditary, but I'd been doing so well.

Lissa glances over at Tim, then me. "Nah...Maybe."

"You are such a bitch." These two are going to be trouble.

"Aren't I adorable?"

And she is, and I'm staring into those green eyes, and there's still all that *je ne sais quoi* stuff going on, and I think there always will be, if we get a chance. If this job, and everything else, gives us a chance.

I hold her face in my trembling hands, and then I'm kissing her. There's so much to be done. So much to absorb, to rage against and mourn the passing of. All of that confusion is inside me, churning madly, demanding attention, and I can't pretend it isn't.

But I get that moment, that kiss. And it's a start.

ACKNOWLEDGMENTS

You only ever get one first book. And, being the first book, I could fill it with a book's worth of people to thank. So here's the stripped-back version.

Off the bat, I'm in no way the first to play with Death. This book is very much a fusion of my love for Fritz Leiber, Terry Pratchett and Neil Gaiman's Deaths, and Charon from *Clash of the Titans*, not to mention Piers Anthony's *On a Pale Horse*. All of these have left a wonderful and, no doubt, influential impression.

Now to the people I know.

Thanks to Marianne de Pierres for getting the ball rolling. Thanks to Travis Jamieson and Veronica Adams for reading early drafts, and to Deonie Fiford for pushing the book to the next level, and giving support at the right time.

And of course, there's my brothers and sisters in writing, ROR. They're the best writing group you could ever want, really.

For the last stages, a big thank you goes to my publisher Bernadette Foley, my structural editor Nicola O'Shea and my copy-editor Roberta Ivers. You've helped make this book better than I thought it could be.

And a thank you to every bookstore I've ever worked in, and the wonderful people I have worked with. Thanks to everyone at Avid Reader Bookstore (and the cafe) for being amazing, and for putting up with the least available casual staff member in the universe (particularly Fiona Stager and Anna Hood). And a massive thank you to Krissy Kneen, and to Paul Landymore, my SF Sunday compadre.

Oh, and there's Philip Neilsen at QUT, my mate Grace Dugan, and Kate Eltham at the QWC, and the SF Writer's group, Vision. And the city of Brisbane, with which I have taken some liberties ... I really better stop—well, not yet.

Thanks to my family, always supportive. And finally, to the one who puts up with everything, and who has never doubted me, Diana, thank you, my heart.

extras

orbit

meet the author

TRENT JAMIESON has had more than sixty short stories published over the last decade, and, in 2005, won an Aurealis award for his story "Slow and Ache." His most recent stories have appeared in *Cosmos Magazine*, Zahir, Murky Depths and Jack Dann's anthology *Dreaming Again*. His collection *Reserved for Travelling Shows* was released in 2006. He won the 2008 Aurealis Award for best YA short story with his story "Cracks."

Trent was fiction editor of Redsine Magazine, and worked for Prime Books on Kirsten Bishop's multi-award winning novel *The Etched City*. He's a seasonal academic at QUT teaching creative writing, and has taught at Clarion South. He has a fondness for New Zealand beer, and gloomy music. He lives in Brisbane with his wife, Diana.

Trent's blog can be found at

http://trentonomicon.blogspot.com.

interview

Have you always known that you wanted to be a writer?

Pretty much. I've wanted to write since I was about five, and it was always fantasy or science fiction. It only took me three decades to sell my first book, but I've been writing in all that time. The only thing I ever really thought I might like to do is be a stage magician, but I don't have the eye–hand co-ordination for that nor the patter.

When you aren't busy writing, what are some of your hobbies?

I like walking—I live next to a fair bit of brush, we have wallabies and koalas in there, and right now the young Kookaburras are learning to laugh, it's a really really horrible sound, until they get it. I love reading, of course, and, occasionally, I'll sketch one of my pets. But I don't really have a hobby, it's that lack of eye–hand co-ordination, I think. When I stop writing I sit in a corner and power down.

Who or what inspired you to write about Death?

Fritz Leiber's Death in the Lankhmar books for starters. The depiction of Charon in the old Clash of the Titans movie. There's a bit of Neil Gaiman's Death in there as well as Pratchett's. Though in my world there are thirteen deaths, collectively called the Orcus, and none of them get along all that well.

I've always had an interest in death, and the brevity of life. It's the wall we all end up hitting. It's fun to imagine various scenarios for what might come after.

I've thrown in a lot of Death folklore as well, though I've mixed it up. Terms like Ankou and Orcus hold slightly different meanings in different cultures' folkstories—an Ankou for instance, is Death's helper, but is sort of death as well.

How did you develop the world of DEATH MOST DEFINITE?

It all started with that first scene. I had no idea what was going on, but it made me want to find out. Pretty quickly in I had the idea of people working for Death, and what might happen if someone starts murdering them.

Of course, at its heart it's still a love story. And Steven always fell in love at first sight.

If death really was run like a corporation, how well do you think it would succeed?

Like any corporation. Really well when everything's working, and utterly terribly when it's not. Oh, and someone would always be stealing the paperclips and pens. And the phones would never work, and we'd all be crashing towards some sort of apocalypse.

Hmm, kind of like the DEATH MOST DEFINITE, I suppose.

Do you have a favorite character? If so, why?

Other than Steven and Lissa, who I see as the heart of the story. I think it's Wal. I never expected to have a plump Cherub show up at all, until, well, until he did. He's part conscience, part troublemaker, and quite tolerant for a creature stuck on someone's arm most of the time.

Oh, but I also love Tim, Don and Sam, Mr D, and Charon. And, in book two there's Aunt Neti. She guards the stone knives of Negotiation, and the secret back ways into hell, and has many eyes and many arms and likes to cook scones—they're delicious, just don't ask what's in them or the jam. (You can tell that I'm deep in edits for book two can't you?)

What can we look forward to in Steven's next outing, MANAGING DEATH?

Well, Steven has to learn how to be Death while organizing a meeting of the Regional Managers called a Death Moot.

You'll meet Aunt Neti, the mysterious Frances Rillman, and the even more mysterious and disturbing Hungry Death. There's betrayals, great battles, an approaching evil god, and scones and jam to be had.

And Steven still has a lot of growing up to do: lucky

he's got Lissa and Tim by his side, and Wal, stuck on his arm. This book is a good deal darker, but I suppose that's what happens when you move up the ladder at Mortmax Industries.

Finally, what has been your favorite part of the publication process so far?

I may sound like a glutton for punishment, but so far it's been the editing. I've loved reworking these stories, making them as tight as I can. I've learnt a lot—the publication process is such a team effort—and I think that's going to really show in book three—but you'll just have to wait and see.

I'm dying to see the books in print. I know how hard I've worked on them, as have my editors at Orbit, and, after thirty years of waiting and writing, it'll be great to finally see one of my own novels in a bookstore!

introducing

If you enjoyed
DEATH MOST DEFINITE,
look out for

MANAGING DEATH

Death Works: Book Two

by Trent Jamicson

There's blood behind my eyelids, and in my mouth. A knife, cold and sharp-edged, is pressed beneath my Adam's apple. The blade digs in, slowly.

I'm cackling so hard my throat tears, and I really didn't have that much to drink last night.

"Gah!" I almost tumble from the wicker chair in the bedroom.

Dream.

Another one! And I'd barely closed my eyes.

Just a dream. Like anything is *just* a dream in my line of business.

These days I hardly sleep at all; my body doesn't need

it. Comes with being a Regional Manager, comes with being Australia's Death.

And I'm a long way from used to it.

But it wasn't the dream that jolted me awake.

Something's happening: A Stirrer, well, stirring.

Their god is coming, and they're growing less cautious and more common: rising up from their ancient city Devour in greater numbers like a nest of cockroaches spilling from a drain.

Christ.

Where is it? I scramble to my feet.

Unsteady. Blinking my eyes, adjusting to the dark.

Stirrers, like their city's name suggests, would devour all living things. They're constantly knocking open the doors between the lands of the living and the dead; reanimating and possessing corpses in the hope that they can destroy all life on Earth and return the world to its pristine—as they see it—state. It's the task of Mortmax Industries, its RMs and Pomps (short for "Psychopomps") to stop them. To make sure that the path from life to death only heads in one direction. We pomp the dead, send them to the underworld, and stall Stirrers. Without us, the world would be shoulder-to-shoulder with the souls of the dead. Without us, the Stirrers would have much more than a toehold; they'd have an empire built on a road of our corpses and despair.

But sometimes the serious bloody business of pomping and stalling can get lost in all the maneuvering, posturing, and occasionally literal backstabbing that modern corporate life entails.

Work in any office and you know that to be true. The stakes are just a lot higher in ours.

My heart's pounding: fragments of my dream are still working their rough way through my veins.

For a moment, I think the monster's in the room with me.

But it's a lot further away than that.

I get to my feet. My back cracks loudly. Lissa's in our bed, still asleep. I don't know why I'm surprised by that; after all, me wandering in here drunk an hour ago didn't wake her. She's exhausted from yesterday's work, all my Pomps are, but she's taken on so much. That's the downside of knowing how things are run, of having the particular skills she has. I feel guilty about it but I need her to keep working: finding and training our staff, not to mention pomping the souls of the dead, and stopping Stirrers from breaking into the land of the living.

Lissa's heart beats loud and steady. Forty-four beats per minute.

One reassuring sound at least, but it's not the only heartbeat I hear. They're all there inside my skull. All of my region's life. All of those slowing, racing, stuttering hearts. They're a cacophony: a constant background noise that I'm better at ignoring some times than others. Mr. D says that it becomes soothing after a while. I don't know about that. Though I've discovered that stereo speakers turned up loud can dull it a little; something to do with electrical pulses projecting sonic fields. Thunderstorms have a similar effect, though they're much more difficult to arrange.

And there are other sensations even harder to ignore. Each reminds me just what I've become.

Someone dies. It's a fair way away, but still in Australia. Perth, maybe, certainly on the Southwest coast. Then another: close on it. The recently dead soul passes through a Pomp, and the echoes of that passage scratch through me. When I was just a Pomp that used to hurt; now it's just a tingling ache, an echo of the pain my employee feels. Just enough so that I can't forget, I suppose.

At least Mortmax Australia is running smoothly; though I wish I could take more credit for that. Our numbers are still low. But with my cousin Tim being my Ankou, my second in command, and Lissa running our HR department as well as leading the Pomps on the field, our offices have reopened across the country. It seems there are always people willing to work for Death. And we've found a lot of them.

Who'd blame them? The pay's good after all, even if the hours can be somewhat... variable.

It used to be a family trade. Used to be.

I leave Lissa to her sleep, stumble to the living room, down a hallway covered with photos of my parents: smiling and oblivious of how it was all going to end. My feet pad along a carpet worn thin by the footsteps of my childhood and my parents' lives. I can smell my mother's perfume. It's lingered; I don't know how, but it has. This used to be their home. I grew up here, moved out, then my house exploded along with most of my life. Now I'm back. And they're dead. And I'm Death. It's pretty messed up, really.

My mobile's next to a half-empty bottle of rum.

I grab my phone, flick through to the right app, marked with the Mortmax symbol—a Bracing Triangle, point facing down, a line bisecting its heart—and open up the schedule. Technically, I don't need to look anymore. All of this comes from me, from some deep knowledge gained in the Negotiation. Still, it's nice to see it written down, interpreted graphically, not just intuitively.

It was definitely a Perth pomp. One of my new guys, Michio Dugan, is on the case. There's another, this one in Sydney—ably handled by a Pomp donated from China—and two in Melbourne. A stall accompanies one of those. The Stir that necessitated that was what woke me.

I close my eyes and I can almost see the stall: the Stirrer entering the body, and the corpse's muscles twitching with this invader's insertion. Eyes snap open. My Pomp on the scene, Meredith, grimaces as she slashes her palm and lays on a bloody hand. Blood's the only effective way to stall a Stirrer, and it hurts, but that's partly the point: We're playing a high-stakes game of life and death. No matter how experienced you are, a Stirrer trying to breach into the living world is always confrontational. And my crew are all so green.

I feel the stall that stops the Stirrer as a moment of vertigo, a soft breath of chill air that passes down my spine.

The Melbournian corpse is just a corpse again.